Rachel a
feat which n

AUTHOR NOTE

I've always been a sucker for a good redemption story. There's a strange kind of appeal in taking a damaged character (or in this case two!) and giving him a second chance to shine. Caleb and Rachel did not disappoint me in this regard. It was great fun putting these two through the wringer and seeing them come out the other side.

SALVATION IN THE RANCHER'S ARMS began its life as my first NaNoWriMo (National Novel Writing Month) book, and remains one of my favourites. I hope you'll enjoy reading about Caleb and Rachel's journey as much as I enjoyed writing about it.

SALVATION IN THE RANCHER'S ARMS

Kelly Boyce

Published in Great Britain 2014
by Mills & Boon, an imprint of Harlequin (UK) Limited,
Eton House, 18-24 Paradise Road, Richmond, Surrey, TW9 1SR

© 2014 Kelly Boyce

ISBN: 978-0-263-90978-4

Printed and bound in Spain
by Blackprint CPI, Barcelona

Kelly Boyce can't remember a time when she wasn't writing stories. In 2002 she joined the RWA and Romance Writers of Atlantic Canada. Shortly thereafter she was one of the featured writers in a documentary about the romance-writing industry entitled *Who's Afraid of Happy Endings?*

A life-long Nova Scotian, she lives near the Atlantic Ocean with her husband and a clownish golden retriever with a stubborn streak a mile wide.

This is Kelly Boyce's amazing debut novel
for Mills & Boon® Historical Romance!

Dedication

In memory of my grandfather, Malcolm Lavers—
a great man and a true hero.

Chapter One

Colorado Territory, 1876

Salvation Falls was like a hundred other towns Caleb Beckett had ridden into over the years, with its faded storefronts and hopeful name, likely conjured up by settlers who had great things in mind, only to be disappointed by the harsh realities of life.

People mixed and mingled on the streets and planked sidewalks as the buckboard he rode jostled over the ruts in the dirt road. A few stopped to glance up at him. He could feel the shift in the air the further into town he went. It was subtle at first, but soon grew to a deep murmur that buzzed like a hive of angry bees.

He guessed that could happen when a stranger arrived in town with a coffin loaded in the back of his buckboard.

Caleb's eyes scanned the storefront signs. They were all the same. Mercantile, hardware, footwear, sundries and saloons. He knew from experience that down near the end of the road he'd find a livery and the butcher, probably a blacksmith or two. It never changed.

He'd spent time in a town just like this, and drifted into even more after leaving it. And if there was one thing he'd noticed, as he moved on from one to the next, it was the similarity of it all. People all wanting the same thing: a decent place to call home, somewhere to belong, a sense of control over their destinies.

He had wanted that once, too. But he'd learned his lesson on that account.

The sheriff's office loomed ahead on the corner where a side street intersected the main road. It wasn't the smartest of choices. Left the jail too exposed, in his opinion. But he would keep his own counsel. It was none of his affair. He had other business here. Business he planned on concluding quickly before moving on. The body in the coffin behind him did not alter this plan in any way.

It simply added a few complications that needed to be dealt with first.

He touched a hand to his chest. Beneath his sheepskin, in the pocket of his wool jacket, a piece of paper crinkled under the pressure.

He never should have played the hand. He should have listened when his gut told him to get up and walk away from the table when the desperation in Robert Sutter's eyes hit a fevered pitch.

But he hadn't.

The price was always hefty when he ignored his instincts. He had the scars to prove it. Both inside and out.

"Whoa." Caleb pulled back on the reins, squinting as the late afternoon sun poked over one of the low buildings and hit him square in the eye. He tipped the brim of his felt hat forward to block the blinding light.

He stopped the buckboard in front of the sheriff's office. He set the brake and jumped down, his muscles protesting after endless hours in the seat. He'd driven straight from Laramie without stopping. He wanted this business over and done with.

Jasper nickered. His horse hadn't much liked being hitched to the back of the wagon for the trip, replaced by a sturdy draft, but Caleb hadn't wanted to tire the paint. He needed him fresh and ready for when he left town.

Caleb left the coffin where it was and, ignoring the stares of those who had stopped to gawk, walked into the sheriff's office.

It took a moment for his eyes to adjust to the sudden dimness.

"Do somethin' for you?"

Caleb blinked and shifted, moving his exposed back away from the open door. Slowly the shadows took shape. The sheriff sat behind a scarred desk, his feet propped up on top and a newspaper in his lap. The tin badge designating his position held a dull sheen in the pale light. Caleb judged the man's age to be close to his own thirty years, though he lacked the hard-bitten look Caleb saw every time he looked in a mirror.

"Afternoon," he said. Flicking the brim of his hat back with one finger, he took in his surroundings. The small office held a desk and chair. In front of the desk were two more straight-backed chairs. A potbellied stove took up the center of the wall he had his back to and it radiated heat, the crisp scent of burning wood almost enough to overpower the smell of leather, bacon and sweat. "I got a body for you."

The sheriff folded the newspaper and unfolded his long limbs. His feet hit the wood floor with a thud. "Come again?"

From the man's reaction, Caleb guessed they didn't get a lot of dead bodies showing up unannounced in Salvation Falls. He hooked a thumb in the direction of the door. He could see a crowd gathering outside. The sheriff noticed, too, and took a few steps forward to peer over Caleb's shoulder. The sun caught his hair, turning the black almost blue. Sharp, dark eyes slid in Caleb's direction.

"Whose body you got in there?"

"Man by the name of Robert Sutter."

Shock registered in the sheriff's expression, a swift tightening travelling down his body like a bolt of lightning, straightening his posture. "Sutter?"

"Man was in Laramie, playing cards." Caleb hesitated, unsure of how much to tell the sheriff. He decided the bare minimum would suffice for now. "Got himself shot."

"Man." The sheriff's hand rubbed at his clean-shaven jaw until the tightness in his expression eased and filled with worry and uncertainty. "You came straight here?"

"Three days' ride." Caleb hesitated again. "Body oughta be buried straight off." The sun had beaten down on him for the duration of the journey, and while April high up in Colorado Territory was a far cry from warm, he didn't guess it did much good to a body stuffed in a pine box.

The sheriff nodded, his attention riveted to the buckboard outside. "I'll send for his wife."

Wife.

Caleb's stomach churned. How had Sutter referred to her? A pants-wearing, mealy-mouthed ball buster.

Great.

He didn't imagine she would be happy to receive the news he had to give. His hand absently brushed against his hip. It almost made him wish he still wore his guns. Almost.

"Might be Rachel can't get here till morning. Their spread is a couple hours' ride out. Be dark by the time someone gets there and breaks it to her." The sheriff rubbed at his stomach, as if the idea of delivering the news that her husband had died in a card game threatened to dislodge his dinner. "You best hole up for the night," he continued. "Mrs. Sutter might have some questions she needs answered. Better if you were here to accommodate her. Might make it easier."

Caleb nodded. He doubted anything he had to say would improve the situation. In fact, just the opposite. But he had to speak to the woman either way. "Hotel?"

"Klein's is the most decent. Pagget's is the least expensive." The sheriff's hand waved in one direction then the other, the rest of him remained focused on the dead body in the buckboard. He seemed unduly affected by the man's death.

"Sutter kin to you?"

The man snapped back to attention. "What? No." He shook his head. "I knew him since we were boys, is all. And Rachel."

"Expect she'll be upset."

The sheriff glanced from the buckboard back to Caleb, his expression unreadable. "I guess any woman would be."

Despite his words, something in the man's tone told Caleb not to expect a bucket of tears when the new widow came to town.

"If you could point me in the direction of the undertaker."

The sheriff walked to the door and plucked his hat off the peg next to it, jamming it onto his dark hair. "I'll ride down with you." He turned before stepping over the threshold into the waiting crowd. "What were you doing in Laramie, anyway?"

Caleb pulled the brim of his hat down to shield his eyes, even though the sun had now dipped low enough to no longer be a bother. "Just passin' through."

Rachel Sutter gripped the edge of the wagon, partly to keep her behind from bouncing out of the seat and partly to keep her hands from shaking, as the large black woman known as Freedom Jones drove hell-bent for leather toward town.

"Slow down, Free." She almost added that Robert wasn't going anywhere, but managed to bite back the last bit, swallowing her anger. A tough pill, at best, and one that left a chalky residue as it went down. She could not believe it.

Robert was dead.

Killed.

The sheriff had delivered the news himself, arriving shortly after supper and pulling her outside where the boys couldn't hear their conversation. The minute Hunter Donovan arrived on her doorstep, Rachel knew it was bad news. Dread filled the empty space inside her and made itself at home.

Breaking the news to the boys hadn't been easy. She did her best to reassure them everything would be fine, but after they had turned in for the night, her numbness gave way, making room for fear to creep in. Curling up on the empty cot in the kitchen where Robert had preferred to sleep, she rocked back and forth with her head buried in her knees. The tears came of their own volition, angering her.

She had cried enough tears during the beginning of their marriage, back when she still believed she could make it work if she tried hard enough. But nothing she did had made a difference.

Robert wasn't interested in her.

He'd had ambitions for her land, but his ambitions for their marriage became a well of empty promises.

Once again, it fell to her to pick up the pieces. But this time, there would be no reprieve. This time, Robert wasn't coming back with yet another scheme for riches or promises of recouping all they had lost.

Rachel shook off her memories of last night and glanced behind her at Ethan and Brody. Both were dressed in their Sunday best, though it was only Tuesday. Brody, at nearly fifteen, had taken another growth spurt. The hem and cuffs of his suit betrayed the evidence that she had let them out as far as they could go. She'd have to get him a new one, but their credit at the haberdashery was overextended as it was.

"Maybe you could wear one of Robert's," she'd suggested. But the idea had been met with stony silence. In the past year, her brother had turned sullen and moody. The sudden distance

between them pained her, but nothing she tried
had bridged it.

"You warm enough, Ethan?" The little boy's
small body was pressed against Brody's, seeking
either warmth or comfort, maybe both.

"Yes, ma'am," he whispered.

Freedom pulled back on the reins and cast a
glance in Rachel's direction. "It'll be jus' fine,
Miss Rachel. Ain't nothin' you can't handle. You
jus' remember, those boys—" she jerked her head
back toward Brody and Ethan "—they be coun-
tin' on you."

Rachel nodded. "I'm fine, Free. Just get us into
town." She would have driven them herself, but
Freedom had insisted. She didn't have the energy
to argue with the woman, who had been with her
since Rachel was Brody's age, coming to help out
when Rachel's mother fell ill.

She'd been a godsend, then and now.

"Hunter says the reverend is making all the
arrangements," Rachel said, peering out over the
jagged landscape. In the distance, the rising sun
hit the mountains, turning their peaks a golden
pink. The early April air still held the bitter nip of
winter here in the small valley. Pockets of snow-
fall had yet to melt away in some spots, but the
promise of spring filled the air with the rich scent
of wet earth.

"Yes, I 'spect everyone in town has heard the
word." Nothing stayed secret in Salvation Falls
for long. No doubt by the time Hunter had reached

her doorstep with the news, most of the towns-people already knew.

"When we get there, take the boys directly to the church," Rachel continued. "Reverend Pearce will be waiting for them. I'll walk to Doc Merrick's from there."

The rushed burial couldn't be helped. Three days had passed since Robert was killed. They had to get him in the ground without delay. Rachel understood. She welcomed it. It would keep her busy, keep her focused. Wouldn't allow her time to stop and think and worry and fret.

If she kept moving, she'd be fine.

A strange sense that she was living someone else's life crawled over Rachel as she walked down the pathway away from the white clapboard church. The structure shone like a beacon in the morning sun, but she turned her back on it once Freedom had taken the boys inside. Rachel had stopped at the bottom of the steps, refusing to go in. She wasn't on good terms with God today.

The cool spring air cut through her thin shawl. She was used to wearing her heavy coat lined with buffalo hide, but it didn't seem appropriate attire for burying one's husband.

Not that Robert had proven to be much of a husband.

She stopped midstride and took a deep breath. That wasn't fair. No, it *was* fair. It just wasn't right. The man was dead. Best let the bad memories and disappointment die with him. It wasn't going to do her any good hanging on to them.

Hunter had had little information to give her about how Robert had managed to get himself killed buying cattle in Laramie, but Rachel had her suspicions. And she suspected that, when she spoke to the man who had brought her husband's body home, they would be confirmed.

Doc Merrick met her at the door to his office. Merrick wasn't a real doctor, at least, not the kind who fixed broken bones and ailing stomachs. Dr. Bolger managed that end of things. Merrick yanked teeth and helped prepare bodies for burial. He might have been a regular doc at one point, but if he was, it was well before Rachel could remember. Either way, she was glad for him. It meant one less thing for her to do. And she'd seen enough death in her life, so she was happy for Merrick's abilities.

"Got Bobby all set, Rachel," he said, taking a deep draw on his corncob pipe. The sweet, pungent smoke wafted around them. "Can't tell you how sorry I am 'bout this. Sad day to be burying a man this young."

Rachel nodded, following Merrick inside to the cramped little room. Small glass bottles lined the shelves against the wall, and oddly shaped instruments, whose purpose she didn't want to think about, hung on hooks near the table. A lump rose in her throat and grew to the size of one of the crab apples growing on the tree next to the barn.

"Sheriff Donovan brought over a suit for 'im." Merrick nodded at the closed pine box coffin sitting atop the sturdy table. The pale wood stood out in the dim confines of the office. Light struggled in through the dirt-encrusted window, adding a weak glow to the room.

"I'll be sure to thank him," she said. No doubt Hunter had given Doc the one suit he possessed straight out of his own closet. She shouldn't be surprised. Hunter and Robert had been friends since they were young boys. They may have had a falling-out years before, but Hunter wasn't the kind of man to hold a grudge past death.

Rachel touched the edge of the pine, letting her fingers trail over the smooth surface. The estrangement had been her fault. Both men had paid court and she'd chosen Robert. She wondered how different her life would have been had she made a different choice all those years ago. Funny how she had known both men most of her life, yet the man she buried today was more of a stranger to her now than on the day they'd married.

Maybe she had never really known him at all. It was a sad thought.

"Can you open it?"

Merrick started. "Open—oh, Rachel, you don't want to do that. It's been three days, and…well…" He shook his head, the bushy white hair bobbing with the movement.

"I know," she said. She knew what happened to a body after death. "But I need to see."

Merrick hesitated but Rachel fixed him with a hard stare until he relented.

"Here." He handed her a stark white handkerchief.

Rachel took a deep breath, the scent of formaldehyde and whatever else the Merrick kept in those bottles, stung her nostrils. She placed the handkerchief over her mouth and nose, and gave him a nod.

It took Merrick a minute or two to pry loose the nails and slide the top toward him, revealing the body within from the chest up. Rachel took a step forward and peered down into Robert's face.

Except it wasn't Robert's face.

At least, not the one she remembered. Robert had had a sense of animation to him, whether he had been angry or excited or somewhere in between. This man, this face, was still and gray, the eyes and cheeks already sinking into the hollows in the bone. Even his pale blond hair appeared stiff and lifeless, darker even, as though the sun's reflection had slipped beneath a cloud leaving it cast in shadow. The body in the box was not Robert. It was an empty shell he'd once filled.

"The sheriff said he was shot." There was no evidence of a bullet wound.

"One to the chest. Straight through the heart. Probably died instantly. Guessin' it would have taken a man handy with a gun to manage such a thing."

Rachel bit down, forcing the lump in her

throat back. At least he hadn't been shot in the gut. Whatever their differences, she would have hated to know Robert had suffered. She closed her eyes and nodded once again, waiting until Merrick hammered the lid back into place before reopening her eyes.

"I'll bring him up to the church," Merrick said. "Reverend said the service would start at ten. I'll have him there before people start arrivin'."

"Thank you," Rachel whispered. Something hollow filled her chest. Sorrow? Regret?

She let out a long breath and straightened her shoulders. She had no time for either.

"The boys and I will be staying at the Pagget tonight. You can send the bill over there." She turned and left the undertaker's office. She'd figure out how she'd pay it tomorrow.

Today, she had a husband to bury.

Chapter Two

Caleb stood against the side wall of the church, closer to the front than he wanted to be. It gave him too clear a view of Rachel Sutter. The new widow sat flanked on either side by two boys. One he guessed was around fifteen, too old to be her son. The other he doubted was more than six or seven. Neither bore any resemblance to her or Robert Sutter.

The church was packed to capacity. It seemed everyone in town had come to pay their respects despite the short notice. Several men lined the walls with him. A few cast glances his way, though none addressed him directly. Just as well. He didn't plan on staying longer than necessary, and the fewer people who remembered his face, the better.

The reverend stood at the front of the church, the pine box to his right. He cleared his throat, signaling he was ready to start the service.

It was easier to think of it as a pine box. Nothing special. Not something containing a body or a man or a life that used to be.

But try as he might, Caleb couldn't erase the image of Sutter's face when the bullet slammed into his chest. There had been an instant, a split second when the shock registered on Sutter's face and he knew he was going to die. Caleb had seen that look on a man's face before, but it still sent a chill straight to his core.

Sutter was dead before his body hit the filth encrusted floor of the Broken Deuce Saloon.

Caleb wished he'd never sat down at the card table. Never witnessed the man's death. Never ridden into Laramie at all.

The reverend's voice droned on. "Thou hast also given me the shield of thy salvation, and thy gentleness hath made me great…"

Caleb recognized the passage. It was from the book of Samuel. His grandfather had spent many nights twisting its words to suit his ends. Caleb gave his head a gentle shake. How many years would need to pass before he could bury those memories?

He closed his eyes and tried to control his breathing, letting the wall take most of his weight. He wasn't sure why he'd come here today. He hadn't been inside a church for so long it was a wonder he hadn't burst into flames the moment he passed through its double oak doors. He didn't know Sutter outside the brief hours before he'd died and hadn't particularly liked what he had known. He didn't know the man's family or the people in this town. He could have ridden in, handed over the body and disappeared into the sunset.

Except he still had business to attend to. And some things a man couldn't walk away from, no matter how much he wanted to.

His attention drifted away from the reverend and rested on the widow. Dressed in black, she wore a small matching hat perched forward on the top of her head. Her hair, a deep mahogany, was twisted into a simple knot at the nape of her neck, but whatever held it in place seemed destined to give in to its weight. Strands had worked their way free and curled down her narrow back.

She stared straight ahead at some point over the reverend's shoulder, away from the pine box containing her husband. Her stoic expression never altered. Caleb tilted his head to one side and studied her, surprised to find her beautiful, though certainly not delicate. Bold, graceful lines and dark, almond-shaped eyes shaded by the short veil of her hat held a man's gaze captive, but it was the wealth of inner strength that radiated from her strict posture and the way she hugged the young boy to her that he thought would endure in the mind long after.

To hear Sutter tell it, his wife didn't possess a single redeeming quality to make a man look twice. Given what a pompous loudmouth the man had been, Caleb should have known his opinion wasn't worth a lick.

She turned, as if sensing his attention. Caleb froze, unprepared for the potency of her dark eyes catching his. For several seconds, he forgot to breathe. Forgot not to stare. Forgot his reasons for being here.

Then, as quickly as her gaze had found him, it slid away. The effect of it, however, lingered like a shadow and he couldn't shake the sense that she hadn't looked at him, but into him. As if in those few brief seconds she had plunged inside the darkest recesses of his heart and taken a good look around.

A shiver crept up his spine and nestled at the base of his neck, making the hair prickle and stand on end.

That's destiny tapping you on the shoulder, his mother used to say.

Caleb shrugged. He was not interested in destiny today. He wanted to take care of business and be on his way. More so now than ever.

"Heard he told her some cockamamie story about goin' to Laramie to buy cattle."

Caleb's ears perked up. The man next to him stood half a head taller than his own six feet but couldn't have weighed enough to matter soaking wet. He'd addressed the man beside him, who stood out of Caleb's sight.

"Geez, Styles. Ain't no way he could afford to be buyin' more cattle in Laramie or anywhere else. 'Course, with Kirkpatrick breathin' down his neck, guess you can't blame the man for trying. Wouldn't have done no good. Kirkpatrick's bought up all of Bobby's gambling debts. Jus' a matter of time before he stops waitin' on gettin' paid back."

Styles shrugged his bony shoulders. "Probably jus' as well he got 'imself shot, then. Save Rachel the trouble when she finds out jus' how much he owes."

Caleb furrowed his brow. It sounded like Sutter had dug a deep hole and was about to drag his whole family down into it with him.

"Ain't that the truth," the other man said. "Still, cain't say I'm surprised much. Bobby always was a gambler. Like my pappy always said, a man is what his past was."

A woman in the pew next to them turned around and shushed the men. Both straightened and mumbled their apologies, but their words resonated through Caleb.

A man is what his past was.

The thought filled him with a deep sense of desolation. If that were true, there was no hope for him.

Rachel sat through the service focusing on what needed to be done rather than the words spoken by Reverend Pearce. If she listened, she would fall apart. Reality would settle in, take root and grow like a weed until it choked out everything else. She had to keep her mind on the future, not on the past or what might have been or all the things she'd done wrong. It couldn't be changed now.

She had to think of the boys. They needed stability, a place to call home, a future to look forward to. Someday, a part of the ranch would be their legacy. Maybe all of it, given that she had no children of her own.

A prickling sensation tickled the hairs at the back of her neck, pulling her away from her ruminations. She turned to her left and scanned the faces of the congregation who had come to pay their respects. Her gaze swept the line of men standing along the wall and settled onto the stranger next to Jeremiah Styles.

He leaned against the wall, and though his manner appeared casual, Rachel sensed a predatory air about him, as if his posture was nothing more than a ruse. His sharp gaze spoke of a man well aware of his surroundings and any threats it might present. Lean and broad shouldered, he maintained an air of readiness, like a mountain cat about to strike. A frisson of unease tangled itself around her.

His gaze bored into hers, steady and unwavering. There was something in those eyes. Something hungry. Desperate. Haunted. It was like looking in a mirror.

Rachel's breath caught and she turned back to

face the front. Closing her eyes, she took a deep breath and forced her heart to slow.

She knew who he was. Strangers were easy to pick out in a town where so few passed through. He was the man who'd brought Robert's body back from Laramie.

He was the one who would tell her the truth about what had happened.

After the ceremony, they convened to the graveyard and lowered Robert's casket into the newly thawed earth. Rachel took a handful of dirt and dropped it into the gaping hole. It fell with a heavy thud onto the coffin. She didn't think she'd ever heard a more lonely sound.

"In sure and certain hope of the resurrection to eternal life through our Lord Jesus Christ, we commend to the Almighty God our brother Robert Charles Sutter, and we commit his body to the ground. Earth to earth…"

Next to her, Ethan gripped her hand and squeezed, pressing his face into her arm.

"…ashes to ashes…"

Rachel's stomach twisted. How had it come to this?

"…dust to dust…"

Eight years ago she had been full of hope. She pulled in her lip and took a deep breath, blinking back tears she refused to let fall. She would not break down. She would not give in.

"…the Lord bless him and keep him, the Lord make his face to shine upon him…"

This was it. It was over.

"...and be gracious unto him and give him peace. Amen."

It was done.

"Amen," the congregation chanted back in subdued tones.

Robert was gone.

And all he'd left behind was questions.

Rachel searched the crowd for the stranger. She needed to understand, needed answers, and he was the only man who could give them to her.

She found him lingering in the shade of the gnarled oak growing in the far corner of the graveyard. He hadn't joined the graveside service, but instead hung back near the road, away from the crowd. His hat, pulled low over his eyes, kept his expression hidden in shadow, but in her mind's eye she could see the clear outline of his chiseled features. The deep-set eyes and windburned cheekbones. The firm set of the mouth against a few days' growth of beard.

He was a handsome man, though not conventionally so. But something about his essence grabbed your attention and held it. This was a man who would be hard to forget, yet she sensed from the way he held back from the others and kept his face half hidden, being forgotten was exactly what he preferred.

Her thoughts were interrupted as the townspeople began filing past her, issuing platitudes and condolences. One by one, Rachel answered with the appropriate, "Thank you....I appreciate it...." And finally, most emphatically, "...no, we'll be fine."

The words had a strange, hypnotic effect, even if she didn't believe them. Standing not too far away on the small crest of the hill, Freedom waited. Rachel sent the boys to her, giving Ethan one last hug before Brody led him away. She watched their retreating backs. What would they do now? The winter had been hard on them, but Robert had promised they had enough funds to replenish their cattle herd at the spring auction in Laramie.

Like a fool she had believed him.

The corner of her eye caught a motion coming toward her. A wall of black wove through the crowd with the determination of the Grim Reaper.

Shamus Kirkpatrick.

Her jaw tightened. Did the man have no compassion?

She could not deal with Shamus, today of all days. No doubt he would come to her dripping of sympathy with all the sincerity of a snake-oil salesman, sizing her up to find her weak spot before going in for the kill.

She had to get away, but panic paralyzed her limbs. The congregation had moved from the grave site to the courtyard in front of the church, leaving her alone.

"Come with me."

The voice was low and husky, and hot breath

tickled her ear. A hand gripped her elbow from behind with firm pressure. The sudden intimacy shocked her, causing her to stumble as she was maneuvered away from Robert's graveside. She glanced up into the chiseled features of the stranger. Up close, the details of his face were even more captivating than from a distance. Tiny lines creased the edges of his eyes, and his full mouth pulled itself into a severe line. There was no give or softness to be found anywhere. He was all harsh angles and rugged maleness. It overpowered her senses, and she let him pull her along without protest.

He led her away from Shamus, down the hill toward the church, his hand solid and firm where it gripped her arm. It had been a long time since a man had touched her. Warmth spread through her and she cursed her body's weakness. So much like her mother.

She gritted her teeth against the thought and found her voice. "Where are you taking me? The boys—"

"Boys are fine," he said, casting a quick glance behind them to where Ethan and Brody stood with Freedom.

So close, his eyes were even more potent, neither brown nor green but a mottled shade of both, and set above a pair of razor-sharp cheekbones burned by the elements. Poking out from beneath his hat, thick brown hair curled up at the ends and whiskers, tinted red where the sunlight touched them, prickled his jaw.

"You're the man who brought Robert home."

"Yes, ma'am."

She waited for more as he directed her around Mrs. Lyngate and her brood of eight children, but the man was silent as a church on Monday morning. She struggled to keep up with his swift gait, gathering her skirts in her free hand.

"Do you mind telling me what my husband was doing in Laramie that got him shot?"

His gaze drifted over her, making her tremble, as if he had reached out and brushed his fingertips against her bare skin. The sensation left her unsettled.

"Maybe that question is best answered at another time. I'll be at the Pagget this evening. Seven o'clock."

Before she could respond, the stranger propelled her into the crowd in the courtyard and the pressure on her arm disappeared, leaving her staring at the broad expanse of his retreating back. Another round of platitudes began. Rachel accepted the condolences, realizing he had left her safely ensconced in the bosom of the mourners where Shamus wouldn't dare accost her.

But Shamus waited, standing near the outskirts of the crowd. His pale blue eyes pierced her. Then he smiled, all arrogance, before turning and leaving. She had avoided him today, but it was a temporary reprieve.

She wasn't as blind as the townspeople believed. She knew all about Robert's gambling debts. Shamus made sure of it. She also knew that, if he decided to call in the markers, she would have no way of paying them back save to sell him her land.

And Shamus Kirkpatrick was not the type of man to let a little thing like Robert's death keep him from taking it.

Caleb sat in the dining room of the Pagget Hotel wishing he had picked another location for his meeting with Mrs. Sutter. He'd chosen it out of convenience, since he was staying there, but the tired-looking décor and even more tired-looking waitress made him rethink his decision. The place had a faded and worn-out feel to it, as though its heyday had come and gone years before.

For himself, he couldn't have cared less. A campfire and can of beans were all he needed, but a lady like Mrs. Sutter deserved nicer surroundings. And given the news he was about to deliver, a comfortable setting was the least he could provide. But it was too late now.

He motioned for the waitress to refill his cup of coffee, hoping this one would taste better than the sludge served earlier. The dark liquid she poured into the chipped mug reeked of tree bark scorched in the fire. He'd seen warmed tar with a more appetizing consistency.

Mrs. Sutter appeared at the threshold separating the small dining room from the main lobby, her hands clasped tightly at her waist. An air of vulnerability lingered around her as she stood on the precipice as if trying to decide whether to continue on or retreat. The urge to protect her against what he needed to do surged up, and he struggled to stuff it down as Mrs. Sutter dropped her hands to her sides, straightened her narrow shoulders and stepped forward.

Caleb stood as she approached his table.

"Evenin', ma'am." He nodded, then remembered his manners at the last minute and rounded the table to pull out her chair. She was already half seated by the time he reached her. Apparently Mrs. Sutter didn't stand on ceremony.

"Thank you for meeting me, Mr.—" She stopped. Confusion marred the clean lines of her face. Again, he was struck by her simple beauty. She shook her head and folded her hands primly in her lap. "I'm sorry. I don't know your name."

He hesitated. He'd had used many over the years. But for some reason he didn't want to lie to her. He didn't delve into why.

"Beckett," he said. "Caleb Beckett."

She smiled, a small, halting expression lost in the dark depths of her eyes. "Mr. Beckett."

The name sounded foreign. Like returning home after years away and finding the landscape had changed shape. Yet, when she said it, her tone and the small hint of a smile made him remember the boy he used to be. For a brief moment, a sense of belonging enveloped him.

He quickly shook it off and returned to his seat across from her. "Would you like something to eat?" A pale cast marred her skin. The shock of the past twenty-four hours had exacted a toll, he suspected, despite her outwardly calm demeanor.

"No. Thank you. I appreciate you taking the time to meet with me." She pursed her lips and two narrow lines formed between her brows. He curled his hand into a fist to keep from reaching over and smoothing them out. She didn't deserve to be put through this worry and distress.

"You're welcome, ma'am." Although he had little choice. They had business to discuss and the sooner he got it done, the sooner he could leave.

Mrs. Sutter let out a slow breath, her shoulders slumping on the exhale. "I am hoping you can give me some answers."

"Answers?" He stared down into his coffee cup and turned the mug around in his hands. This was the part he had dreaded.

"Do you know why my husband was in Laramie? He told me he was purchasing cattle at the auction, but…"

But purchasing cattle didn't get a man shot in the chest and stuffed in a pine box.

Her gaze did not waver; even without looking at her, he could feel it on him. Despite Sutter's unflattering description of his wife, Caleb found her straightforward manner appealing. He found *her* appealing, a fact that disturbed what little peace he had. He chose his words with care.

"Could be he did attend the auction."

"But that's not where you met him." She lifted her chin. "I would prefer if you would be honest with me, Mr. Beckett. Do not feel you need to spare my sensibilities or protect me from the truth. I'm quite capable of handling it, whatever it is."

He didn't doubt it for a second. Rachel Sutter didn't strike him as the type to shirk from the storms life threw her way.

"I met your husband at the Broken Deuce. There's a poker game held there every year during the auction. A lot of money can change hands. Fortunes won or lost at the turn of a card."

"And my husband," she said, her voice dropping to a whisper. "Was he—?"

Caleb nodded. "He played at my table, ma'am."

A muscle in her jaw twitched. "Did he win?"

He could tell from the way she stared down at the table with a hard set to her mouth she already knew the answer. Caleb didn't bother to sugarcoat it for her. He doubted she would appreciate being pandered to on top of everything else.

"No, ma'am."

A bitter laugh shot out of her as her head dropped back. She stared at the ceiling for a moment before letting out a long breath and recapturing his gaze. "No. Of course he didn't." She licked her lips, the motion mesmerizing him for a moment, shooting heat to parts he tried not to think about.

She had plump, full lips. Again he was struck by the contrast between the vision sitting before him and the wife Sutter had described. Had the man been blind as well as stupid?

"I'm sorry, ma'am."

She waved off his apology. "How did he get himself shot?"

Caleb rubbed at a stain on the tablecloth and debated glossing over what had happened. No woman should have to hear the details of this. But she had asked him not to hold back, and he figured he owed her that much. "Your husband got upset when the game turned against him. He accused a man of cheating. I think by then he had lost so much, maybe he figured he had nothing left to lose. He made a move to draw his gun, but…"

He peered across the table at her. She stared at the spot on the tablecloth he had been rubbing with his finger. When he stopped speaking, she filled in what he left unsaid, her voice quiet. Beaten.

"I take it whoever he planned on shooting was a faster draw."

Caleb nodded. "Yes, ma'am."

"Who?"

"Beg pardon?"

"Do you know the name of the man who shot my husband?"

He debated lying. Nothing good could come of this. But, she had asked him for the truth and again, he felt compelled to give it. "A man by the name of Sinjin Drake."

"What happened to him?"

Caleb arched an eyebrow. "Drake?"

"Yes. Did they...did they hang him?" Her bottom lip quivered, the first breach in the stone wall she had built around her emotions. She pulled the errant lip into her mouth catching it with her teeth.

"No. They said the shooting was self-defense."

"Was it?"

Caleb shrugged, wishing she would let it go. It did her no good to hear this. And it did him no good to tell it.

She stood abruptly, the chair scraping against the hardwood floor. Caleb rose to his feet.

"I thank you for your time, Mr. Beckett. For bringing my husband's body home—" her hands fisted together in front of her until he could see the white of her knuckles "—and for telling me the truth."

He said nothing.

"Will you be staying in town long?"

He wasn't sure why she asked. Politeness perhaps. Although she had risen to leave, she now seemed uncertain of where to go or what to do.

"Unlikely."

She gave a curt nod. "Well then...I should—"

"There's another matter I need to speak to you about."

Confusion flitted across her features. "Another matter?" Then it cleared and realization dawned in her eyes. "Oh. Oh, of course. You wish payment for—" She let out a small laugh and pressed her fingertips to her forehead. "How stupid of me."

"No, ma'am. I don't expect payment." He wished she would sit down. She was looking paler by the minute and what he had to tell her was not going to improve matters. "Please." He motioned to the chair.

She waved him off. "If you don't expect payment, then forgive me, but I see nothing else we would have to discuss."

Lord help him, but there was no easy way to do this other than telling her straight out. He reached inside his jacket and pulled out the folded papers. He set them on the table and slid them toward her.

Rachel stared down at the folded papers, her heart pounding. She reached out a tentative hand and picked them up, unfolding them with deliberate slowness. The words swam before her eyes and a strange buzzing rang in her ears. This wasn't happening.

It couldn't be.

"He put your land up as collateral."

Except it was.

"It appears I'm the new owner of the Circle S ranch."

The room swayed and tipped and swerved.

"Ma'am?"

Mr. Beckett sounded far away. She tried to find him, but it was hard to keep her eyes focused. She couldn't catch her breath. Why couldn't she catch her breath? Blackness encroached at the corners of her eyes and her legs turned weightless.

"Ma'am?"

Something scraped loudly across the floor. A blur passed before her eyes before something solid enveloped her.

Then there was nothing.

Chapter Three

Caleb shoved the table out of his way. The coffee cup crashed to the floor, rendering the chip in the rim redundant as pieces scattered across the hardwood. He caught Mrs. Sutter under the arms and hauled her against his chest, but the impact was not enough to revive her.

"Aw, hell."

He scooped her into his arms and headed for the lobby, ignoring the gaping stares of the waitress and the sorry excuse for a chef who lumbered out from the kitchen, a stunned expression on his face and a dripping ladle in his hand.

Caleb took it all in with one sweeping motion, sizing up the situation and ruling both of them out as able to offer assistance. The pimply faced boy behind the front desk, with his wide-eyed expression, didn't fit the bill either.

What was he supposed to do now? It served him right. He had watched her growing paler, noticed the way she wavered. He'd offered her food, such as it was here, and tried to get her to sit down. When she didn't, he should have stopped. She'd been through enough today. His news could have waited. *He* could have waited.

"Sir! Sir!" The boy jumped out from behind the counter and ran up the stairs behind Caleb, slipping in front of him as he reached the first floor landing.

"Out of my way," Caleb snarled. He was in no mood to be polite. This day—heck, this week—had gone from bad, to worse, to downright catastrophic. "You want to make yourself useful go get the doc and send him to my room."

"Your room? Wouldn't…uh…" The boy had yet to clear out of his way and the way he was fidgeting back and forth raked across Caleb's taut nerves.

He bit the words out. "Wouldn't I what?"

The boy's eyes widened and he flattened his back against the wall. "Her room is over there," he said with a jerk of his head pointing in the opposite direction to where Caleb was heading.

"Her room?"

"Y-Yes, sir. Mrs. Sutter and the boys. They're in room 205. T-To your right."

Caleb blinked. He hadn't realized Mrs. Sutter was staying at the same hotel. He wasn't sure why her being here made him uncomfortable. Part of him didn't like the idea of her in such squalid surroundings. The other part…well, the other part didn't like it, was all.

He turned toward room 205. "Open the door," he ordered.

The boy obeyed without argument. "I'll go get the doc," he said, then disappeared, his clumsy footsteps echoing down the hallway.

Caleb walked to the narrow bed in the center of the room and placed Mrs. Sutter in the middle of it, settling her limp body against the horse-hair mattress. He was surprised by how light she was curled in his arms and how reluctant he was to let her go. He sat on the edge of the bed and tapped her cheek with his hand.

"Mrs. Sutter?" Her skin was smooth and soft beneath his calloused palm. "Mrs. Sutter?"

A sudden movement caught the corner of his eye. Caleb spun away from the bed, his hand instinctively reaching for his gun but coming up empty.

The young boy he'd seen in the church stood frozen in place next to a cot pushed against the far wall. Wide gray eyes stared up at Caleb.

When he spoke, the boy's voice barely made it to a whisper. "Is she dead?"

Caleb shook his head, willing his heartbeat to return to normal. "Just a faintin' spell."

To her credit, Mrs. Sutter stirred, adding credence to his words. The boy relaxed, and for the first time Caleb noticed the raggedy toy in his arms. A dirty old rabbit sewn together out of canvas. The kid clung to it as if it were a lifeline.

"She'll be fine," he added. "It's been a rough day, burying your pa and all."

"Mr. Sutter weren't my pa." The boy pulled the rabbit up under his nose and hugged it tighter.

Caleb absorbed the information but couldn't make sense out of it. Maybe the widow had been widowed before Sutter.

Mrs. Sutter stirred again, and the young boy crawled out of the chair and drew closer to the bed. A tentative hand reached out and touched hers, little fingers curling inside her palm. "She doesn't get sick. She said she don't have time for it."

Caleb nodded. Sutter had been dead wrong about his wife. In the few short hours Caleb had known her, she'd proven herself capable of withstanding tragedy and facing ugly truths. This was a woman who knew the harsh realities of life. A sense of reluctant kinship filled him. He knew what it was like to have your life destroyed.

He pulled a rickety chair out from a corner, lowering his aching body into it. It had been a long few days.

"You got a name, son?"

"Ethan."

Caleb nodded and scanned the room. "Where's the other boy?"

Ethan crawled up onto the bed and laid his head down on the pillow next to Mrs. Sutter. It bothered Caleb how motionless she was. He didn't have much experience with fainting, but he found it worrisome she still hadn't woken. He watched her expressionless face. Beneath the black wool dress, the gentle swell of her small breasts rose and fell. Relief made him breathe easier.

A minute had passed since he'd asked his last question. The boy, Ethan, stared at him over the top of the rabbit's head. He tried again.

"Where's your brother?"

"Brody ain't my brother, he's hers." A small finger released its hold on the rabbit and pointed at Mrs. Sutter. Another mystery solved.

"Where is Mrs. Sutter's brother, then?" Caleb knew when someone was evading a question, and this boy was doing a brilliant job of dancing around its edges.

Silence.

"Son?"

The boy's gaze met Caleb's then slid away. Unease itched at the back of Caleb's neck and he rubbed at the spot. He did not want to get involved with these people any more than he already was.

"Ethan, tell me where he is."

"Brody told me not to. He made me promise."

Caleb pursed his lips. If Brody made this kid promise not to give up his whereabouts it was a sure sign he was up to no good. He glanced at Mrs. Sutter. She'd been through enough today without someone else adding to her misery.

He leaned forward and rested his forearms on his knees. "Ethan, if your ma was awake right now—"

"She ain't my ma. My ma's dead."

Caleb hung his head. This was one convoluted family tree. He straightened and took a breath. "If Mrs. Sutter was awake right now, what would she ask you to do?"

Ethan hesitated then scowled. "Tell the truth."

Caleb raised an eyebrow at the boy and waited. After a minute of ruminating, Ethan let out a frustrated huff then lowered the rabbit from his mouth, as if that's what kept the secret in.

"Brody said he was gonna go to the Seahorse Saloon to win some money to pay off Mr. Kirkpatrick."

Caleb cursed under his breath. Great.

The pimply faced boy from the lobby arrived with the doctor. Caleb explained what had happened—well, at least the fainting part. He kept what had led up to it to himself. The deed was no one else's business, at least until he determined what he planned to do about it.

All the way back from the funeral, Caleb had mulled over his prospects, none of which left him satisfied. His original plan of signing it over and walking away had been knocked about good with the insertion of Kirkpatrick. If what he'd heard was correct, signing over the deed to Mrs. Sutter would only result in her losing the property to Kirkpatrick in payment of her dead husband's debts.

He rubbed a hand over his face and took one

last look down at the woman unconscious on the bed. When had this become so complicated?

Caleb left Mrs. Sutter in the doctor's capable hands and slipped out of the room.

It seemed he had to go collect a boy from a saloon.

It was easy enough to find, as the Pagget was at the same end of town. Caleb followed the sound of the tinny piano. There were three saloons in all. The Seahorse had a faded sign hanging from the second-floor balcony. The slight breeze made its hinges creak as it swayed back and forth. Caleb pushed through the swinging doors where the stench of watered-down whiskey, sweat and cheap perfume rose up and assaulted his nostrils. Desperation permeated the sawdust strewn about the floor and soaked into every crack in the wall.

He hated places like this. They brought a man to his lowest then dug the hole a little deeper. The patrons here wouldn't think twice about letting a kid buy his way into a game. Hell, they'd probably encourage it, seeing him as an easy mark.

Brody wasn't hard to find. The room was small, the crowd sparse. One back table had a game going. A few others were occupied by solitary drinkers who looked as though they'd taken root in their seats with no intention of leaving any time soon.

The boy was facing away from the door. Dumb move. A man should never leave himself exposed in such a manner, especially in a place like this.

Fastest way to take one in the back. A motley crew of men flanked the edges of the table. They paid scant attention to him, save for one old-timer who glanced up long enough to down a shot of whiskey before pouring another and returning to the game.

The pot in the center of the table was meager by most standards, but he guessed the high stakes games didn't happen in a place like this. The Seahorse appeared to cater to the dregs, picking up whatever the other two saloons had cast out.

Caleb sauntered up to the table and stood at the boy's shoulder. It didn't take long for the kid to glance up as the game came to a stop.

"You lookin' to git in?" the old-timer asked, his voice thin and reedy. What few teeth he had left were nothing more than tobacco-stained stumps.

Caleb gave his head a slow shake. "Come to take the boy home."

Brody stiffened and threw Caleb a hostile glare before turning back to the cards. "I ain't goin' nowhere. I got me a game here and—"

Caleb's hand came down firm and heavy on the boy's scrawny shoulder. "The game's over."

Showing more balls—or stupidity—than most men, Brody tried to shrug his hand off, but Caleb held firm.

"I don't know you, and I sure as shootin' ain't leavin' here with you, mister."

Caleb applied more pressure, gripping the ill-fitting wool coat with his fingers. Brody flinched beneath his hold. "Your sister is ill and needs you," Caleb said in a low voice.

The boy's stiff posture registered his shock. Caleb didn't hesitate. He hooked his foot around the leg of the chair and pulled it back, hauling Brody to his feet in one swift movement. The boy grabbed what few coins were in front of him. It went against Caleb's instinct to get involved like this, but responsibility for Mrs. Sutter's current predicament weighed on him. He might be a lot of things, but he wasn't the type of man who shrugged off his honor when it became inconvenient. Much as he would have liked to.

"Gentlemen, if you'll excuse us." He tipped his hat to the men sitting down. No one made a move to stop him.

He led Brody through the saloon, pushing him past the swinging doors and dragging him down the steps. Once they hit the street, the boy turned surly again and yanked his arm from Caleb's hold.

"Get your hands off me! I was winning. You had no right!"

"You were losing," Caleb told him. "You think for one second the pair of twos you were holding would stand up against the set of jacks the old timer had ready to play? You think every man at that table wasn't markin' you to take a fall?"

"I knew what I was doing." But the telltale surprise widening his eyes told Caleb different. The bravado was all for show. The kid didn't have a clue he was being played.

Caleb shook his head. "You don't know nothin', kid. You're so wet behind the ears you might as well have just had a bath in the creek. You don't think your sister's got enough to worry about without you gallivanting around acting the fool?"

"We need the money. I'm the man of the family now. It's my responsibility to watch out for us."

"There's better ways to put bread on the table—" Caleb stepped down off the sidewalk, his boots landing in a pile of muck and horse dung. "Aw, crud!"

"It ain't about bread, mister." Brody rounded on Caleb while he stomped the dung from his boot. "Maybe my sister believes Robert was in Laramie buying cattle, but I know better. He went to gamble and he lost. It ain't the first time he's done it, either."

"I'm guessin' it's the first time he got himself shot dead." Caleb stepped around the kid and kept walking, heading across the street. He could feel the rain coming. The moisture sank deep into his bones. He didn't care to be out in it, even if it meant sleeping at the Pagget, a lousy excuse for a hotel. At least the rooms were big enough so that he didn't feel the walls closing in on him. He'd pass the night under a dry roof and worry about everything else tomorrow.

Brody caught up with him. "We owe money. And if we don't pay it we're gonna lose everything. Kirkpatrick bought up Robert's gambling debts and he was pressing him to pay off the markers or sign over our land for payment. Why do you think Robert went to Laramie? Figured he could make a big strike at the tables and come back and save the day. Instead he got himself shot."

"And you think you can walk into some hole of a saloon and make all your problems go away?"

"Ain't none of your business!"

"You got that right." He didn't want to hear anything else about their problems. He had enough of his own. All he wanted was to go back to his room and sleep this day off. Although having to face Widow Sutter again tomorrow to iron out the news he had dropped on her tonight didn't bode well for things improving any time soon.

"And my sister ain't ill. She don't get ill. Says she doesn't—"

"—have the time. So I've heard. But she passed out cold in front of me, so I guess she found a few spare minutes."

Brody stopped, the last of his bravado falling away. "You ain't foolin'?"

"You ever say anything other than *ain't?*" Caleb shot the kid a glare and kept walking. Let him figure it out on his own whether he wanted to follow or not. He'd done his part. He got the kid out of the game before he lost money the family didn't have. He was done with it. He'd deal with the rest tomorrow. Maybe between now and then he'd be hit with some brilliant epiphany showing him a quick way out of this mess that wouldn't stress his conscience.

Brody hurried to keep up. "Is she okay?"

Fear edged the boy's voice, erasing his earlier anger. "Doc came over. I suspect she's fine. Shock and exhaustion, is all."

At least he hoped it was nothing more. It sure would be a terrible thing if she were to find herself in the family way now, with no husband to provide for her. His honor might have dictated that he drag her fool brother out of a saloon, but it didn't extend so far that he'd be taking on the responsibility for a dead man's family by offering up marriage.

He wasn't anybody's idea of a good husband.

He wasn't anybody's idea of a good man.

When they reached the hotel, Brody bolted up the stairs ahead of him and ran down the hall, bursting into Room 205, letting the door slam against the wall. Caleb followed at a slower pace, feeling every last one of his thirty years. The life he'd been living all these years was starting to catch up with him. Sooner or later the time would come when he'd have to stop drifting and start thinking about settling somewhere.

But now was not the time.

And Salvation Falls wasn't the place.

Chapter Four

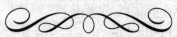

Rachel cracked open her lids. Warm sunlight pierced her eyes and sent a sharp shooting pain straight through her brain. She bit down on her back teeth to keep from cursing. She sensed Ethan hovering nearby.

"Rachel?"

The mattress depressed and his small body crawled onto the bed. She moved her arm and let him nestle into her side.

"I'm all right, sweetheart. Don't fret. It was a bad day, is all." Dr. Bolger had come by and given her the once-over and announced the same thing. She'd decided not to contradict him. She didn't know how many people Caleb Beckett had spoken to since arriving in Salvation Falls, but it only took one person to spread the word. The news that she and her family were homeless and penniless would travel like wildfire.

Then what? Would they expect her to behave as her mother had, bartering herself to make life easier? The idea made bile burn at the back of her throat. It would be a cold day in July before she ever stooped that low, prostituting herself in such a way. And to what end? Her mother's actions had done nothing more than make their situation worse, wrecking her father and destroying their family beyond repair. Were the pretty baubles she'd earned worth that?

Rachel pulled her mind away from the dark memories. She was not her mother. Every decision she made, every action she took was painstakingly made to ensure that.

But what could she do now to improve her perilous situation? Her land, the land her father had left her, belonged to a man she didn't know. Who knew what he would decide to do with it? She'd had no time to ask and he'd given no indication.

The man possessed an enigmatic edge and an even more dangerous touch. Through the haze of last night, the memory of her body pressed against his survived in her memory. The touch of his hand against her face had almost been enough to rouse her from the darkness she'd fallen into.

None of which answered the critical question: What would happen to her family now? The ranch hands—Len, Stump and Everett—could find work on another spread. No doubt Shamus would take them on if Mr. Beckett didn't see fit to. Maybe she could even convince Shamus to hang on to Foster, though he had grown too old to do more than load up the chuck wagon and be a general nuisance.

And Freedom. Well, no doubt she'd pack it in and follow Rachel wherever she went with the boys. Question was, where would they go? She didn't have a cent to call her own without the land. She had no family left to turn to. She owed money all over town, and even if the stores were willing to float her for a little while longer out of respect for her current situation, they wouldn't do it forever. Eventually she'd have to pay the piper.

But how?

There were few ways a woman could make an income in this town and, short of marrying, fewer still were respectable. Her mother had taught her that.

"Can we go home?"

Rachel hugged Ethan tighter and kissed his tawny hair. "Sure, sweetheart. I have some business to take care of first and then we'll go home."

Unless Caleb Beckett had other ideas on the matter.

Rachel looked across the room to the chair where Brody still slept. He'd come rushing into the room a few minutes after she'd come to. She didn't know where he'd been and he hadn't offered up the information. She would deal with him later.

"Where'd the man go?"

Rachel pulled her attention away from Brody's quietly snoring form. "What man?"

"The man that brung you upstairs when you fainted. He was nice. I liked him."

"*Brought* me upstairs," she corrected. "And you like everybody." The poor boy had spent the first four years of his life in a brothel. By the time Rachel took him in, he'd been starved for male influence.

"Is he comin' back?"

"I'm not sure where Mr. Beckett is, Ethan. I expect he's going about his business." Or her business.

Resentment toward her situation and the man who had turned her life upside down boiled in her veins. She pushed it away. She needed to conserve her energy for what was to come.

"He told me you weren't bad sick." Ethan smiled up at her with an innocence she didn't remember possessing at his age. "He was right, too. You're all better now, right?"

She hugged him close. "I'm all better now."

At least for the moment.

"Mr. Beckett? A moment of your time?" On the planked sidewalk outside of his office, Sheriff Donovan stood, hands on his hips. The fact that he used Caleb's name, the one he'd given to Mrs. Sutter, made him wary.

He halted and looked toward the livery at the end of the street. The day was just getting started and the sun had barely had time to creep up from the horizon. What was the sheriff doing up so early? Did he sleep in his office?

"I won't keep you long," the sheriff promised, as if sensing Caleb's hesitation.

Caleb scowled. He didn't know what the sheriff wanted and he didn't like walking into things blind. It made his stomach work itself into knots and raised his guard. But he guessed there was no avoiding the conversation. Donovan struck him as the determined type. Letting out a sigh, he stepped out of the street and up onto the dryer sidewalk. It had rained overnight and the streets had turned to muck.

The sheriff motioned to his office and Caleb followed. Probably better to not have this conversation outside, even though only a few souls had started milling about. Inside, warmth radiated from the potbellied stove, hitting him full force. The sheriff went over to it and stirred at a pot of beans and bacon.

Caleb hadn't eaten since sunrise the day before. With all the commotion of yesterday, he'd simply not had the time to find a decent meal and Mrs. Beckett's fainting kept him from his supper. The scent of the bacon made the knots in his stomach twist tighter. Hunger gnawed at his backbone.

Sheriff Donovan scooped a helping onto his plate. "You hungry?" He didn't sound enamored of the prospect of sharing his breakfast.

Caleb lied and shook his head. He wasn't sure breaking bread with a lawman would start his day off on the right foot, and given the run of bad luck he'd had of late, he didn't want to do anything to keep the string going.

The sheriff appeared relieved. He walked back to his scarred oak desk and dropped down into the chair behind it, motioning for Caleb to take an empty seat in front. Then he reached inside his desk drawer and produced a basket covered with a checkered napkin. Beneath it, the comforting smell of freshly baked biscuits rose up and assaulted Caleb's senses.

Donovan shrugged. "Minnie from the bakery brings these over every mornin', but if I leave them out my deputy makes short work of them. You sure you don't want one?"

Caleb shook his head, clenching his back teeth. He wondered what the penalty was for knocking a sheriff out cold and stealing his meal. "You want something in particular?"

Donovan tucked the cloth napkin into his collar and glanced across the desk. "Got your name off the hotel register," he said, explaining how he knew Caleb's name. "Signed it yourself, so I take it you can read and write?"

"You takin' a survey?"

The sheriff shrugged and spoke around a mouthful of beans. "I find it a bit curious, is all. Not many drifters can."

"What makes you so sure I'm a drifter?"

Donovan glanced up from plate. "Got that look about you."

"That a fact?" Caleb couldn't fault the sheriff for his powers of observation, though they hardly told the whole story. But looking at the surface of a man rarely did. Most of what he was lived deeper than that, hiding out in the places people couldn't see.

"I believe so. But given you can read and write, I'm guessin' there's more to you than meets the eye."

"Glad to have satisfied your curiosity." Caleb's grandfather had made sure he could read and write. He wanted his grandson to be able to recite verbatim every passage in the Bible pertaining to sin and damnation. All these years later, and Caleb was still trying to scour the words from his mind. He pushed his chair back. "If that's all...?"

The sheriff held out a hand and motioned for him to stay put. "Not quite. You'll forgive me, Mr. Beckett, but it isn't every day we get a stranger riding into town with a body in the back of his buckboard. Rachel's important to us. We want to make sure there's nothing we need to worry about."

We. As if the town as a collective had decided to take her under their wing, and he as the outsider was considered a threat. But where were these people when Sutter was gambling his family out of house and home? Where were they when Kirkpatrick started pressuring Sutter in the hopes of getting his land?

The threat to Rachel didn't come from an outsider like him, it came from the inside.

"Do we need to worry?" the sheriff asked outright.

Caleb gave his head a slow shake, his eyes never leaving the sheriff, who returned the silent perusal, his beans and bacon forgotten.

"Then I expect you're on your way out of town, Mr. Beckett?"

"Currently I'm on my way to the end of the street. Beyond that, I can't say it's anyone's business but my own where I go or when I get there."

The hard look on the sheriff's face indicated he was not satisfied with the answer, but the man's satisfaction, or lack thereof, was the least of Caleb's concerns this morning.

"What were you doing in Laramie, Mr. Beckett?"

Caution invaded Caleb's veins.

"Just passing through," he said, searching the sheriff's face for clues as to what the man was fishing for.

"How'd it be you came to bring Robert's body home?"

"I was there when he was killed." He kept his tone even, gave nothing more away.

"Who killed him?"

"Man by the name of Sinjin Drake."

Something in the lawman's face altered. "Sinjin Drake?"

"You know him?"

"By reputation only. Not a lawman north of Tucson who doesn't, I expect. Man's said to be one of the fastest draws in the west with a body count to prove it."

"That so?"

"Did you meet the man?"

"We sat at the same table. Can't say we shared much conversation."

"Did they arrest him?"

"Drake? No. The law said it was self-defense. Sutter went for his gun."

The sheriff's gaze sharpened. "His guns weren't on the body."

"I said he went for his guns. I didn't say he was wearing them at the time."

Shock registered on Sheriff Donovan's face. "What do you mean he wasn't wearing them?"

"A man needed at least fifty dollars to sit at the table. Word was Sutter sold everything but the clothes on his back to raise the capital."

"And Drake shot him anyway?"

Caleb didn't answer. He didn't need to. Robert Sutter had come home in the back of a wagon with a hole through his heart. That was all the confirmation needed as far as he was concerned.

"We done here?"

"For now."

Caleb headed for the door but the sheriff's voice stopped him cold.

"You won't mind if I wire out to Laramie and verify your story?"

Every fiber in Caleb's body stilled. He glanced at the sheriff out of the corner of his eye. "Don't matter none to me."

Chances were he'd be nothing more than a fading memory in the minds of Salvation Falls residents by the time the sheriff got news back from Laramie. And that suited him just fine.

After Rachel managed to get the boys fed and Freedom tracked down, she arranged to send them back home in the wagon. She'd get back on her own after she conducted her business with Mr. Beckett and figured out where things stood. She would need the time to formulate a plan, determine what to do.

Did the man plan on kicking them off their land—his land, now? A sick sense of displacement filled her, followed by burning frustration. Her entire world had been pulled out from under her and there wasn't a thing she could do about it.

Rachel took a deep breath and smoothed a hand over her skirt. She still wore her widow's weeds, but she didn't plan on making it a habit. She didn't have time to dye her meager wardrobe black to mourn a man who didn't deserve her tears.

She made her way down Main Street. When she'd inquired about Mr. Beckett this morning, Cletus at the front desk told her he'd left for the livery thirty minutes earlier. She picked up her skirts and hurried her steps. The last thing she needed was him showing up at the ranch ahead of her, announcing his ownership before she had a chance to explain it to her family herself.

She needed to talk to him, to settle this thing. She couldn't live in a sickening limbo land wondering what would happen. She had to keeping moving. If she stopped…

Well, if she stopped everything would catch up with her and she'd end up passing out again from the weight of it all.

Her skin burned anew with the humiliation of succumbing to such weakness, a luxury she could not afford. Muriel, the waitress who'd brought her breakfast, had told her Mr. Beckett moved with lightning speed, shoving the table out of the way to get to her before she hit the floor.

The woman all but swooned retelling the story, as if it were some romantic tale from a dime novel and not the most embarrassing thing to happen to Rachel since…well, since she didn't know when. Last night's debacle left her mortified. One minute she was standing to leave and the next…

The next she was swooped up in a pair of strong arms.

The memory came unbidden. She tried to remember specifics, but the entire episode was hazy, save for the sensations his touch had conjured. The strong arms carrying her, the solid chest where she'd rested her head. The rapid beat of his heart as he rushed her upstairs. And the gentle way he had laid her upon the mattress, his palm touching her cheek. She'd tried to answer him when he called her name, but she'd been too weak to respond.

She shook her head. No doubt her state of mind tainted the truth. She sincerely doubted a man like Caleb Beckett could be considered a romantic hero in any way, shape or form. He had the edge of an outlaw rather than a shining knight.

Not that Rachel believed in shining knights. She had disabused herself of their existence a long time ago.

Taking a deep breath, she straightened her shoulders and marched into the livery.

She stopped inside the door, letting her eyes adjust to the dim light. The scent of hay, horses and manure mingled in the air around her, but she had spent too much time in her own barn to pay it much heed.

She found Mr. Beckett brushing long strokes down his horse's back in one of the stalls. The horse, a beautiful paint, nipped playfully at the brim of his hat. He chuckled and spoke in low tones. She couldn't make out the words, but the sound surprised her, drew her in. She stood silently for a moment and watched. He'd removed his sheepskin jacket and tossed it over the edge of the stall door. His broad back shifted with each stroke of the brush, mesmerizing her. There was a fluidity to his movements, and while one hand brushed in a rhythmic pattern, the other rested on the animal's neck, petting it. The horse nickered in response to the sound of its owner's voice.

The unguarded moment surprised her. She had expected to arrive to find him glaring down at her, arms crossed, impatience stamped into every ruggedly handsome feature while he counted the hours before he could toss them off the ranch. This hint of good humor threw her.

Then again, who wouldn't be in good humor after the boon of winning a prime piece of land through no more effort than the turn of a card?

The muscles in her neck tightened.

"You gonna stand there all day?"

She jumped. "I…I…how did you know I was here?"

He peered over his shoulder. Whiskers shadowed his square jaw. The brim of his hat hid his eyes, and still she could feel the force of his gaze through every inch of her body. There was something about this man. Something beyond the rugged face and strong body. He had a presence, commanding and vibrant. No doubt she could have walked into a room blindfolded and known instantly if he occupied the same space. The awareness irritated her.

"I could sense you there."

Rachel swallowed. A shivery tremor swept through her veins as his answer echoed her own thoughts.

She fought to get her voice out without trembling. "I wanted to talk to you. About last night."

"Figured." He rested an arm on the short stable wall and stared at her. Hot liquid poured through her veins from the strength of his full attention.

She gripped her hands in front of her and forced her spine straight, ignoring the strain on her muscles. He was not going to make this easy. "I guess I owe you some thanks for catching me when I—" She couldn't say the word, couldn't admit to the weakness.

"Fainted?"

She squinted into the dimness. Was he smiling? His mouth quickly resettled into an unreadable line and she wondered if it had just been a trick of the light.

"Yes, I suppose. Thank you."

"Not necessary."

"Well…either way." She shifted on her feet. "I think we need to speak about the deed to my land. Am I to understand you now believe you own it?"

He didn't answer right away. He made one last stroke down the paint's neck and walked out the back, rounding the stalls and coming up behind her. She spun on her heel to face him, surprised to find him so close. Her body's response to his nearness hit her square in the stomach and she took a quick step back.

There was a hard-bitten practicality about the man. It showed in the efficiency of his movements and the economy of words he used to convey an opinion. But his eyes held something different, something softer that gave him a sense of humanity. She wondered what his story was. Had he always been this way? Or, like her, had life hammered away until the person he became was far different than the one he had started out as? Perhaps she could talk reason with him, convince him to—

"No believing about it," he said. "Your husband put the deed in to meet the raised stakes. I won the hand."

So much for reason.

"A-And that's legal?" Could she contest it? There had to be a law to prevent people from doing something as colossally idiotic as throwing away every last acre they owned on a stupid card game!

"Yes, ma'am. It's legal."

And, even if it wasn't, by the time the circuit court judge made his way to town for her to plead her case, Mr. Beckett could have parceled off sections of land, sold them to the highest bidder and been long gone.

Her heart sank into her worn leather boots, taking her hopes with it. She stared at Mr. Beckett's chest, absorbing what he told her. The tiny red checks on his shirt had faded until the color barely existed and one buttonhole was empty, the frayed remains of thread poking through the hole.

Caleb Beckett owned her land. She had lost everything. The room swayed around her.

"No, you don't." He reached out and closed the

gap between them, placing a hand on either elbow to hold her steady. "None of that, now."

His voice reached deep inside of her. She closed her eyes, fighting the uncomfortable ache his touch created and allowed herself one brief moment of respite where someone else took the burden and she did nothing more than hang on.

She opened her eyes and stared at his chest again. "You're missing a button," she whispered.

"Beg pardon?"

"On your shirt. You're missing a button." This was what she noticed. Her entire world was collapsing around her and all she could think about was how his shirt was missing a button. She must be losing her mind.

He let go of one arm and reached for the front of his shirt, pulling it out far enough to see the damage. His forearm brushed against her breast and her body tightened involuntarily. He didn't apologize. The touch was so brief and light perhaps he hadn't even noticed. But she had. An unexpected jolt shot from her breasts to the tips of her toes, hitting every place in between.

"Guess I'm not much of a seamstress."

She nodded and pulled away, walking farther into the livery to put space between them. It was hard to breathe when he stood close. She almost preferred passing out over the strange commotion his nearness created. It made no sense. She didn't know this man, this stranger, yet she responded to him like a common harlot.

Like her mother.

She threw off the thought and held her ground. She could not afford to weaken. "If it isn't too much to trouble you with, Mr. Beckett, perhaps you could tell me just what it is you plan to do now that you own my land."

Caleb mulled the question over in his mind, trying to clear the storm that touching her had stirred. His shoulder still held the phantom imprint of where her head had rested the night before when he'd carried her to her room. His arms still bore her weight.

What *were* his plans?

All night he'd lain awake wrestling with the question. It had seemed cut-and-dried as he rode out of Laramie toward Salvation Falls. He would sign the deed back to Sutter's family and leave. As much as having a place to call home appealed to him, he knew that kind of life was not meant for him. He had learned his lesson on that account the hard way.

But watching Mrs. Sutter hold herself together while her life fell apart, threw him off balance, a sensation he didn't much care for. Sutter had left his family in a bad way financially, then gone and got shot before he could make reparation. But it was obvious his wife had carried the burden of his ineptitude for far longer than the few days Sutter had been dead, and it had worn her down until she teetered on a sharp edge.

The easy thing would be to give her back the land as planned. Easy, but wrong.

From everything he'd learned so far, that would accomplish nothing more than throwing her from the pan to land in the fire. This Shamus Kirkpatrick had a bead on her land and the means to demand it as payment for debts owed. From the glimpse Caleb had of the man at the funeral, Kirkpatrick didn't strike him as the type who would back off when his quarry was in a weakened state.

If Caleb signed the deed over to her, he would be leaving her at Kirkpatrick's mercy.

It made him wish he'd handed the deed over to the sheriff upon his arrival in town and kept on riding. Then, he wouldn't know the particulars and wouldn't be bogged down by this unwanted sense of responsibility.

But nothing about this godforsaken situation was straightforward. He was halfway up the creek and his paddle was still sitting on the shore. If he was smart, he'd jump out and swim to it. But like a fool, he was letting the current take him farther upstream.

"Guess maybe I'd like to see the ranch."

Tension tightened her rose-tinted lips and robbed her cheeks of color. Her dark eyes grew starker in contrast. "Yes…of course."

"We could ride out this morning. If you feel up to it," he added. Last thing he needed was her fainting again, tumbling to the hard ground and injuring herself. He didn't need to add anything more to his already full conscience.

"I will require transportation. I sent Freedom and the boys on ahead with the wagon."

"I have mine. We can take that. I can pick you up at the hotel in an hour."

She nodded absently, wandering over to the stall. Jasper greeted her with a bob of his head before nestling his muzzle into her outstretched hand.

"It's a beautiful horse." She stroked the bridge of his nose. Jasper nickered in response, arching his neck. The horse was a world-class Romeo. Next thing, he'd be rolling over in his stall and expecting her to scratch his belly.

"I won him in a card game," Caleb said, without thinking.

She stopped mid-stroke. "Of course you did."

Her hand dropped away and she stepped away from Jasper. The horse glared in Caleb's direction, holding him responsible. He couldn't fault the horse, he supposed. Mrs. Sutter was a beautiful woman, a strange mix of resilience and vulnerability that made a man want to—

He stopped the thought there. He would not be falling into that trap again. Marianne had taught him where that kind of thinking got a man. His business with Mrs. Sutter was just that—business. He'd do well to keep that in mind and not let himself waver while he figured a way to get them both out of this mess.

"I will be ready to leave in an hour," she said, brushing past him without a second glance.

Caleb closed his eyes, his resolve shaken by the sweet scent of violets left drifting in the air after she passed.

What had he gotten himself into?

Chapter Five

Caleb had never been to this part of the country before, and as they rode out of town toward the mountain range rising against the sky, he was staggered by the beauty that surrounded him. Tree-lined horizons with purple peaks stretched heavenward, while endless meadows of determined wild flowers poked their heads out of the raw earth anxious to erupt into full bloom.

They followed a winding creek, the sound of the gurgling water a balm to his battered soul. For a few blissful seconds Caleb closed his eyes and allowed himself to breathe deeply, taking in the fresh air and the feel of wide open spaces and peace.

A man could die happy here.

Why Sutter, who'd had everything a man could ask for, had gambled it all away baffled Caleb. A man like that didn't deserve a good woman like the one sitting next to him. Then again, neither did Caleb.

Man is born to trouble. And you most of all.

Caleb opened his eyes, his grandfather's words lingering in the air around him. It galled him to admit the old man had been right.

As much as the land called to him, staying would lead to problems he couldn't fix. He might hold the title to the Circle S ranch, but it didn't belong to him.

It'd be best all round if he got himself gone.

Out of the corner of his eye he caught Mrs. Sutter looking at him. He gritted his teeth. He'd let his guard drop.

She watched him as if she were searching for something in particular. Caleb resurrected his defenses. There was nothing there she needed to see, nothing that would give her any ease.

Mrs. Sutter turned her attention back to the rutted road and pointed to her right when they reached a divide. "This way."

He steered the buckboard, shifting the reins in his hands. He tilted his head in the direction they hadn't taken. "Where's that lead?"

"Shamus Kirkpatrick's land."

Kirkpatrick. He guessed the man would be in for a bit of a shock when he realized his plans for getting the land had been undercut. Caleb considered the outstanding debt owed Kirkpatrick by the widow. Likely he could pay it if she'd let him. He'd accumulated a fair bit of savings between winnings in card games and odd jobs as he traveled from town to town. With no home of his own and no one to spend it on, he'd socked money away and let it grow. He may as well put it to good use. Maybe the good turn would help atone for past sins, balance the ledger slightly.

"I understand Kirkpatrick was pressing you to sell him your land to pay off debts," Caleb said, venturing into territory the firm set of her mouth told him she didn't want to tread. The scowl did nothing to detract from her beauty.

"Where did you hear that?"

Caleb shrugged and adjusted the reins in his hand. "People talk."

"Does no one in this town know how to mind their own business?"

"Might be they're concerned."

"*Could be* they need to pay more attention to their own affairs and less to mine." Her voice turned hard, but underneath he recognized a current of shame. She had a lot of pride, likely it was the only thing keeping her going right now.

"Planned how you're gonna pay that?"

She turned to face him, her dark eyes smoldering with unspent anger. "My only source of income was my land, Mr. Beckett. Without it I'm left with nothing and no means to pay anyone anything."

"Will Kirkpatrick forgive the debts?"

The muscle near her jaw twitched. "Shamus is not a man to relinquish what he's owed."

Shamus. Her use of his given name made Caleb

wonder how close their relationship was. "Then he'll want his money."

"He'll want something," she whispered, her composure slipping enough to reveal what that something would be.

A cold, animalistic anger clenched its sharp claws around Caleb's chest. Would Kirkpatrick expect her to pay off her debt with her body? The very thought rankled him in a way he couldn't shake. She deserved better than that.

"I could pay the debt—"

"You've done quite enough already, thank you. I don't want or need your charity."

The unspoken truth hung heavy in the air. She may not want it, but they both knew she needed it.

"Do you have family?"

"Just the boys. Robert's parents passed away several years back."

"And your own people?"

Her features tightened. "Dead as well."

Just his luck. Rachel Sutter had no one to turn to.

Save for him.

The weight of obligation settled on his shoulders like a yoke.

They rode in silence. Caleb tried not to think about the woman sitting beside him or how things were about to change for the both of them, whether they liked it or not, thanks to one man's greed and desperation. There had been no reason for Sutter to put his ranch up that day, but the fool wouldn't listen to reason. Now, here they were, trying to sort through the consequences. The buckboard crested a hill and in the distance he could see a small home. So small Caleb wondered how everyone fit inside. It must have made for some cramped quarters.

Over to his right, a short distance away, were a few more outbuildings placed in what could only be described as a haphazard manner that made little sense. It was as if no forethought was put into where things should go. He noted a barn, two tiny cabins, one close to the house, the other closer to the barn, and a larger cabin further up the rise. As they drew closer, he picked out a chicken coop, a corral and a freshly tilled garden. Closer to the house, a gnarled oak crept upward toward the midday sky, the first hint of buds dotting its branches. Come summer, with the leaves in full bloom, it would cast a welcome shade across the narrow porch lining the front of the house.

Despite the odd configuration of buildings, it was a pretty spot. Homey.

He didn't belong here.

Next to him, Mrs. Sutter stiffened, the movement bringing her leg against his. A shock of sensation shot through him. He bit down on the sudden rush of unwanted desire. He should have taken care of that in Laramie, but Caleb had never developed a taste for whores. And he hadn't the time to find himself a lonely widow.

Until now.

But this widow was strictly off limits.

"Company?" He nudged his chin in the direction of the black horse tethered next to the porch. Something told him his day was about to become even more complicated.

Mrs. Sutter spoke through gritted teeth. "Shamus Kirkpatrick."

It said a lot about the man that he had the audacity to show up the day after she'd buried her husband.

"I could ask him to leave if you—"

She cut him off, a frantic edge to her voice. "Don't say anything about the deed. Please. The boys don't know yet, and I need time to figure out how to tell them. I know this isn't any of your concern but..." She sent him a pleading look. "Please."

He stared at her a moment, an unwanted need to protect her welling inside of him. He knew he would regret getting involved, but he couldn't tell her no. Not when she was looking at him with those soulful dark eyes and one of her hands rested on his arm, a fact he was pretty sure she was completely unaware of.

"Reckon I could do that."

Mrs. Sutter glanced down at her hand and snatched it back, curling the fingers into her palm and resting it against her belly, holding it in place as if she were afraid it might reach out voluntarily and touch him again.

"Thank you."

Caleb nodded and pulled up on the reins, irritated with his reaction. The absence of her touch was far too noticeable. When they reached the house, he set the brake and jumped down from the buckboard, patting Jasper's rump as he passed behind him. He'd kept Jasper tied to the back of the wagon for the ride up, letting the draft horse he'd purchased in Laramie do the work of pulling them. By the time he reached Mrs. Sutter, she was about to jump down. He reached up and grabbed her around the waist, lifting her to the ground.

"I don't need—" She didn't have time to finish her reprimand before her feet hit the ground.

"Nothin' wrong with a man helpin' a lady down."

She glared at him. It disturbed him how much he enjoyed it. So much so, he let his hands linger at the curve of her narrow waist. Once again he was struck by how small she was. One stiff mountain wind and she'd all but blow away. Yet he had no doubt her deeply rooted resilience would beat back the wind until it regretted ever making the attempt.

Her hands curled into fists on his shoulders. Mere inches separated their bodies, and God help him but he liked the feel of her in his hands. He watched her swallow, avoiding his gaze.

"You can take your horse down to the barn and stable him there."

"Think I'll come inside first."

Her hands pushed at his shoulders and she

slipped out of his grip, stumbling slightly before catching herself.

"That isn't necessary."

"I think it is." He wasn't about to let her face Kirkpatrick alone. The man would be less inclined to browbeat her for the money if Caleb was there, and if Kirkpatrick tried, Caleb would put a stop to it. His hand brushed his hip. He wondered how long it would be before he got used to not finding his Colt strapped there.

She inched away from him and started toward the porch, keeping her voice low. "I appreciate your silence on the matter of the deed until I figure things out, but my business with Kirkpatrick doesn't concern you."

Caleb shrugged and caught up with her on the step. "My house. My concern."

"Mr. Beckett—" But whatever admonishment she meant to deliver was lost as he opened the door and motioned her inside with a sweep of his hand. She shot him a glare as she marched past.

He walked in behind her and turned his back away from the door. The house had a strange unfinished feel to it, as if whoever built it had given up partway through. The front room served as kitchen, dining room and sitting area with little room left over to maneuver. It held a cookstove, a kitchen table large enough to sit eight and a narrow cot that rested against the far wall. A door next to the cookstove exposed a narrow hallway he assumed led to a bedroom. The whole setup gave the house a cramped feel and he itched to set it right.

The large black woman he'd seen at Sutter's funeral stood, arms crossed, near the counter, her expression angry and apologetic all at once.

Kirkpatrick set his coffee cup down with slow deliberation and rose from his seat to greet them, as if it were his kitchen they had walked into. Tall and broad, dressed all in black, he made an imposing figure. Caleb guessed him to be closing in on fifty, given the lines around his eyes and the threads of gray marring his coal-black hair. Though his smile was congenial, his eyes held the cold flatness of a snake's.

Kirkpatrick ignored him, addressing Mrs. Sutter. "Rachel."

Caleb didn't much care for the familiarity the two shared. Instinct told him their relationship went beyond just being neighbors, and the notion disturbed him for reasons he chose not to explore too closely.

Mrs. Sutter acknowledged Kirkpatrick with a short nod before conducting the introductions. "This is Shamus Kirkpatrick. Mr. Beckett is the one who brought Robert home."

Kirkpatrick nodded in his direction. "Much obliged," he said, as if Caleb had done him a favor, then turned back to Mrs. Sutter. "We should talk."

"The woman just buried her husband, Mr.

Kirkpatrick. I'm sure whatever business you have can wait a few days."

Mrs. Sutter's back went rigid. He guessed the widow wasn't used to having someone speak up on her behalf.

Kirkpatrick's pale eyes met his gaze. "Won't take but a minute."

"It can wait," Caleb repeated, more firmly this time. He would deal with her umbrage later.

Kirkpatrick fell silent and tension smothered the air in the room. He turned to Mrs. Sutter and smiled. The gesture held no warmth. "Got yourself a new protector, do you now, Rachel? You certainly wasted no time. But, then again, neither did your mama."

Her swift intake of breath, as if the words had inflicted a deep wound, were all Caleb needed to end the conversation.

"You'll be leaving now." He walked in front of Mrs. Sutter to get to the door, blocking her from Kirkpatrick with his body. He didn't know what that reference to her mother had meant, but he wasn't about to stand around and let the man land another verbal strike. With one swift shove the door flew open. "I'll see you out."

He followed Kirkpatrick, leaning his hip against the porch railing to ensure the man had no intention of lingering. Kirkpatrick untied his horse from the hitching post and swung up into the saddle, settling himself before looking down at Caleb. "You'd best not get yourself involved in this, Beckett."

Caleb raised an eyebrow at the threat.

"I guess I'll be the judge of what I should and shouldn't get myself involved in." Not that he had much of a choice. Like it or not, he *was* involved.

He'd grown careless. Ignored his instincts that Mrs. Sutter was a danger he would do better to avoid. But his reaction to her had hit him unaware and now, in the span of a day, he had become entangled in her life.

Worst of all, he could not become quickly untangled without leaving her and her family at the mercy of this villain.

And that, he realized, watching Kirkpatrick ride off in the direction of his own land, was something he could not do.

Rachel dropped hard into the chair vacated by Kirkpatrick, her head collapsing into her hands. Part of her hated the way Caleb Beckett had stepped in and taken over. Another part of her was secretly relieved. Shamus's barb about her mother had turned her tongue to lead. Usually his references to her mother were veiled, subversive, and made when only the two of them could hear, his little way of letting her know he had not forgotten. Today he had brought their secret into the open, with a stranger standing in the room. Humiliation had raced through her veins and stolen her voice.

"We're in trouble, Free," she whispered into the still silence of the room.

"'Cause of the debt?"

Rachel pushed herself to her feet and walked to the door, looking through the screen. Mr. Beckett was halfway to the barn with the buggy, but she didn't expect he'd linger there for long. He still hadn't told her his intentions and not knowing made a restless nest of eels roil in her belly. She placed a hand against it, hoping they would settle, but it did no good.

"He owns the land."

She heard Freedom approach her. The older woman's arms wrapped around her protectively. "Kirkpatrick don't own anything, baby girl. We'll figure a way out of this. You been tendin' this land since you was Brody's age, and ain't no one goin' to take that from you."

Rachel shook her head, the reality of her situation pounding into her with each heartbeat. "Someone already has. Robert put our land up for collateral in a card game. He lost it to another man."

Freedom's head turned, following Rachel's gaze toward the barn.

"Mr. Beckett?"

Rachel nodded.

"Oh, baby girl. What we gonna do now?" Freedom's arms tightened around her, and Rachel was glad for their support.

"I don't know, Free. Like you said, we'll figure out something." But what that something was, she couldn't say. She was plum out of ideas. "I guess I best go talk to Mr. Beckett and try to figure this mess out."

Rachel extricated herself from Freedom's motherly embrace to head in the direction of the barn and an uncertain future.

Chapter Six

Rachel found Mr. Beckett in the barn pulling his saddlebags off the wall of the stall where he'd settled the paint he called Jasper. The draft horse was in the next stall over, munching on oats. Mr. Beckett slung the saddlebags over his shoulder and glanced at her when she walked in. At least this time she didn't embarrass herself by dawdling in the doorway watching him like a love-struck schoolgirl. Still, the effect of his presence had not diminished. If anything, it grew each time she saw him. The man had the annoying ability to muddle her thinking, and she didn't like it one bit. Right now, she needed all her wits about her.

"You come all the way down here to scold me for kickin' that mudsill out of your house?"

Rachel was certain she detected a sparkle in his eye, but it must have been her overtired mind imagining things. Mr. Beckett did not strike her as the sparkling type. She pursed her lips and took in a deep breath, letting it out slowly in the hope it would lessen the sway the low cadence of his voice had over her. It did little good. She cursed her body's weakness, wrestling with the fear Kirkpatrick was right—she was just like her mama.

"I came here to determine what your intentions are."

"My intentions?" One eyebrow arched and disappeared beneath the low brim of his hat.

Rachel lifted her chin, determined to keep a businesslike manner. "Mr. Beckett, you own my land. I have the boys, Freedom, my hands, and they all need considering. I need to make arrangements as to where they are going to go and how they are going to live. If it doesn't tax you overly much, perhaps you could let me know how much time I have to accomplish that before you send us packing."

"And yourself?"

"I beg your pardon?"

Mr. Beckett let his saddlebags slide down his arm to the floor. She wondered what kind of life a man led where he could contain all his worldly possessions within the confines of two saddlebags and a bedroll strapped to the back of his horse.

"You've listed everyone under the sun and how you have to make arrangements for them. Where do you fit on that inventory of bodies?"

He shifted his weight and leaned against Jasper's stall, looping an arm over the low wall and crossing his feet at the ankles. His lean form was relaxed, yet she couldn't shake the impression that it could change in a heartbeat.

"Well...I..." Her gaze searched the corners of the barn as if the correct answer was hidden amongst the bales of hay and bridles. She didn't have time to think of herself, she had a family and they came first. "What does it matter to you?"

He shrugged, his steady gaze unnerving her. "Suppose it doesn't."

"Then perhaps you could answer my original question with respect to your intentions."

"I have no intention of running you or your family off your land."

"It isn't *my* land anymore, Mr. Beckett." The words caught in her throat. She swallowed, determined not to break down in front of this man. Fainting was bad enough, but to cry? She wouldn't have it.

"Caleb," he said. "Since it appears we're going to be spending plenty of time with each other for the current duration, I see no point standin' on ceremony."

She bristled at the notion. It made her nervous. Already the short time she'd spent in his company had left her twisted in knots that had nothing to do with losing her land. The more distance she could keep between them, the better. But that would be hard to do if he planned on settling in for a while.

"I think for the sense of propriety it would be

best if we kept our relationship more…formal. And how much time will you give us?"

"And I'll call you Rachel," he said, as if she hadn't spoken. "Propriety don't mean a hill of beans when there's no one around to judge how proper you're being."

"Mr. Beckett—"

"Caleb."

She gritted her teeth. The man was as irritating as he was handsome. It was a shame one didn't cancel out the other.

"Unless you're worried callin' me by my given name might make you like your mama. Is that it?"

Rachel sucked in a mouthful of air but still couldn't breathe. Mr. Beckett's suggestion rendered her lungs useless. "What do you know about my mama?"

Had someone in town said something? Rachel had hoped the rumors about her mother's behavior would have died long ago when they buried her. Rachel had done everything within her ability to live a proper and respectable life, to erase the tarnish her mother's actions had put on their family. Living with a gambler and cheat did little to aid her, but it did not stop her from trying. Had the attempt been wasted effort?

"Don't know more than what Kirkpatrick said to you, but it seemed to hit a nerve so I'm putting two and two together."

Relief swept through her. She glared at him, resenting the ease with which he leaned there, not a care in the world. And why would he care? He wasn't the one who had lost everything. Everything she had lost, he had gained.

"I would appreciate it if you would stop trying to add up things you don't understand. All I want to know from you, *Mr. Beckett,* is what your long-range plans are."

He smiled at her emphasis on his name and she was struck by the sudden transformation in his features. Years peeled away, and for a brief instant, she had a hint of the young boy he might have been. But as quickly as it appeared, the smile vanished, and the enigmatic stranger returned.

"I don't make long-range plans, *Rachel.*" Her name slid over her, awakening areas that had long been dormant. He pushed away from the wall and stalked toward her. Each step swallowed the space between them, drawing him closer until she had to fight the urge to run away, to find one of those dark corners she'd searched out earlier and hide in its shadows.

He stopped a few feet from her, and when he spoke next, she had to struggle to hear him over the rapid beat of her heart. What was wrong with her?

"For the short term, I can tell you I have no intentions of sending your family packing. If your husband had lived, I would have fixed this somehow."

Rachel forced her legs to move, a feat that took more will than she wished. She walked to the open barn doors and stared unseeing into the yard beyond. She needed distance. She couldn't think with him up close. He was like a strange poison that flooded her bloodstream and invaded her mind.

It was ridiculous, this unwarranted response to him. She didn't know this man from Adam. He had barged into her life, a stranger she knew nothing about, bringing the worst news possible, and yet...yet he was the only lifeline she had.

Wasn't that just her luck?

She heard his footsteps growing closer. She spoke to ward him off, in the hope her words would stop him in his tracks. "Fixed it how? Were you going to give it all back? Do you expect me to believe you would hand over a prize piece of land out of some misplaced sense of honor?"

"Honor is never misplaced."

She whirled on him, anger fueling her movements. "I wouldn't know. I've seen so little of it."

He sank his hands into the front pockets of his faded wool pants and stared at her for a long time. "So I gathered."

Rachel crossed her arms over her chest and dropped her gaze to the floor. The way he looked at her, through her, made her feel naked. Exposed. She wanted to wrap herself in a safe cocoon far away from his probing eyes, before he realized how deep her fear went, how unsure she was that she could save her family this time.

"Look," he continued, his broad shoulders relaxing slightly. "I didn't plan on this either. When I sat down to that game in Laramie, I didn't want to do anything more than pass the evening playing a round of poker. I didn't expect to walk away a landowner. Settling down isn't something I cotton to. If your husband hadn't—" He sighed and rubbed a hand over his face. For the first time, Rachel considered the possibility he, too, had been worn out by the day's events.

She hadn't anticipated this side of things. Hadn't considered he too might have mixed feelings about the sudden change his life had taken.

"Then what do we do?"

He rubbed at the several days' growth of beard along the edge of his jaw. "We can tell people, your family included, you've hired me on."

"What?"

"With your husband gone, you'll need someone to run the ranch—"

"I run the ranch, Mr. Beckett—"

"Caleb."

"Caleb," she amended through clenched teeth, too tired to argue. "I run this ranch. I have since my father passed. Do you plan on replacing me?"

"Do you want me to?"

Mr. Beckett—*Caleb's* question surprised her. What surprised her even more was her response. *Maybe.*

She was tired. Bone dead tired. The past decade had worn her down and wrung her out until there was nothing left. In the past few years, every day had become a struggle to make it to the next. Yes, she loved the ranch. Loved the idea of making a go of it and the sense of accomplishment she got from an honest day's work. But trying to do that and care for Ethan and Brody while looking after the house, the garden, the animals…

She was one person and she couldn't do it all.

The idea of not having to carry the burden alone seemed inconceivable. And far more appealing than she would ever admit aloud.

Rachel massaged her forehead with her fingertips.

No. She could not think like that. She couldn't allow herself to hope someone would swoop in and her problems would magically dissolve. Caleb Beckett's arrival didn't herald any of these events. If anything, it brought an end to the one thing she had left. The only thing keeping her family safe and intact.

Caleb stepped closer. His nearness surrounded her. She was overcome with a sudden longing to fall against his broad chest and drop the burden at his feet. But she couldn't. This was not a trusted friend. And he was definitely not family. He was nothing more than a handsome stranger who had ridden into town and could ride out at any moment.

She needed to remember that.

"I don't know what I'm going to do about the deed," he told her, his voice low and enticing. Lord, how she ached to give in. To let go. Now that he'd put the idea in her head it did not want to leave, like a weed she couldn't kill. "And until I do, there's no sense upsetting your family. You and the boys can stay at the house. I'll—"

"I can't let you live here on your own land like some kind of hired hand."

"If we're gonna perpetrate the myth I am a hired hand, I can't rightly be bunking up at the house, now can I? Besides, if it's my land it should be my say on how I live on it. Or who I let live on it."

Rachel straightened, her pride gaining a foothold. "I won't live here on charity."

"I'm not asking you to. If you're working, I'll pay you a wage."

She stumbled back a step. Had she heard him right? He was going to…pay her? "A wage?"

"Can't have you working for free. Wouldn't be right. Besides, last time I checked, you got debts to pay, and unless I'm readin' things wrong, Kirkpatrick is lookin' to collect. Way I figure it, you have two choices. You can let your pride march you right off this property without two cents to squeeze together, or you can keep things as they are until we figure it all out and pay off Kirkpatrick in the process."

We. There was that word again.

She shook her head. "Shamus doesn't want the debt paid in cash—he wants the land and he wants it now. He's threatening to take the matter before the circuit judge if we don't pay up."

"Doesn't matter. The debts were your husband's to pay, not mine. Now that I own the land, Kirkpatrick has no claim to it. Simple as that."

Except there was nothing simple about it.

One of the horses nickered from the depths of the barn as if agreeing with her thoughts.

"I can give you the money to pay him off," Caleb offered.

"Like I said, I don't take charity."

"And I don't give it. Think of it as a loan. You'll work it off, repaying me instead of Kirkpatrick. No one needs to be the wiser."

She scoffed at his naiveté. Obviously this man had never lived in a small community before. "Everyone in town knows I don't have that kind of money. They'll question where it came from and how I'm earning it."

"Tell them your husband won the money in Laramie."

"They won't believe it. Robert was never any good. He lost far more than he ever won." The fact Caleb was standing here with the deed to her land proved that.

"They'll come to in time if you stick to your story. People believe what they want to. Seems to me people in this town have a good opinion of you. If you say it's true, and I back you up, they'll accept it in the end."

Rachel stared at him long and hard trying to find his angle and coming up empty. "Why would you do that? What's in it for you?"

"Don't matter."

It was an ambiguous answer at best, revealing nothing of his motives. Try as she might to see behind the guarded green-brown eyes, she couldn't. But she knew one thing for certain—people didn't extend such a favor without expecting something in return. But what did Caleb Beckett want? And how high a price would she have to pay?

A vision of her mother, wasting away from guilt and disgrace, entered her mind. She quickly backpedaled away from his suggestion. Some prices were too high.

"No," she said firmly, knowing her answer could be the final nail in her financial coffin. "I appreciate the offer to extend the loan, but it would never be believed. I'll use my wages and repay Shamus in installments. If he objects and gets the circuit judge involved, then we can reveal the truth of ownership. In the meantime, if you're still amenable, we'll act as if nothing else has changed."

Except that everything had.

And they both knew it.

"Suit yourself," he answered, letting the matter drop.

"I will. Now, if you're determined on playing the part of hired hand, I'll show you to the bunkhouse."

Chapter Seven

They walked in silence, Rachel leading the way. She tried not to stumble, an attempt made more difficult by the fact that she could feel Caleb's eyes boring into her back. As crazy as it seemed, she could feel his silent perusal travel over every inch of her like a caress. She was thankful it was a short walk from the barn to the bunkhouse.

"What's this?"

Rachel glanced behind her. Caleb pointed to a low pile of stone boarded over.

"The old well. We dug the new one when we built the new house."

"Where was the old house?" Rachel pointed to a spot nearby. "What happened to it?"

"It burned down. We ended up boarding up this well when Brody was small to keep him from falling in, but lately Ethan's taken to pestering it. He's convinced there's gold at the bottom and it's the end to all our problems."

"Could get dangerous."

"I keep an eye on him." Her anger spiked at the implication she failed in her duties. She turned and kept walking.

"Never said you didn't. You always this ornery?"

She turned and glared at him over her shoulder. He made her ornery. She didn't like the strange feelings that crept up whenever he was near. Not that she'd be telling him that. "Here's where you'll be staying." She stopped in front of the wooden structure. It wasn't much to look at, but it was solid and well made.

A flicker of something she didn't recognize skittered across Caleb's expression with such speed she wasn't sure she'd seen it at all. Was he regretting letting her have the house?

"It's small, but it's clean. The men built the bigger bunkhouse when we took on more hands. You, Brody and Foster will share this one."

"Where do the other hands stay?"

Rachel pointed to the larger bunk on the rise. "Len, Stump and Everett stay there. Freedom has the smaller cabin closer to the house." Caleb didn't respond, just continued staring at the door. To break the silence, Rachel opened it and stepped inside.

A tiny window on the side wall over Foster's bed let in a hint of light through the calico curtains. She'd hung them in the hope it would add a homey feeling. They were new, replacing the ratty old blue ones that had been there for an age.

She had tried to spruce the small bunkhouse up as much as she could, but there wasn't much to be done. There was barely room to move. Foster's single bed and a set of bunks were against two walls with a narrow walk space in between. A chest of drawers sat at the foot of the bunk beds, and a potbellied stove and bucket of wood filled up the space at the other end of the living space.

On the top bunk, Brody lay reading a dime novel he held pried open hiding his face.

"Brody?"

He moved the book just enough to glance around its edge. Rachel didn't wait for him to acknowledge her verbally. He rarely did these days, preferring sullen silence. Foster and Freedom both promised her he would grow out of it, but Rachel worried it was more than that. What if he pulled away from her and would not return? The thought saddened her. Her family was the most important thing and, right now, all she had.

"Brody," she said, injecting a sense of false optimism into her voice. "This is Mr. Beckett—"

"We met," her brother said, moving the book to block his face once again. His rudeness appalled her, but drawing attention to it would do no good. She'd tried that approach in the past with less than stellar results.

"Mr. Beckett is going to stay on for a bit to give us a hand." The lie tasted bitter on her tongue, but she pushed on, determined to maintain the ruse until she came up with a better solution. "He'll be bunking with you and Foster."

This got his attention, but any hope that the news would be received in good spirit was dashed when her brother snapped the book shut and slapped it onto the bed next to him, sliding off the bunk in one swift motion. His booted feet hit the ground with an angry thud.

"What the hell do we need him for?"

Embarrassment welled up inside of her. Where had the sweet boy she remembered gone? "Watch your language, Brody, and show Mr. Beckett the courtesy he deserves."

"He don't deserve nothin' from me. We don't need an extra hand, and we sure as shootin' don't need some interloper taking up space in here."

She couldn't necessarily fault Brody on the space issue. The bunkhouse didn't allow for much room outside the beds and stove, but she wouldn't tolerate such behavior. The last thing she needed was for her brother's moody temperament to cause Caleb to rethink his decision to allow them to stay here.

"That's enough from you, young man. Apologize to Mr. Beckett this minute and—"

"That ain't never going to happen," her brother said, pushing past her and glaring at Caleb as he stalked through the door. Caleb shifted slightly to make way for him, having yet to step inside the small confines of the bunkhouse.

"I'm sorry."

"Guess he's not much interested in having a new roommate. Why isn't he sleeping in the house?"

She turned at the sound of Caleb's steps on the wood floor. He'd come up behind her, filling the bunkhouse with his presence. He stood close enough that she could feel the heat generated by his body and every last inch of her jumped to attention.

Her heart beat an unsteady rhythm.

"He and Robert didn't get on well. Keeping the two of them under one roof became a less than pleasant situation. We had planned to expand the cabin, but..." Rachel shook her head. It was another job Robert had promised to do that never got done. "Last year Brody decided to move out here with Foster after one of our hands married and moved on."

She pursed her lips. She didn't know why she'd told him that. It was none of his affair why Brody slept where he did, and she wasn't in the habit of discussing her personal business with others.

She cleared her throat and motioned behind her, her back brushing against the wood frame of the beds. "Anyway, you can take the bottom bunk."

Caleb didn't move, didn't step away from her. Granted, there was little room to maneuver without backing out of the bunkhouse entirely or stepping up onto Foster's bed. He glanced down at her with an unreadable expression and shrugged one shoulder. The saddlebags slipped down his arm to be caught in his hand. He reached past her to toss them onto the bed. His arm brushed hers as he leaned in, his chest almost touching her. Her breasts ached for the contact. An unexpected need raged through her without warning and without mercy.

She couldn't breathe. Heat flushed her face.

She needed to get herself under control. She couldn't let her physical reaction to him rage on like this. It was ridiculous. He was a stranger. A drifter. There was no telling what his character was or what his habits were. Maybe that was it. It was just fear and…and…exhaustion. Yes, of course. She was exhausted and her mind was not working properly. After a good night's sleep she would be fine and—

"You alright?"

Lord help her, even his low masculine whisper turned her nerves to liquid and raced through her veins like an out-of-control brushfire.

She nodded. She needed to get out of this bunkhouse. To breathe in fresh air untainted by the musky scent of leather and outdoors that clung to his skin and clothes. The small confines of the bunkhouse closed in on her.

"I need to see to supper."

"It's just past noon."

"Then I need to…" Her mind blanked. At any given time she could rhyme off a list as long as her arm of things that needed doing, but now, when she truly needed the information, her memory failed her.

"To?" Caleb's eyebrows arched upward and the spark of humor she'd witnessed earlier revived itself, robbing her of what few wits she had left.

She swallowed. "There's plenty to be done here. I can't be standing around idle."

"Don't let me keep you, then."

Despite his words, he didn't step aside. Rachel willed her legs to move, faltering when her hip grazed his hard thigh as she squeezed between him and the bunks. She hurried out the open door, nearly tripping off the step in her rush to escape Caleb Beckett and the foolish emotions he set off inside of her.

When she glanced back, he stood leaning in the doorframe, all six feet of him stretched out to fill the entrance, making her feel small and insignificant in comparison. She picked up her skirts and turned in the direction of the house, fleeing on wobbly legs, feeling his gaze on her back the entire way.

Caleb couldn't move. Couldn't do much of anything save watch Rachel's gently curved hips sway back and forth as she scurried to the main house as if the devil nipped at her heels.

What the hell had just happened?

His body still hummed, every fiber strained to go after her to see if he could ease the craving that standing so close to her had brought on.

She had him addled to the point he hadn't even noticed he was standing in what amounted to little more than a stuffy, dark box with barely enough air in it for a mouse to breathe. He hadn't noticed anything except how the dingy light from the midday sun set off the fiery highlights in her mahogany hair and made it appear soft as silk. He'd been mesmerized by the golden glow of her skin until all he could think about was drawing her down onto the bed and peeling away the layers of clothes she wore to discover what treasures hid beneath. The intoxicating smell of violets hung heavy in the air. A man could drown in that scent. And in that sweet little body with those delectable curves.

This was going to be a problem.

He stared back into the bunkhouse to divert his attention but it did no good. Without Rachel in the bunkhouse, it returned to what it was—a dark, suffocating little box. Already he could feel the walls closing in on him. His throat constricted. He'd never be able to sleep in here.

Caleb walked outside and sat down on the step, staring at the house and wondering for the umpteenth time what he'd gotten himself into.

If he had a lick of sense he'd hightail it out of town before sundown.

"Gone? What do you mean, he's gone?" In one swoop, Rachel's heart soared to the heavens then plummeted to back to Earth. Caleb Beckett was nowhere to be found.

Brody shrugged and shoveled another mouthful of scrambled eggs into his mouth. Len, Stump and Everett had already been and gone, taking their morning meal and splitting up the work for the day between the three of them. Once he finished his breakfast, Brody would be meeting Len near the north end of the property to fix a section of fencing that had been knocked down. Likely by one of Shamus's men.

"I mean he's gone. Wasn't there when I got up. Didn't even look like his bed been slept in." Brody smirked. "Guess your hired hand didn't cotton to hard work and decided to leave."

Rachel's mixed emotions told her it would never be as simple as that. Caleb Beckett owned the land. He wouldn't just walk away.

Would he?

She took the empty plate Brody handed to her as he made his way out the door without so much as a goodbye. At least he'd waved in Ethan's direction, showing the little boy a token of affection. Rachel barely registered the slight. It happened every morning now, and today her mind was too occupied with Caleb's disappearance to deal with Brody's moodiness.

"You think he's gone for good?" Freedom thrust her strong hands into a mound of dough in front of her and kneaded it once before flipping it around for another thrust.

"Aw, no," Ethan said, his mouth half filled with oatmeal. "I like him."

Rachel set the plate on the counter and crossed the room to the cookstove, tousling Ethan's hair as she went, hoping the boy would not sense her agitation. "Perhaps Mr. Beckett woke early and rode out to start working before Brody woke up, is all."

The words echoed hollowly in her breast. Without consulting with the other men, how would he know what was required of the day or which section of the property to head to? And Brody said it didn't look as if his bed had even been slept in. Had he left in the night?

Rachel placed a hand over her stomach where it twisted with worry. She didn't think Caleb Beckett was the type of man who would pull a midnight run, but obviously her ability to judge men had failed. Her marriage was a stark reminder of that.

"Maybe if I catch him a fish he'll come back. Foster said he'd take me out to the creek today." Ethan's hopeful smile broke her heart. The boy had lost too many people in his short life. It made her angry to think Caleb had made an impression on him in such a short time and that he could become another name added to the list.

"Put your dishes on the counter and go find Foster. I'm sure we would all like to eat a nice big fish for dinner tonight." It was as noncommittal an answer as she could give. She didn't have the heart to watch the crestfallen expression on Ethan's face if it turned out Caleb didn't return.

The very thought left her as boiling hot as the chili simmering on the stove in front of her. She gave it a vigorous stir. If he had left for good, what did that mean for them? Would he drift to other parts and sell the land to someone else, or gamble it away as Robert had? Then what? Would another stranger ride in one day, deed in hand and run them all off the land?

She had assumed he would be true to his word, a mistake she'd made all too often. What made her think she could trust the word of a man she knew nothing about? He had drifted into town with Robert's body after riding into Laramie to play a game of cards. He had no apparent past and did not seem overly concerned about where he spent his future. An air of danger pulsated from him, and she suspected he was a man with something of a murky history. Everything else remained mired in mystery.

The way her body responded whenever he came near was the biggest mystery of all.

Even now, remembering the way he had looked down at her in the bunkhouse, the way her skin sizzled where their bodies brushed together—

"If he does return, you should marry the man on the spot," Freedom said, kneading another section of dough.

Rachel's hand slipped from the spoon. It continued to spin around the pot of its own accord.

She stepped back, the heat from the stove causing her skin to flush.

"I should what?"

"Marry the man."

The idea left her sputtering. "I…I know nothing about him."

Freedom shrugged, as if that were inconsequential. "Maybe so, but he didn't send you packin' and that speaks good to the man. Shows more consideration than that dead husband o' yours, God rest his useless soul. Did he make any untoward suggestions about you earnin' your salary by layin' on your back?"

"Freedom!" Heat pooled low in her belly, then lower still at the suggestion. Rachel stalked to the counter and grabbed the dirty dishes, moving them to the sink, anything to keep her mind away from the images Freedom's words conjured in her mind. Maybe it was better Caleb had disappeared, after all.

"Don't you 'Freedom' me. A strong, strappin' man like that is bound to have needs. But if'n he didn't ask you to fill them then that says something positive to his character. Still, I'm guessin' he wouldn't be indifferent. He's got needs, you need a place for yourself and the boys. Seems a natural fit to me."

Rachel scrubbed hard at the oatmeal caked to Ethan's bowl and wished even harder that Freedom would stop talking. Each word she spoke made the images in Rachel's mind even clearer until she ached in places she had long forgotten existed. She had put her own needs so far down on the list they'd fallen off completely. She'd simply stopped thinking about them. But, in the span of two short days, Caleb had managed to resurrect them with a vengeance. It embarrassed her how little it took. A brief glance, an accidental brushing of bodies.

Embarrassment turned to disgust. No matter how hard she'd tried to stop the feelings from coming, they would not be squelched. Well, maybe some things were just born into a body, but that didn't mean she had to act on them like Mama had. She was a stronger woman than that, and while she might have a far sounder reason than Mama ever had for prostituting herself, she still possessed too much pride to fall so low.

"I could not possibly marry the man, Freedom. It's a ludicrous idea and not one I care to entertain, thank you."

"Don't see why not. You could do a lot worse. Hell, you already done a lot worse."

Rachel scowled at the reminder. She'd married Robert young, too young to know enough about men to judge his true character. She would not make the same mistake again.

Freedom dropped the dough into a pan and turned, brushing the flour from her hands. She fixed Rachel with a hard stare. "I know it sounds crazy, and I know there be a hundred reasons not to do it. But simple fact is, you's got nowhere to go. At least if you marry Mr. Beckett you got yourself a home and the boys got some stability."

"I am not marrying Caleb Beckett. Either way, he doesn't exactly strike me as the type of man anyone could put a claim to." His unexplained absence at the ranch this morning spoke volumes.

"Well, you best do something 'afore Mr. Kirkpatrick come sniffing back around here."

"I have done something. I told you, Mr. Beckett is giving me a salary—to continue doing what I normally do, overseeing things and such. I'll use that to pay off what we owe Shamus."

Freedom snorted. "You'll be working till you're sixty to save up enough for that! And how's Mr. Beckett gonna pay you if'n he ain't even here? You marry him, and he's got reason to stay."

"He owns the land. That's reason enough," Rachel said. Or it should be. But what if it wasn't?

She scrubbed harder. This situation grew worse by the minute. What would she do if he didn't return? If Shamus showed up demanding the land as payment and Caleb was nowhere to be found, what then? Once Shamus discovered the deed had changed hands he'd track down the circuit judge in a heartbeat and demand…what? Could the judge give Shamus the land if the owner was absent and considered to have vacated the area? Fear painted her worry with dark strokes.

Rachel stepped away from the sink. "Can you finish the dishes, Free? I'm going to change and head down to the barn to start to work there."

She needed some distance from everyone. Especially Freedom's crazy ideas about how to solve her problem. And she needed to determine what the heck they were going to do now that Caleb had seen fit to drift off to parts unknown and leave her in the lurch.

Chapter Eight

In the distance, Rachel heard the sound of a wagon rumbling toward the house. She stopped brushing down Old Molly and listened. The paint snorted as her attention strayed to the window across from his stall. She couldn't see anything from inside the barn. Likely it was Foster and Ethan done at the creek and loading the wagon up to take a hearty lunch out to the men. Rachel knew they could easily have packed something in their saddlebags to tide them over until dinner, but she liked doing this for them. They worked hard and deserved a decent noontime meal, and it gave Foster something useful to do now that he was getting older and could no longer spend hours in the saddle like the younger men.

Rachel took an extra minute to enjoy the feel of the afternoon sun radiating a welcome warmth through the window before giving the paint a swat on the hindquarters and backing him out of the stall.

Seeing Caleb's horse when she arrived a couple of hours earlier filled her with relief. Although the buckboard and draft horse were gone, she was certain Caleb wouldn't have left the paint behind. So long as Jasper remained, Caleb would return.

Though this knowledge did not quell the anger growing inside of her. With each passing moment it grew in proportion to the worry Caleb's potential desertion had evoked.

Rachel pitched her shovel into the stall and scooped up a pile of horse dung and trampled hay, tossing it into the waiting wheelbarrow. The constant physical motion did little to sooth her jangled nerves.

Did Caleb not consider how she would feel if, upon waking, she discovered he'd gone? No message, no note, nothing to indicate his whereabouts or his intentions. Did he not think how she might worry, contemplate what it meant, fear the worst?

Of course he didn't. Why would he? They were nothing to him. It was ridiculous to think otherwise. Whatever he had agreed to thus far was for his own benefit, not because he put other people's troubles ahead of his own wants and needs.

She shoveled faster.

He was a drifter, for crying out loud. A gambler, obviously. Heck he could even be an outlaw wanted in several territories for all she knew, and here she was forced by a turn of the cards to stay here with him until she managed to pay off Kirkpatrick and start over, or until Caleb decided they were no longer welcome.

She set aside the shovel and picked up the pitchfork, replacing the old hay with fresh.

The whole situation was maddening! This limbo she now lived in put her emotions through the wringer like every day was wash day. How much of this could she stand, wondering every minute if today would be the day Caleb changed his mind and left her and the boys high and dry? He didn't owe her a thing. They were here on his largesse and how could she determine how far that would stretch?

Maybe he did own the land, but she at least had the right to know what his intentions were with respect to how it affected her family. She would give him a piece of her mind and force him to draw a clearer picture of those intentions, and if he refused, then…then…

The last bit of hay slid off the end of the pitchfork onto the floor of the stall.

Then there was still nothing she could do.

Rachel slumped against the stall. She hated this sense of impotence. How was she supposed to care for her family if at any moment they could be cast out? They would have nothing but the clothes on their back and a huge debt owing to Kirkpatrick hanging over their heads.

She rested her head on the wooden post and took a deep breath as worry and anger seesawed back and forth.

* * *

Caleb drove the buckboard through the open doors and into the barn, walking into the ray of sunlight coming through one of the side windows. Dust motes danced in its beams and he felt the warmth on his skin as he passed through. Riding to and from town, he had been struck once again by the beauty of the land, the richness of its promised bounty as spring erupted all around him, filling him with a sense of renewal. It called to him, urging him to put down roots, dredging up old memories best left in the past. He had tried settling down once before, and it had ended in betrayal and a bullet in his back. What made him think it would be different this time?

He shook the dark memory off. Truth be told, he'd figured he'd end up on the wrong end of a bullet long before the need to settle down pulled at him again. So far fate had spared him, though he wasn't sure if that made him a lucky man or not. But riding through the woods, listening to the music of the forest, breathing in the fresh mountain air, well, he felt pretty lucky indeed.

He just wasn't fool enough to think it would last. He'd learned his lesson on that account and knew better than to allow his mind to veer too far down that path. No, he would figure out a way to set things right and keep Rachel safe from Kirkpatrick's machinations. Then he would get gone, preferably before the sheriff dug up more about the events in Laramie than Caleb needed him knowing.

Sensing he wasn't alone, Caleb jumped down from the wagon and scanned the length of stalls. A young boy dressed in trousers and a floppy old hat stood with his back to him, scratching Jasper's nose. He was too small for Brody, too big for Ethan.

"You there," he called out. "Can you tell me where I might find Mrs. Sutter?"

He'd looked up at the house when he'd unloaded the lumber he'd purchased, but no one had been around.

He barely managed to keep his jaw from hitting the hay strewn floor when the boy turned around.

Rachel tilted back her hat and gave him a direct look. "I see you decided to return."

Caleb grasped at his scattered wits. Now that she had fully turned toward him, he could see how the trousers skimmed over the enticing curve of her hips. Tendrils of dark hair curled gently against the line of her jaw, bobbing with each subtle movement. The shirt she wore did little to keep his mind on the straight and narrow. It fit against breasts pushed upward by her corset, their soft roundness straining against the material. Despite her light frame and the clothes she wore, there was nothing boyish about her.

"Return?"

"As in you were away and now you have come back." There was an edge to her voice.

"Right. I…uh…went into town." He struggled to get his brain working again, to move away from wondering what lay beneath that shirt, but his mind wouldn't ponder why she appeared angry with him. It was busy speculating whether Rachel Sutter was the type to wear one of those frilly lace-type corsets, or if she was all utilitarian and plain. Caleb suspected the former. It was always the ones you didn't suspect that surprised you.

"To town? For what?"

He wasn't sure what business it was of hers where he went or why, but she sure seemed irate over him being gone. There was no denying the severe tone in her voice or the hands planted firmly on those hips he was trying his best not to think about.

"Thought I'd purchase some lumber to expand the house. Place is too damn small to fit all of you. Figured I'd expand it, maybe add an extra bedroom."

He thought she'd be pleased at the prospect of having more space, but her full lips pursed into a tight line, telling him he had read the situation wrong. Blast it, if this woman wasn't hard to figure out. One minute she was all but begging him to keep quiet about the deed, the next she was refusing his help as though she'd rather strip naked and run through town than take one cent from him. He was trying to do her a favor, expanding the house.

"I understand this is now your property, Mr. Beckett, and you can do with it as you please, but out of courtesy, do you think it remotely possible you could inform me of such changes beforehand?"

He raised one eyebrow. "Inform you?"

"Yes, inform me."

"Like report to you, get your permission?" He rolled a finger in the air. The idea rankled him. He wasn't used to having anyone vet his decisions, nor did he see any reason to start now. If he had to discuss with her every thought or idea that popped into his head, he'd never get anything done. Not to mention the less time he spent in her company the better. She had the ability to draw a man in and addle his thinking. He didn't need to have his thinking addled. He needed all his wits about him to come up with a solution to this confounded problem he'd found himself in so he could get the heck out as soon as possible.

"I'm not asking you to get my permission—"

"Good thing, seein' as how I don't need it."

The muscle in her jaw danced beneath her smooth skin and fire sparked in her eyes. The sight spread quickly to his groin. He had the sudden urge to touch her skin and see the fiery anger turn into something else. He shifted uncomfortably. This really needed to stop before he embarrassed himself.

"Thank you for your oh-so-gentle reminder of my situation, Mr. Beckett."

"Thought we agreed you were going to call me Caleb."

"*You* agreed. But seeing as how you don't require my permission to do whatever you want with this property, I see no reason why I'm required to call you whatever you dictate I should."

"You have to if you're in my employ." He didn't know what made him say such a thing. Last thing he wanted was her feeling indebted to him. Though he certainly did appreciate seeing the spark in those deep brown eyes fire up again and the flush color her cheeks as she tried to hold her anger in check.

Rachel Sutter did not like losing control, and yet there was nothing else at this particular moment Caleb would like to see more. Besides, he liked how his name sounded when she said it, even if she spit nails as she did.

"Are you suggesting—"

"That I make it a mandatory condition of your employment that you call me by my given name? Yes, I think I am."

"You can't be serious." She stared at him in amazement. The kind of amazement that made him feel like an annoying bug she wanted to stomp on with her boot.

He shrugged. "If I let you call me anything you feel like, my guess is you'd be callin' me a horse's ass—"

"You got that right."

"And seein' as how I don't particularly like being called that, regardless of how much I might deserve it, I'm thinkin' it best I insist you call me Caleb. It's better than whatever alternative you might come up with given your current state of mind."

Her nostrils flared and she glanced down at the bucket of oats near her, then over to him. No doubt she was contemplating dumping it over his head, but given her restraint, he didn't fear she'd actually go through with it. He almost wished she would. Just a glimpse of her letting go would be worth wearing Jasper's dinner.

"Fine," she said, taking a step toward him, smiling sweetly. "I will call you by your given name. But please be aware, that every time I utter it, it's the other name I'm thinking of."

She turned slightly and bent to pick up the bucket of oats, giving him a clear view of her shapely backside. The image of fitting that derriere against him made the temperature in the barn rise exponentially.

Caleb cleared his throat and gave his head a shake. "Great. Good. Glad we got that all cleared up."

He turned his attention to unhitching the draft horse from the buckboard and tried to scrub his mind of the pictures it kept producing about his enticing new employee. He was treading on dangerous ground here. The question was, how long before the ground gave way and sent him hurtling down a landslide, bringing her along for the ride?

The mournful strains of music derailed Rachel's train of thought, pulling her away from the worry over her family's future and mollifying her fears. She stopped wiping down the kitchen counter and closed her eyes. The music washed over her as it drifted in through the open window carried on a light evening breeze.

The sound reminded her of her father, of happier times before he left to work on the railroad. Before her mother turned traitor to their family and sought the company of another man. It took Rachel to a time when she would sit by her father's knee on a warm summer's eve and he would play his harmonica. Sometimes it would be a lively tune and she and her mother would clap and dance, and the house would be filled with laughter. Other times, he would play a quiet, sorrowful ballad and her mother would hum along.

It had been a long time since she'd heard anyone play the harmonica in such a way. Foster often played his fiddle, but it was a much different sound than—

Rachel's eyes snapped open and she leaned over the counter to see out the window. Who was it? None of the other men played the harmonica. Her gaze searched through the fading light, squinting at the two figures sitting outside the bunkhouse, one on a ladder-back chair, the other on the narrow step.

The music stopped abruptly and the two bodies leaned close as if deep in conference.

"What on earth is Caleb doing?"

Rachel debated confronting him. She had avoided Caleb as best she could for the past few days, ever since he insisted she call him by his given name. In truth, she had no trouble referring to him as such. What she took issue with was being ordered to do so. In her own home. Which was not her home any more.

"Oh!" She threw down the dishrag in a fit of anger. "Well, you might own this place, *Mr. Beckett,* but a few things are still my domain."

And that included the other member of the little powwow. One seven-year-old boy who needed to get himself ready for bed and didn't need to be spending time with a stranger who had blown into their lives and was just as likely to blow out at the drop of a hat, leaving said boy devastated by his departure.

Rachel let the door bang behind her as she started toward the bunkhouse wrapped in self-righteous anger and intent on retrieving Ethan. A shrill blast of noise rent the air. She winced at the sound, but the sudden laughter that followed stopped her in her tracks. And the low chuckle accompanying it nearly took her knees out from under her.

She stared at the scene, close enough to see

them but still far enough away to escape their notice as they bent head to head and conferred. She slowed her approach.

"You have to breathe, gentle like. Doesn't take much force to make it sing for you."

Caleb took the harmonica from Ethan and demonstrated what he meant. Again the mournful sound reached up and tugged at Rachel's memories. She lifted her skirts to keep them from rustling in the grass and alerting them to her presence.

Caleb was teaching Ethan to play the harmonica. This man, who had gone out of his way to distance himself from everyone on the ranch, taking his meals alone, choosing chores that required only one man, keeping his conversation to single words and staying silent whenever anyone dared ask anything personal, was now sitting here teaching a little boy how to play the harmonica and showing the patience of Job as he did.

None of this matched the hard-edged, remote stranger who had all but bullied her into calling him by his first name and who set about making changes to her house without giving her fair warning he planned to do so.

"So, I blow like I'm talking to someone?"

Caleb handed the small instrument back to Ethan. "Like your whisperin' in someone's ear, tellin' them a secret."

Something about the way he said it, or the small quirk of his lips as he did, sent a sizzle of sensation through Rachel's veins. She wondered what secrets he would whisper, what they would tell her about this man who had turned her life, and her sense of well-being, on its ear. The sudden need to hear made her careless and she stumbled over a rut in the path caused by last week's rain.

Ethan's gaze jumped from Caleb over to her and a huge grin splayed across his sweet face. "Caleb's showing me how to play the harmonica!"

Caleb hadn't reacted to her presence at all. She remembered how he had instinctively known she was there watching him when she went to confront him in the livery the day after he announced he was the new owner of the Circle S ranch. The man had the uncanny ability to be totally aware of his surroundings at all times. In his excitement to show Rachel his new skills, Ethan blew hard into the organ, making it screech.

"Oops. Sorry." He scrunched up his face, glancing at Caleb. "Whispering?"

"Like you're tellin' a secret."

"I don't have any secrets."

Caleb reached over and tousled Ethan's tawny hair. "Then you're one of the lucky ones."

Rachel straightened, struggling not to let the affectionate gesture soften her opinion of the man. "I came to collect Ethan for bed."

"Aw, but we was just startin' to learn stuff."

As much as Rachel loved the boy's thirst for knowledge and inquisitive nature, indulging it at this particular time did not seem the best course of action. It was clear that avoiding Caleb over the past few days had done little to lessen the disconcerting effect his presence had on her. Being near him now, with memories of the past stirring up her emotions, and seeing a side of him she had not been prepared for, made the ground beneath her shift unexpectedly.

"Can we stay for one more song?" Ethan gave her a pleading look, his hands with the harmonica fisted beneath his chin. "Please!"

She let out a slow breath. Ethan had had so little good in his short life she had trouble refusing him anything that brought him joy. His requests were generally small, inconsequential things most people would have taken for granted, but to him they meant the world. Would it really do any harm? She ignored the whispering *yes* her heart issued, telling herself that, for Ethan, she would make the sacrifice.

"Fine. Scoot over." She meant to put herself as far away from Caleb as possible.

Ethan thrust the harmonica toward Caleb, who wrapped his much larger hand around the instrument, dwarfing it. "Play a long song," he whispered loudly.

Again Caleb chuckled, and the incongruous sound startled Rachel to such a degree she didn't have time to stop Ethan as he crawled into her lap, erasing the extra body between her and Caleb.

She leaned her back against the closed door of the bunkhouse, sneaking a gaze heavenward, wondering if she was being tested.

If so, she had a sinking feeling she was failing miserably. As much as her mind resisted Caleb's sudden presence in her life, her body responded to him in ways she had no remedy for. Is this what her mother had suffered?

The somber tune Caleb chose to play reverberated through her, the tender vibrations strumming against her taut nerves. She closed her eyes against the onslaught and beat back the memories of happy, easy times. She rarely visited those memories. It was too painful, remembering everything they'd had and how quickly it had fallen apart. The knowledge of how easily life could be taken away from you if you didn't hold tight to what was important was a lesson she'd never forgotten.

The music lulled her, easing her anxieties and soothing the tension gripping the muscles of her neck and shoulders. She relaxed, comforted by Ethan's warm body curled into hers. She wrapped her arms around him, holding him tight. All too soon the song ended, and the echoes of the music died away.

"Don't move."

Caleb's quiet instruction intruded. Rachel snapped her eyes open, mortified she had allowed herself to let go so easily in front of him.

He nodded toward her arms and she glanced down at Ethan. In a matter of minutes, the boy had fallen asleep.

Chapter Nine

"I can't remember the last time I did that," Rachel whispered, the words escaping before she could call them back. She blushed at the admission, unable to look at Caleb.

"He do that a lot? Fall asleep at the drop of a hat?"

She nodded, thankful to turn attention away from herself. "Hard to imagine, after all he's been through, that he can find solace in a solid night's sleep, but he does."

"If he doesn't belong to you, where'd he come from?"

The inference raised her hackles. Robert had refused to consider Ethan a member of her family, a wound that still cut deep. "Make no mistake, *Caleb,* he belongs to me every bit as much as if I had given birth to him myself."

Caleb held up a hand, shaking his head. The dying strands of sunlight caught the edge of his jaw, turning the whiskers a glowing red, contrasting with the dark brown of the hair poking out from beneath his hat. "I meant no disrespect. He's a fine boy. Anyone would be proud to call him son. I only asked out of curiosity. He said you weren't his natural ma, and I just wondered how he possessed the good fortune to end up here."

His words surprised her given his propensity to avoid her as much as she had been avoiding him. She pulled her mind away from that path, refusing to explore it further, and focused on Ethan, whose deep breathing indicated he was well into dreamland and not likely to wake any time soon.

"Ethan's ma and pa rode in from the east, coming with a small wagon train. It had been larger when they set out, but they'd encountered one hardship after another, and their numbers had dwindled to less than half their original size."

Rachel adjusted Ethan in her arms, a wave of love enveloping her as he snuggled closer.

"His pa died shortly before they reached Salvation Falls. They hadn't meant to stop here but to pass by farther up on the trail. But Alma, his ma, couldn't manage the wagon without Ethan's pa, so she pulled in here, hoping to find work to support her and Ethan."

"And did she?" The low timbre of his voice matched the still night air.

Rachel shook her head. "I suspect you know there aren't too many respectable options available to a woman left on her own. And, by then, she had taken to the laudanum to dull the pain of her loss. She needed to feed Ethan and her ad-diction. She ended up at the Seahorse, trading her body for cash. Cyrus, the owner, he let her keep Ethan there in one of the back rooms, but she had to pay extra, which meant less money in her pocket and less chance of escaping that way of life."

"What happened to her?"

"Same thing that happens to most of the women forced into that line of work," Rachel said. "Their bodies wear out, they get diseased, or they simply give up and take the only escape they can find by ending their own lives."

Caleb leaned forward in his chair. He reached over to her and Rachel froze, unsure of his inten-tions. His knuckles grazed Ethan's sleep-flushed cheek. The tender ministration touched her some-where deep. The breach in her defenses made her want to bolt, but Ethan's body kept her rooted to the stair. If Caleb was aware of the effect he had, she couldn't tell. His sharp focus remained honed on Ethan.

"Which one of those things happened to Ethan's ma?"

"All of them." Rachel forced the words past the constriction in her throat. "She was a fragile little thing to start with and barely twenty when she arrived here. Between the laudanum and the harshness of that life, it's hard to say which made her give up in the end. Cyrus found her one morning hanging from one of the rafters in her room. Ethan was sleeping on the bed."

"Did he see what happened?"

Rachel shook her head. "I don't know. He never talks about it. He was only four at the time. My hope is that if he did see anything, he was too young for the memory to take hold."

"Terrible thing for a young'un to witness."

"Don't judge her harshly for it," Rachel said, fearing her story cast Alma in a poor light. "She was a good girl brought down by circumstance. Sometimes a body can only stand so much hurt before it just can't take anymore."

His gaze transferred to her. The air stirred around them, brushing against her like a soft touch. She wanted to look away, to break the current of electricity his gaze elicited, but she couldn't. Or wouldn't.

"You sound like you know what you're talking about."

Rachel clamped her lips shut. What was it about this man that made her reveal the things she did? She needed to watch herself. He was not her confessor, he was a man who had turned her life upside down and thrown her emotions into turmoil.

"What happened to Ethan after his ma died?"

Rachel finally looked away, but the effects of his gaze lingered, taunting her. "Cyrus took what little money she had saved and used it to bury her, then dumped Ethan on Hunter—"

"Who?"

"The sheriff," she said. "I was in town running errands when it happened. Hunter said that if he couldn't find a family to take Ethan in he'd have to find an orphanage. Hunter was a bachelor, ill-equipped to be looking after a small child. I knew with Ethan's background—he practically grew up in a whorehouse—I worried there wouldn't be a lot of decent families willing to bring him into their homes."

"So you took him."

She nodded. "What else could I do?"

Caleb had no answer to her question. He wished someone had cared that much about him when his own ma had passed, instead of leaving him in the care of his grandfather, a mean and bitter man who preached the word of God to others then twisted those words to excuse his cruel behavior at home.

He understood Rachel's reasoning. Everybody had their own limit for the amount of hurt they could stand before it became too much. His mother had reached her limit. Caleb often wished he had reached his, as well, but each time he thought he had, the limit extended itself. He knew more awaited him down the road. Some people thought surviving hurt made you strong, but Caleb had decided long ago that it just made you unlucky. Plenty of times he'd wished he could will himself to die, but each time death eluded him.

"It was a good thing you did, taking him in." How different would his own life have been had someone done him such a kindness?

"Robert didn't think so," she said, staring out into the streaks of orange fading from the sky.

"But you did it anyway."

For a fleeting moment, he thought he saw her chin tremble, but she took a deep breath and regained her composure. "Just because something's the right thing doesn't mean it's the easy thing, but you do it anyway."

"Like stayin' here, pretending to your family nothing has changed to keep them from worryin' while you shoulder the burden yourself?"

Her dark gaze found his, searing into him until he felt it through every inch of his body. "I would do anything for my family, Mr. Beckett."

He didn't correct her on the use of his name. Any other time he would have enjoyed getting a rise out of her and watching the fire dance in her eyes, but at that moment all he wanted to do was pull her into his lap and hold her against him, protect her from the vagaries of the world the way she did Ethan. It was doubtful she would ever allow such a thing. He'd seen enough to know she didn't lay her burden on others with any great ease.

Just as well. He had a sinking feel if she did, he'd pick it up and carry it for as long as she needed him to. And that was a risk he couldn't take.

He stood and motioned toward Ethan. "Here, let me carry him back to the house for you."

"I can—"

He didn't wait for her to complete her refusal. He leaned down and scooped Ethan into his arms, taking in a lungful of violet-sweetened air as he did. The boy didn't even stir, though something deep inside of Caleb did. He wished now he had kept his mouth shut, hadn't asked so many questions. The more he knew of Rachel Sutter the harder it became to remain immune to her and her situation.

How could he not admire a woman who showed such steadfast loyalty to her family and courage in the face of such odds?

Though it was not her loyalty or her courage he admired as she walked the path in front of him, her hips swaying with each step.

Blast it! This was getting out of control.

He'd do well to steer clear of her whenever possible. No more asking questions about her family or delving into her history. He didn't need to be admiring her—any of her—and he sure as heck didn't need to be thinking about or worrying over what would happen to her. All he needed to do was figure a way out so he could turn Rachel Sutter and her delectable little body into nothing more than a fading memory.

Until then, he'd be sure to keep as much distance between her and him as possible.

Rachel hesitated at the doorway leading into the newly constructed addition Caleb had built. Shafts of yellow sunlight wound around the beams and columns, painting the honey-colored floor with a warm, inviting glow. On the front wall, catching the afternoon sun, the frame for a large window gave her a view of the old oak and the road that led to town.

It would be beautiful once completed. A real home. She couldn't wait to see—

Her thoughts skidded to a stop, and the fear she tried hard to hold at bay pounded frantically at her heart's door. Likely she wouldn't be around to see the finished product or to enjoy it. Despite Caleb's decision to let her family stay in the home, she knew eventually his patience would wear thin living in the small bunkhouse. And once he decided to move into the house she would have no other choice but to move out. She'd yet to puzzle out where she would move to, however.

It both amazed and worried her how much work he'd accomplished in such a short period of time. His strong and efficient work ethic stood in stark contrast to his drifter ways, a strange dichotomy. The man possessed too many layers to count, and each one seemed to contradict the one that came before it.

Rachel set the tray filled with a bowl of steaming hot chili and fresh biscuits on the makeshift workbench. She could have called Caleb into the kitchen to take his noon meal, but he had so far been disinclined to share meals with the other men and her family. She also had a few things she wanted to say without Freedom's watchful gaze taking it all in.

Caleb's back faced her as he made measurements along one of the wooden posts running floor to ceiling. She watched for a moment, taking in the full length of him, from the breadth of his shoulders to the trim waist, watching the subtle movements as he made a few marks with a pencil. Engrossed in his work, she didn't think he was aware of her presence, yet she'd been duped before.

"I brought you lunch."

"Much obliged." He didn't turn around or glance over his shoulder to acknowledge her in any way. He moved the triangular apparatus in his hand down several inches to a lower section of the post and made a few more marks. The rebuff rankled, though she was even more irritated by how much it bothered her in the first place.

"I thought we might speak briefly."

"Kinda busy at this particular moment."

Rachel pulled her lips inward and breathed deeply through her nose to calm her churning emotions. She did not care for his casual dismissal. She had something to say, and she needed to say it before her nerve faltered. She feared saying anything that might prompt him to throw her and her family off the only place they called home.

"It's rather important. It won't take long."

The loud sigh and way the sweeping expanse of his shoulders slumped did not bode well. The fear residing inside of her since this ordeal began twisted in her belly, whispering that she should reconsider, scuttle back to the kitchen and keep her mouth shut. But she'd never been one to back down from a confrontation, and she wasn't about to start now. She swallowed her fear and stiffened her spine.

Caleb carefully set the pencil and triangle on a cross beam and turned around. For a brief moment her throat constricted. She was not yet accustomed to seeing him without his hat shading half his face. On the rare occasions he came into the house and automatically removed it, showing he at least had learned some manners, Rachel made a concerted effort to look the other way. Eye contact with this man causes her more problems than it was worth, setting her mind reeling in all kinds of unwanted directions.

But now she had little choice. She could hardly have a conversation with him while staring at the ceiling and she couldn't allow him to work while she spoke and risk him not hearing her. Although the way he stared at her with those hazel eyes, stubble grazing the sharp angles of his jaw, his lips sensual and strong, made her wish she was addressing his back.

"You had somethin' you wanted to say?"

The tone of his voice conveyed his displeasure at being interrupted. It threw her. Yesterday evening, he had seemed completely content to sit outside the bunkhouse while she regaled him with the tale of Ethan's origins and her own decision to take him in. Now the distant drifter had returned. What had changed?

She pushed the question out of her mind. Perhaps it was better this way. Easier. She wouldn't worry so much about hurting his feelings. Most likely he wouldn't even care.

"I wanted to speak to you about Ethan."

He said nothing. Only one eyebrow arched upward, leaving Rachel unsure if he was amused or annoyed.

She cleared her throat, reciting the speech she had spent the better part of the morning constructing. "While I appreciate the time you took showing him the harmonica, I would appreciate if in the future you curtailed the time you spent with him."

The eyebrow slowly lowered back to its original position, the only indication he had heard her. Maybe he had simply grown weary of holding it in place. The man was impossible to read.

"That it?"

She had expected—well, in truth, she had no idea what type of response she had expected. She had been prepared for an argument, if one came, but she had not prepared for this apathy.

"As we will not be in each other's company for an extended period, I would prefer Ethan not grow attached to you. As I explained last night, he has suffered much upheaval and loss in his life, and I do not want to add to it by having him lose one more person."

"Fair enough."

His indifference irked her. Did he care so little? He had taken such time with Ethan the previous night. She saw with her own eyes the tenderness he showed toward the boy. Had she imagined it? Misread what she saw?

She continued to babble as if her words could sneak past his barriers and draw out the man she'd met last night, the one who took the time to show a lonely little boy attention. The man who had touched his cheek with a surprising tenderness. She didn't stop to think about the consequences of breaching such a fortress.

"He has a tendency to grow attached quickly and then become upset when people leave."

Caleb shrugged. "I'll be sure and leave the boy alone."

Unexplained frustration welled inside of her.

"I'm not saying to cut yourself off completely or ignore him if he approaches you. Of course, if he speaks to you I expect you to respond with kindness. I am simply requesting you don't court his attentions."

"Fine."

Rachel's spirits drooped. The fortress was impenetrable. The man from last night just a hazy mirage. "That's it? That's all you have to say?"

The eyebrow edged upward again. She had the sudden urge to smack it with the heel of her palm to cut its ascent short, but she didn't dare get close enough. Even at this distance, even with indifference holding her at arm's length, she could feel the pull he had over her. She took a step back.

"Why do I get the sense it isn't just Ethan you want me to avoid?"

Her body stilled until the only movement remaining was the rush of blood through her veins. "I don't understand your meaning."

Caleb took a few steps toward her, each one slow and deliberate, the way someone would approach a skittish animal they were trying not to scare away. She felt ready to bolt, but her limbs would not cooperate. He stopped, close enough that she had to look up to meet his gaze.

"You get right hitchy whenever I'm around—"

"I most certainly do not."

"Like you can't decide if you want to run off or…" He shrugged.

Rachel should have let it go, but the words were out before she could haul them back in. "Or what?"

He looked at her and she swore she could feel his gaze travel from the tips of her toes all the way to the last hair atop her head, teasing every inch in between and leaving his mark. He was right. She did want to run away. Being close to him made her want things, things she refused to allow herself. She knew better than to lose control and give in to such desires. How giving in ended in pain and disaster. But Lord have mercy, something about this man made her want to court disaster.

"You tell me," Caleb said.

Rachel tried to read his expression. His hazel eyes burned into her, but the rest of his features remained carefully schooled. She swallowed, keeping the answer inside of her. Letting it out was not an option. Not with him. It opened too many doors she was determined to keep shut.

"I do not get...hitchy, and I am most certainly not afraid of you."

"Didn't say you were afraid of me. I said you wanted to run away."

"From what?" She lifted her chin, trying to show bravado she didn't own. His nearness, the way he looked at her, made her head swirl and her body tingle until she felt downright...hitchy.

"From this, maybe."

He reached up and his work-worn knuckles grazed her cheek, slowly drawing a path downward until she ached so badly it took all of her willpower not to beg him rid her of it. Her breathing grew labored. She needed to step away. Freedom could walk in here at any moment, and the last thing Rachel needed was more suggestions that she should marry Caleb. But her legs wouldn't work.

His gaze intensified and her knees grew weak. "You deserve more than this."

She swallowed. "More than what?" Her voice was breathy and quiet, barely recognizable.

"More than scrabbling every day to make ends meet. Working yourself to exhaustion. Worrying about everyone else's needs and never tending to your own." Caleb's hand slid to her throat, his thumb teasing the edge of her jaw. She trembled, her body barely able to contain the feelings stirring inside of her.

"Are you offering to tend to my needs?" Heat flushed every inch of her the moment the words left her mouth and she realized what she has said.

"Do you want me to?"

The sound of the door banging on its hinges jolted Rachel back to reality and she jumped back, guiltily glancing at the opening that led to the kitchen. Voices drifted toward them.

Her hand flew to her face. The heat of humiliation scalded her skin. She stared at Caleb. He stood there watching her react, any opinion he had on her bold behavior carefully locked away.

"I didn't mean that," she whispered, backing further away from him, as if the distance could turn back time and erase what she had done, the things she'd said.

"No?"

She closed her eyes briefly and took in a deep

breath. It didn't help. She needed to get out of there, away from him.

"Your lunch is growing cold." She waved a hand at the tray as she inched her way toward the door. He ignored his lunch and continued to watch her, studying her like an ant under a magnifying glass. She reached out and felt for the newly constructed archway leading to the kitchen. She spun on her heel and hurried through it.

Freedom glanced over her shoulder from where she stood at the counter chopping potatoes for the supper stew. Ethan sat at the table eating a plate of beans.

"What is wrong with you, child? You're so flushed you look like you was conversin' up close with the devil hisself."

"I think I may have been," Rachel said, for surely only the devil could tempt her in such a way that she forgot all about the years she'd spent keeping her desires in check so as not to turn out like her mother. Only the devil could cast one look and break open the vault where those emotions were kept and bring them racing to the surface until everything else faded into the background.

"I'm going out to the garden." She needed more than one room's distance between her and Caleb, and the temptation roiling between them.

Chapter Ten

Once Caleb finished eating Freedom's tasty beef stew, he set the empty dish outside on the porch and made his way down to the corral. As usual, he'd taken his supper alone, avoiding the boisterous mix of hands and Rachel's family that surrounded the supper table each evening. Only, this time, his avoidance had nothing to do with wanting to dodge potential questions about who he was and where he'd come from, and everything to do with trying to forget his foolhardiness of this afternoon.

What had he been thinking, egging Rachel on like that, prodding her to acknowledge the strange chemistry sizzling between them whenever they were in the same room? He'd made a promise to himself to leave it be, ignore it. Ignore her. A promise he conveniently forgot the moment he turned around and saw her standing in the newly built room, shoulders squared like a seasoned general and hands gripped together at her small waist like a green soldier. One look, and every promise he'd made fled for the hills, sent packing by the desire that rushed through his body and left no room for anything else.

He couldn't stop himself from touching her. Or from wishing there had been more. Especially once she'd started talking about taking care of her needs. He was pretty sure she hadn't meant it exactly the way it came out, if the crimson stain on her cheeks had been any indication, and Lord knows she'd backed out of there fast enough when he suggested taking her up on that offer.

He puffed out a breath and leaned against the railing of the corral. He was in way over his head on this one.

"C'mere, boy," he called to Jasper. The horse stopped nibbling at the grass, nickered, and then ambled over to where Caleb stood. He gathered a section of the horse's mane and gently led him back to the stables. His questionable behavior dogged his every step.

What would he have done if Rachel had said yes? Take her right there amid the lumber, in full view of anyone who passed by? He'd told her she deserved more, better, yet he was neither of those things. He'd stepped out of bounds and heaven only knew what Rachel would think of him now. He was no better than Kirkpatrick, holding power over her and using it against her.

Not that she was immune to his touch. He could tell from her rapid breathing, the way her expression softened and her lips parted in invitation. He'd almost taken her up on it. Almost waved goodbye to all his common sense and pulled her into his arms and kissed her so soundly they both would have felt the effects long after the kiss ended. If she hadn't stepped back, he would have done exactly that.

He was a dang fool!

He'd almost walked directly into a trap of his own making. A trap he swore he would never be caught in again.

Caleb shook his head as he stabled Jasper and filled his trough with oats. He couldn't afford such a lapse in judgment. He'd done that once before, thinking he could have the type of life where a man settled down comfortably in a home with a wife and a family.

Marianne.

It'd been a while since he'd thought of her. The pain of her betrayal, once a sharp knife through his heart, had since dulled, turning to disappointment more than anything else. He couldn't fault the choice she'd made, but it served as an ominous reminder. Some men weren't meant for settling down. Some men had a past, and that past didn't care one whit about dreams or wants or desires.

He couldn't allow himself to give in to whatever feelings were developing for Rachel. Feelings that grew with each passing day as he watched the strength with which she kept her family going and the limitless love she surrounded them with. He could not deny an overwhelming need to know what it would be like to be a part of that circle any more than he could deny the urge to protect her, the way she did everyone else.

But he was not the right man for the job. Eventually, his past would come calling. It always did, one way or the other. And it never left empty-handed.

By the time Caleb returned to the bunkhouse he could feel the dampness in the air. Daylight had given way to darkness, but gray clouds still smothered the stars. The others had already turned in. The lights in the main house had been extinguished.

He quietly opened the bunkhouse door and was greeted by Foster's snoring. Brody, sleeping on the top bunk, had rolled over to face the wall, his blankets pulled up around his ears. The woodstove radiated a stifling warmth and filled the small space with the scent of burning wood.

Each night, Caleb hoped his opinion of the bunkhouse would change, but it never did. It was still a small, dark room, even more so with the sun long set.

He sat on the edge of the bottom bunk, his bedroll next to him. His heartbeat had picked up the minute he'd stepped inside and the sheen of sweat on his forehead had nothing to do with the heat from the stove. He closed his eyes and tried to picture himself somewhere else. The trail leading along the creek with the breeze teasing the hair at his neck. The sound of the rushing water. Birds warbling overhead, calling out to each other in song. Rachel, her long hair dark against stark white sheets, spread out over naked shoulders—

His eyes snapped open. No. Not that.

Sweat trickled down his back.

Breathe.

Like every night before, the walls closed in.

Just breathe.

His throat constricted.

It was no good. Caleb stood, grabbed his bed-roll and slipped out the door, closing it quietly behind him. A straight-backed chair leaned against the outer wall. He sat down and stretched his legs out, covering himself with the bedroll. Overhead, the sky rumbled. A few minutes later, the first few raindrops splattered against the toe of his boots.

He sighed and surveyed the dark, starless sky. "You don't like me much, do you?"

As if in response, lightning split the sky and the rain increased in force. He twisted his mouth into a scowl.

"Thought not."

He pulled his hat lower and the blanket higher. It was going to be a long night.

Rachel lit the candle on the kitchen counter and worked the pump until water filled the kettle. The rolling thunder and her memories of the afternoon made it impossible to sleep.

She had crept from the room, careful not to wake Ethan, who had curled up next to her. He had his own bed tucked in the corner of her bedroom, but the rain and thunder had driven him to hers.

She'd spent half the night tossing and turning. Every time she closed her eyes she saw Caleb's image dancing beneath her lids, tormenting her in the same way his touch had teased her earlier. She was mortified by her response. Horrified she hadn't immediately pulled away. Shamed by how much she wanted to experience it again.

How had she come to this? Her whole life she had done her best to keep her wanton desires under lock and key. It had never been too difficult. Certainly, on occasion, she had felt the stirrings of wanting…more, but she'd never fully understood what *more* meant.

Until now.

And now she could not erase the shocking visions that mocked her each time she closed her eyes. Visions of herself with Caleb, naked and writhing beneath the ministrations of his hands and mouth as he explored every inch of her body until—

Thunder cracked and rumbled, blessedly interrupting her thoughts. She placed a hand to her forehead and stared out the window over the sink. She was hanging by a thread, and if she didn't get control of herself it was going to snap.

Forks of lightning flashed across the sky,

stretching its spindly fingers and illuminating the outbuildings and the landscape beyond. Rachel hadn't realized what she'd been staring at until the sudden light revealed the bunkhouse in the distance. What she saw there was unexpected, but the eerie glow dissipated before she could be certain it was nothing more than the result of her overtaxed imagination.

A few seconds later thunder rumbled, shaking the foundation of the house beneath her bare feet. She continued to stare out the window, waiting. Within a minute, another flash of lightning gave her a second look.

What was Caleb doing out there?

Rachel grabbed her coat from the peg by the door and pulled her shawl over her head to protect it from the driving rain. The man had obviously gone mad. She shoved her feet into her boots and turned up the wick on the lantern as she headed out the door.

Sidestepping as many of the puddles forming on the pathway as she could, it took her only a few minutes to reach the bunkhouse. She held the light up to eye level, still in disbelief.

Caleb poked a finger out of the edge of the soaked blanket covering his body and tilted the brim of his hat back far enough to glance up at her and scowl. "What in tarnation are you doing out in this?"

Her mouth fell open. "What am *I* doing out in this? I'm not the one sleeping in the rain. Have you lost your mind?" The question seemed redundant. Obviously he had. No man in his right mind would sleep in such conditions when a perfectly warm, dry bed awaited him on the other side of the door. Brody complained of Foster's snoring, but surely it wasn't so bad that being soaked to the skin was preferable.

"I wasn't sleeping."

"You were perhaps enjoying the lovely weather?"

His scowl deepened. "Get back to the house before you catch your death."

"Me?" Did the man think he was immune to Mother Nature's wrath? "I'm not going anywhere until you get back inside."

"I'm not going back inside."

"Then I'm not going anywhere."

To prove her point, Rachel sat down hard on the step leading up to the door.

She didn't sit for long. Caleb's strong hand wrapped around her arm and lifted her to her feet. She barely had time to grab the lantern before he propelled her forward toward the house. Her legs did double time, two steps for every one of his long strides. He was far less careful about missing the puddles than she had been, and the water splashed up beneath her soaked nightdress to chill her bare legs. He didn't say a word. It wouldn't have mattered if he had. The rain and thunder would have drowned him out. He let his actions do the talking, and they spoke volumes.

Rachel didn't protest. She didn't particularly care for the manhandling, but ultimately she was getting what she wanted. Him out of the rain. He didn't slow until he had her inside the house. She set the lantern on the kitchen table and swiped at the water on her face. When he turned to leave she called after him, stopping him before he reached the door.

"I'll only follow you back out."

He turned, slowly, his hazel eyes piercing through the dim light. A chill made goose bumps dimple her skin. "You'll stay put." His voice brooked no argument.

"You might own this land, Caleb, but you don't own me. I'll do as I see fit."

He pointed a finger at her. "Stay put," he repeated, biting the words out one by one. He turned and walked out the door.

Lips pursed, Rachel followed. His mule-like tendencies aside, she was not about to let him sleep out in the pouring rain. It had nothing to do with concern over his well-being, she told herself. She simply didn't have time to play nursemaid when he fell ill.

He spun on his heel at the sound of the door slamming shut behind her. Rachel barely had time to get her bearings in the dark when she was lifted up and over his shoulder, and carried back into the house.

"Let me go!" She beat at his back and kicked her legs.

"Shh! You'll wake the boy," he whispered harshly, throwing open the door as thunder shook the earth, drowning out her curse. He headed straight for the cot pushed against the far wall. One minute his broad shoulder bounced against her belly and the next she was falling through the air, her rump landing on the feather mattress Robert had insisted upon when he left her bed for good.

She leaned back as he loomed over her, one hand planted on the wall next to her head. The lantern danced light and shadow across his hard features. She inhaled his scent, a heady mix of fresh rain and cold air.

"Stay put," he repeated, holding a pointed finger under her nose. His expression possessed a hard edge. This was not a man accustomed to being defied.

"No."

His mouth flattened into a grim line and he looked away, resting his forehead against his outstretched arm. "He said you were hard-headed."

"Who said?"

His gaze swung back to her but he didn't answer. He didn't have to. Humiliation burned through her.

"What else did Robert say?"

Caleb said nothing.

"Tell me. I have a right to know!" She shoved at his wet sheepskin jacket but her small fist proved ineffective against the solid wall of muscle beneath.

"It doesn't matter," he said.

But it did matter.

The stress of the past week welled up inside of her and bubbled to the surface.

Hurt surged through her. One hand twisted into the wet hide of Caleb's jacket, while the other pummeled his chest in anger and frustration. "That isn't fair! I tried to be a good wife. I tried to understand Robert's failings and help him be a better man, the man I thought I'd married. But did he care? No. He was too busy gambling and whoring!"

Caleb's cold hand grabbed hers and held it tight. "I'm sorry. I shouldn't have said—"

She didn't want to hear his platitudes. She had gone into the marriage determined to create a home filled with love and laughter. She'd failed miserably. Year after year she'd watched her silly, romantic dreams get stomped flat until there was nothing left. Robert hadn't cared. He'd gotten what he'd wanted. Her land.

"What did Robert expect me to do? Stand around while we lost everything? This is the only home I've ever known. It's all my family has. I had to save it. He wasn't doing it. I had no choice. I had Brody and Ethan and I had…I had…"

She took a shuddering breath. She didn't want to cry. She had made it this far without crying. She tried to swallow back the tears but it was too much. They lodged in her throat then tumbled out in a sob, wracking her body.

"Aw, hell." Caleb eased himself onto the bed and pulled her onto his lap like a small child who'd had a nightmare. "Shh…don't cry," he whispered into her damp hair.

She shivered. Damn fool woman. What had she been thinking going out in this weather after him? He didn't need her concern. He'd slept in the rain before. He'd survived. He was less sure he could survive the sobbing woman shaking in his arms. Nothing kicked a man in the guts harder than a crying woman. It shot past every last defense he had and brought out all the things he'd tried hard to bury.

Worst of all, he couldn't escape how good it felt to cradle her in his arms, cold, wet clothes and all. He knew he had crossed into dangerous territory. She stirred something in him. Something he thought had died long ago. Something he worked hard at keeping dead.

"Shh…it's okay."

Her small body shook with a bitter sob. "It's not okay. My land is gone and my family is going to be without a home."

"I won't let that happen." The promise was out before he could catch it.

"We're not your burden to bear. And we can't keep pretending with you sleeping in the rain and me in here like I still have any claim to this place. Your rightful place is in my bedroom."

He bit down and closed his eyes, trying his best to erase the enticing image of her laid out naked on crisp sheets, her hair curling down over bare breasts—

Her head shot up, disrupting the image, and he found himself staring down at tear-stained cheeks and shiny eyes dark as midnight. "I mean...that's not what I meant. I mean, without me in it. Because it's your bedroom now, not mine. I don't mean that I would be in—"

He nodded and reached up, pulling her head back to his shoulder. The more she talked about it, the more vivid the vision became.

"I know what you meant." He tried to keep the disappointment out of his voice. A man like him didn't possess the kind of luck required to put a woman like Rachel Sutter in his bed.

He loosened his hold on her. The worst of the crying had abated, reduced now to the occasional sniffle and hiccup. He moved to set her off his lap.

"Wait." Her hot breath whispered against his neck. He suddenly wished he'd shaved so his rough whiskers didn't chafe her soft skin. "Can I...would it be okay..." She let out a long sigh and her weight pressed into him a little more. "Can I stay here a minute more? Would that be all right?"

Caleb swallowed. He knew what such a request cost a proud woman like her, and despite every sensible part of him telling him to refuse, he couldn't do it. For a brief moment in time she needed him. He knew it wouldn't last, but he couldn't deny how good it felt while it lasted. It had been a long time since someone had needed him.

"Sure."

He tightened his hold, thankful for the barrier of their jackets, yet even that wasn't enough to keep his mind from wandering to places it shouldn't be going. He couldn't help imagining easing her back onto the mattress, peeling the wet clothes from her body and covering her with his own. He couldn't help wondering if the rest of her was as soft and warm as the face nestled into his neck, or if her curves were every bit as alluring when bared to the lamplight. He wondered about her taste, her touch, her scent. He wondered if the sunrise set off the deep red in her hair and if she would turn into him and hide her face from its rays, snuggling in deep the way she did now.

He wondered about it all.

He just didn't want to wonder about it.

He didn't need that kind of complication.

"Why were you sleeping in the rain?" Her voice saved him from the disturbing effect his wayward thoughts had on his battered soul.

"I don't much care for small spaces." Funny how easily the admission tripped off his tongue. He'd never told anyone before.

She lifted her head, her eyes heavy with exhaustion. "How do you know how small it is if you're sleeping?"

A strand of hair had come loose from her wet braid and plastered itself to the side of her face. He reached up without thinking and drew his finger across her cheek, tucking it behind her ear, lingering near the soft curve of her neck. Her lips parted slightly and the warm exhalation of her breath touched his skin.

"I, uh…" What had she asked?

His hand slipped from her ear and cupped her face. Despite her cool skin he could feel the flush of warmth beneath. He needed to stop. This instant. He could feel the madness creeping up on him, the desire she kindled being stoked by the weight of her body and the dim light. Her lips, those full sensuous lips, taunted him until reason deserted him and he leaned forward just enough to take a small taste.

She inhaled sharply as his mouth softly touched hers.

Chapter Eleven

Rachel's earthy sweetness robbed Caleb of breath. He lingered there, cherishing the touch and the taste and the purity of her response as her mouth opened slightly and she breathed him in. Her hand lifted and slipped around his wrist, but she did not pull his hand away. Instead, she leaned in, ever so slightly, and accepted the kiss.

Every ounce of his being immediately hungered for more. For the past week he'd been quietly lusting after this woman, trying desperately to deny the fire she stoked within him. It had taken all of his considerable will to stuff those needs down and pretend they didn't exist. All it had taken was a few tears and a quiet request, and all of his good intentions had come undone.

He shifted slightly, tilting his head to take in a little more of her mouth, taste a little deeper without causing her to shy away. He didn't want to let go, not yet. He knew he should, that he had to. This couldn't last. He needed to pull away, apologize. Swear it would never happen again and make her believe it, even if he didn't. How could a man experience such sweetness and sensuality, and not want more?

But more was something he couldn't have.

With great reluctance, Caleb gently broke the kiss and rested his forehead against hers. Her rapid breaths brushed against his skin.

Her hand slipped away, and she straightened but made no move to leap out of his lap and throw him back out into the rain. He chanced a look at her. Her eyes were bright with surprise but did not possess a hint of disgust at the liberties he had taken. She touched her fingertips to her still parted lips, the motion taunting the thread of decency Caleb hung by.

"I apologize. I didn't mean to—"

She shook her head. "It was an accident," she said, her voice a soft whisper.

"It won't happen—"

"No, of course not."

Through the haze of emotion the kiss had created, he tried to remember what they had been talking about, anything to restore a sense of normality. He came up empty. "You had asked me something."

She nodded but avoided his gaze. "You said you didn't care for small spaces. I asked how you would know the room was small if you were sleeping."

"Right." Lord, she was beautiful. Even though she was soaking wet and wearing a coat two sizes too big he was still certain he had never seen anyone look so good. "I can't get to sleep if the room is small."

She looked up then, curiosity breaking past the awkwardness that enveloped them. "Why?"

He stopped the words before they escaped. He couldn't talk about that. "Can't a man have some secrets?"

"You're nothing *but* secrets. It seems you know a lot about me, but I don't know anything about you," she said, searching his face for answers. Every instinct he possessed told him he was treading on risky territory and it was time to retreat. Sharing intimate secrets with this woman had already led to one grave lapse in judgment. He could not chance another. Yet he made no effort to dislodge her and move away.

"You know my name," he said. It was more than anyone else knew. He'd changed it countless times over the years until he'd almost forgotten what it sounded like. It sounded good. At least, it did when she said it.

"Where are you from?"

He shrugged and the movement caused her to readjust her position. Her hip nudged against his groin, adding an emticing pressure against a painful swelling. He swallowed.

"I'm a drifter," he told her.

"I don't think you are," she said, resting her

head on his shoulder once more. The motion surprised him. He had expected that, once her senses returned, she would want to put as much distance between them as possible. Instead, she continued the contact, behaving as if the kiss had never happened.

He didn't know whether to be relieved or insulted.

"What do you mean?"

"I think you're just a man who's been drifting."

"What's the difference?"

It was her turn to shrug. When she spoke, he could tell the exhaustion of the past week had caught up with her, and the heat from the stove and their bodies had begun to lull her to sleep. "You don't seem to like it much…drifting. I saw your face when we rode up to the ranch. You looked like a man who…" She took a deep breath and relaxed further into his arms.

"Looked like a man who what?" What had she seen?

"It feels really nice here," she whispered, her voice fading. Was she still talking about the ranch? Or her current position on his lap?

"Rachel?"

She had grown pliant in his arms. Caleb pulled his head back and glanced down. Her eyes had closed. Dark shadows smudged beneath the crescent shape of her long lashes.

"Mmm?"

He moved to ease her off him, but her fingers

clung to the front of his coat. "Don't go," she mumbled. "Just for one more minute."

Her request touched a part of him so deep he hadn't even been aware it existed until her words landed there and stoked the embers. How long had she been deprived the luxury of a good night's sleep, without worry or fear invading her dreams? How long since she'd had the chance to lie protected in a man's arms without having to worry everything she'd worked for would fall apart in the morning light?

Could he deny her that?

His arms tightened around her. *No.*

"You need to get out of this wet coat," he whispered.

She nodded but didn't move.

Drawing on what little sanity he had left, Caleb reached between their bodies and fumbled with the buttons on her coat, releasing them one by one, then doing the same with his. He shrugged out of his before coaxing her out of hers, all the while trying to ignore the soft press of her breasts against his wool shirt, or how quickly her body heat permeated the thin cotton of her nightdress where his hand rested against her back.

This was his penance for his rash behavior. This slow unyielding torture.

But unless you shall do penance, you shall all likewise perish.

Caleb shook the verse from Luke out of his head and reached for one of the blankets behind them. He pulled it over her and eased her down against the pillow. One of her hands curled in his shirt, aware of his presence, refusing him the option of slipping away. Resigned, he tucked the blanket tightly around her then lay down next to her.

She nestled closer, furthering his torment. Caleb slipped his arm around her and rested his chin on top of her head. Within minutes her breathing deepened and he knew she had succumbed to sleep.

He wished he could be so lucky. He couldn't remember the last time he'd experienced a restful night's sleep.

One thing was for certain—he wouldn't this night.

Rachel stirred in her sleep, aware something was...different? She tried to awaken, to drag herself away from the warm comfort of sleep that left her groggy and disoriented. But sleep did not want to let her go without a fight. An even snore lulled her back into the intoxicating dream she'd had—

Snoring?

Rachel opened one eye and stared. Directly in front of her was an expanse of skin dusted with a light smattering of hair visible through the undone buttons of a worn shirt.

She blinked and tried to move, but a heavy weight held her legs in place and an arm had been flung across her waist, pinning her arms in front of her. Between them.

She flattened one hand against a wall of unforgiving muscle. Beneath her touch she could feel the even rise and fall of breathing, the steady beat of a heart. Her own thumped erratically against her ribs.

She pushed her mind past the veil of sleep, searching for an explanation. The previous night rushed back. Caleb sleeping in the rain. Carrying her back to the house. Her insistence he stay, hold her. Not let go.

The kiss.

Shame scalded her skin. She'd behaved wantonly, allowing him to take such liberties, giving in to the kiss the moment his lips had touched hers, setting off a firestorm of sensations she was powerless to resist. Her defenses had crumbled and she'd embraced her desires, disregarding every reason she had ever given herself for not becoming like her mama.

Was such behavior passed down like the color of her eyes or the shape of her nose? Would she always fight and fail in the attempt to suppress such craven desires? And why had this unrepentant need waited until Caleb's arrival to make itself known with such a vengeance?

Humiliation welled up inside of her. How would she face him? What would he think of her? She took a deep breath and tried to remain calm. The last thing she needed was to lose her composure again and throw herself at Caleb as if he was a safe harbor in the middle of a raging storm. There was nothing safe about him. If anything, he represented a brand new danger she apparently lacked the ability to resist.

It took her a moment to realize his breathing had changed, and the even buzz of his snoring had fallen silent.

"You angry about last night?" His voice held the roughness of someone who had awakened from a deep, satisfying sleep. He made no attempt to remove his tangled limbs from hers. Worse still, she made no attempt to make him.

"I'm not angry."

"The way you're twisting my shirt tells me different."

She looked down at her hand where it clenched the worn material over his heart and realized he was right. She let go.

"Sorry." She peeked up at him. His mouth twitched. The whiskers were getting thicker. At this rate he'd have a full beard in no time. She remembered the way it had tickled her skin as his mouth pressed into hers. "You need a shave."

"That I do."

She needed to get up. It shouldn't feel so right to lie here in Caleb's arms. She knew nothing about him, other than the fact that he considered himself a drifter and didn't care much for small, dark spaces. And that his kiss revealed a surprising tenderness that stole her breath.

Stop it! "I need to get up now."

If she didn't, she ran the risk of staying there all day wrapped in the safety of his arms, shutting out the rest of the world. It was a tempting idea. But a quick glance out the window showed the first hints of gold coloring the horizon. Soon Freedom would arrive and Ethan would awaken. She couldn't risk them finding her in such a compromising position.

Caleb exhaled, his warm breath ruffling the stray hairs loosened from her braid through the night. She must look a sight. With slow, languorous movements he removed his leg from hers and slipped his arm from her waist, sliding it beneath the pillow.

Rachel quickly pulled herself up into a sitting position, the sudden absence of his warmth hitting her like a cold blast of winter air.

"Thank you...for staying last night." The words choked out of her.

He closed his eyes. He had surprisingly long lashes for a man. Dark at the roots, then turning pale at the tips, where they brushed against his cheek. "You're welcome."

"I—I—" Heat crept up her neck and invaded her face. "I haven't slept that well in a long time."

Two vertical lines appeared between his brows. "No...me either."

"We'll have to find you other accommodations if the bunkhouse doesn't suit." She pulled her mind to more practical matters. Anything to stop her thinking about what had occurred last night and what would change now that morning's harsh light threatened. "Ethan suggested you could sleep here."

He opened his eyes when she gave the mattress pat. "Wouldn't be right."

"It's your house."

"I'll bunk out in the barn." He stretched, his long limbs dwarfing the narrow cot.

"I can't have you—"

"If it's my place, I'm guessing I can pretty much sleep where I want, don't you agree?"

She pursed her lips, the reminder of her precarious living situation hitting home once again.

"Fine. Sleep in the barn." She stood up, suddenly conscious of how little she had on. The thin nightdress left little to the imagination. She reached down and grabbed her coat off the floor, wrapping it around her shoulders. His gaze traveled over her, starting at her toes and slowly making its way up until their eyes met.

Perhaps the barn wasn't such a bad idea after all.

"I'll get dressed and start breakfast."

He nodded and looked away, making a hard study of the far wall. "I'll go get myself a shave."

"Thought you might be hungry."

Caleb glanced over his shoulder to find Freedom's tall frame silhouetted in the doorway of the kitchen, a well-stocked plate in one hand and a steaming mug of coffee in the other. The aroma from both wafted into the newly constructed room, competing with the strong scents of pine and cedar. His stomach rumbled.

"You thought correctly." He set down his tools and approached her, suppressing the wave of disappointment that washed over him. Rachel usually delivered his noon meal, but she'd taken to avoiding him since the night of the rainstorm. Just as well. He was finding it exceedingly difficult to put the kiss they'd shared out of his mind. Nor could he budge the memory of how good it felt waking up with her body nestled into his. He couldn't remember the last time he'd slept so soundly or woken up feeling so content.

Freedom placed the food on the same bench Rachel had a few days earlier.

"Thank you kindly, ma'am." He picked up the plate and took a bite of tender fried chicken.

"Don't you be *ma'am*-ing me. You's call me Freedom, jus' like the rest."

Caleb swallowed and smiled. He'd call her whatever she wanted if she kept bringing him tasty fare like this. "Yes, ma'am. Freedom."

"Mmm." Freedom's sharp eyes studied him. She didn't look in a hurry to get back to the kitchen and he sensed he was about to have company with his meal.

"Care to sit?" He'd constructed a makeshift table to lay out his hand-drawn plans of the addition. He'd wanted to show them to Rachel, in the hope she would be pleased, before he realized that doing so was like rubbing salt in a wound. She didn't believe she would be here to enjoy the extra space, and Caleb couldn't figure yet if she was right or not. If she wouldn't let him pay off Kirkpatrick, maybe the best course of action would be to send her away. Lord knew the two of them couldn't stay living here on this ranch together for a whole lot longer without another incident occurring. The atmosphere between them was combustible, and he for one did not care to get burned.

Freedom pulled out one of the stools he'd brought in and plunked her ample form on the small seat. She remained silent while he scooped in a few more bites, but Caleb knew he was on borrowed time. Freedom Jones was working up to say something and he suspected he'd have no choice but to listen when it came.

He didn't bother trying to stop her. Maybe it would help divert his thoughts from continually straying to Rachel's sweet taste.

"It was a good thing you done, bringin' Miss Rachel's husband home."

Caleb nodded. There wasn't anything good about it and he knew it. The man should have come back of his own accord, not stuffed in a pine box and dropped in the ground the day after he arrived.

"Can't say he'll be sorely missed 'round here, but a man deserves to be buried near his kin jus' the same." She waved a hand at Caleb as if he had been about to speak past the mouthful of biscuit he'd just taken. "And don't go tellin' me I should be respectin' the man now 'cause he got hisself shot dead. That man don't deserve my respect no how after treatin' Miss Rachel like he did."

"Treating her how?" Caleb's guts clenched around the food he'd just swallowed. Had the man abused her?

Freedom scrutinized him from head to toe, as if judging how much she could trust him. "Turns out he wasn't wantin' a wife when he married Miss Rachel, jus' her land. Wanted to make hisself up like Mr. Kirkpatrick with his high-falutin' attitude and fancy clothes, 'cept Mr. Robert didn't have the gumption to get off his sorry behind and do the work required. Thought he could gamble his way to riches. And he treated Miss Rachel like an afterthought while he was doin' it, like she wasn't worth his attention. Broke her heart, though she'd never admit it. Had all these romantic ideas in her head 'bout bein' a happy family. Guess she was tryin' to make up for how hers had ended up."

Kirkpatrick had made reference to Rachel's mother, but Rachel had never elaborated. It seemed a painful subject and not one he wanted to pry into. Now curiosity whetted his appetite, and he couldn't resist the lure.

"How did her family end?"

"In a bad way." Freedom shook her head

and resituated herself more comfortably on the wooden seat before she continued. "Rachel's daddy kilt himself when she was jus' fourteen and left the land to her. After his passin', her mama got sick. That's where I come in. Kirkpatrick done hired me to care for the woman, but he wanted me to spy on Miss Rachel, too, tell him everythin' she was doin' and thinkin'. Well, I ain't no spy and I told him so. I quit that day and Miss Rachel took me in. But ain't nothin' we did could save her mama. That woman had more things weighin' on her than she could carry. When she passed away two years later, that left Rachel with Brody. He was a small boy, younger than Ethan is now. That's when Mr. Robert and the sheriff came callin'. Sheriff is a good man. He'da been the right choice, but Mr. Robert jus' dazzled her till she forgot everyone else, makin' promises he never kept."

"You said her pa left the land to her, not Brody?" Seemed to him a man would pass the land to his son, regardless of the boy's age.

For a moment Freedom said nothing, her face void of expression. The silence was punctuated by birds warbling just outside the window. Sunlight poured into the room and pressed against Caleb's back.

"Her pa left the land to her, and rightly so," Freedom said. It wasn't much as far as explanations went, but Caleb knew it was all he would get.

"And how does Kirkpatrick figure in all of this?"

"Kirkpatrick wants her land. They share a border, but he needs more space for his cattle and Rachel's land is rich for grazing. He offered once to marry her, 'afore she settled on Mr. Robert, but she turned him down. I'm guessin' he'll start sniffin' around again now."

The idea set his teeth on edge. He'd only met the man once, but it was enough to know he was a first class bastard who would no doubt take great pleasure in breaking someone as strong and spirited as Rachel.

"I take it Mrs. Sutter doesn't want to marry Kirkpatrick?"

"Might be she don't have a choice now, seein' as she don't own the land no more and has no way to pay off the debt she owes." She gave him a pointed look.

Caleb set the plate down on the table and stood, walking over to the window. He stared out into the yard beyond. It wasn't hard to see why Rachel mourned losing this land. The valley was rife with rich soil and the snow-peaked mountains in the background took your breath away. It was like a small oasis in the middle of a harsh land. He closed his eyes and breathed in the fresh air, letting a sense of calm sweep over him.

If things were different, this would be a nice place to call home.

But things weren't different. He needed to keep that in mind.

He opened his eyes and turned back to Freedom.

"She told you about me ownin' the land."

"She did."

"Why are you telling me all this?" Freedom didn't strike him as a gossip, and he'd known when she walked into the room she had a point to make.

"Figured if'n you had a good sense of what Miss Rachel has been through you'd do right by her. She's suffered enough misery."

He nodded. Freedom was right. He knew it. He'd known it from the first moment he laid eyes on her at Sutter's funeral and watched the stoic strength with which she held things together, only to be brought down when he told her the news of the deed. The yoke of responsibility hung heavy on his shoulders.

"I plan on makin' things right."

"Mmm. And how you plan on doin' that, Mr. Beckett?"

Caleb placed his hands on his hips and let out a long, slow breath as he watched Ethan chase a stray chicken around the yard, trying to corral him back into the coop.

"Damned if I've figured that one out yet," he muttered.

His plan to make his sojourn in Salvation Falls a brief one crumbled with each passing day. He should have signed the deed over to Rachel on the first day and ridden straight out of town as he'd planned. Before he knew about Kirkpatrick, before he'd met her family. Before he'd known what type of woman she truly was. If he'd left before he learned all that, his conscience would have been clear. Ignorance would have been his bliss. But he hadn't done that. Instead, he'd lingered too long, and now, knowing the scope of what Kirkpatrick wanted and sensing Rachel's vulnerability, well…

He couldn't walk away. Not yet. She needed help, whether he liked it or not.

He would do what he had to.

He owed her that much.

Chapter Twelve

Rachel stacked the last of the supper dishes on the shelf. Next to her, Freedom hummed an old spiritual, filling the quiet kitchen with her rich voice. This used to be Rachel's favorite time of the day. The men had been fed and the lively energy of the late dinner hour had dissipated as the hands and Brody went off to their respective bunkhouses. With the work of the day completed, Rachel could put up her feet, maybe read Ethan a story from the book of fables her father had given her years ago.

This was the time of day when she could relax.

At least it had been, before her world had been turned upside down. Now, when she finally had time to stop working, her mind filled with worry and she started fretting over what she would do.

It didn't help matters that Caleb had ignored the call to supper, as was his habit, and continued banging away. He'd framed up the roof with Foster's help, but when Freedom rang the dinner bell only Foster hurried his old bones to the table. The hammering continued, competing with the whine of the harmonica Ethan abused each night in an attempt to learn to play properly.

Rachel rubbed at her temples. If she wanted quiet, likely she would have to hike well into the mountains at this rate. As for peace, well, she had given up on that elusive item. Especially since, any minute now, Caleb was bound to make his way into the kitchen and pick up the plate she'd set aside, warming on top of the stove.

Rachel usually tried to ensure she had removed herself from the kitchen by then, retreating to her room, but there had been potatoes to scrub and beans to soak and time simply got away from her. But if she sneaked away now and let Free—

"I's be headin' off to my own bed," Freedom said. "You be sure and see to it Mr. Beckett get his supper. Man been workin' hisself to the bone all day. He'll need a full belly lest he drop over from lack of sustenance."

"You're leaving?" She couldn't leave. Freedom always stayed behind to ensure Caleb got his meal. If Free left then…well, then Rachel would have to face him, and that was the last thing she wanted. Her eyes strayed to the cot and heat flushed her skin.

"Been a long day. These ole bones are right weary tonight. I'll take Len his plate." Len had missed supper, sending word back with Brody that he planned to complete his work on the fence while there was still daylight left.

"I can do that." Anything to avoid being left alone with Caleb.

Freedom waved her off as she headed to the door, taking the spare lamp with her to light her way. "He's right on my way. Poor fool must be starvin', waitin' so long on a meal. You mind Mr. Beckett get his too. Cain't have my good cookin' goin' to waste."

Rachel didn't have a mind to do anything save run into her room and hide. She didn't want to lay eyes on Caleb. Every time she did, she was reminded of the expression she'd seen in his hazel eyes seconds before he'd kissed her. They had been filled with compassion and desire and loneliness. She couldn't shake the sense he had needed to kiss her every bit as much as she had wanted him to.

She touched her lips. At times, she swore she could still feel him there. The gentle pressure awakening things inside of her she'd left dormant for more years than she cared to count. And other things she hadn't even known existed before his kiss. As much as she fought against it, as much as she hated the thought of turning out like her mama, she couldn't stop imagining what it would be like to be kissed by him again. Couldn't help wanting it deep in her bones, until every thought she'd had since then somehow led back to him.

Rachel gave her head a quick shake. That was

the kind of perilous thinking that got a girl into trouble, and she already had more trouble than a body could handle.

"This mine?"

Rachel jumped and spun around, too deep in her thoughts to have noticed the hammering had ceased.

"Yes," she said, taking a step back, even though Caleb was on the other side of the room. The more distance the better. "Be careful," she warned as he reached for the plate. "The dish is still—"

"Dang it!"

"Hot."

"Son of a—" Caleb winced, shaking his hand as if he could agitate the burn right off it.

"Come here." Rachel crossed the room and took him by the wrist, leading him to the sink. She cranked the pump handle and stuck his hand under the rush of cold water.

"I'm fine." He tried to pull his hand away, but Rachel held firm, tucking his arm against her ribs to hold him in place.

"Don't fight me. You don't want it to blister." But even as she said the words she became overly mindful of his body next to hers. The feel of sinew and strength in the arm pressed against her ribs. The rough calluses on the hand she held beneath the stream of water. He'd stop trying to pull away, and when the water petered out he made no move to step back.

Rachel froze, awareness pulsating through her with each heartbeat. She had no idea how to gracefully extricate herself from this position. Worse, she wasn't sure she wanted to. It surprised her how good it felt to simply stand next to a man, this man, and have his presence surround her, to feel the weight of him leaning into her. If she turned, they would be face to face. Close enough to kiss.

Her breath shuddered in her chest and she closed her eyes, savoring the moment as much as she wished it away.

"Thank you." The low rumble of his voice vibrated into her.

She opened her eyes and gripped the edge of the counter. Her knees had become inconveniently weak. "You're welcome."

In the window over the sink, she watched their reflection. He tilted his head toward her. "You smell like violets, you know. Did anyone ever tell you that?"

She shook her head. He'd shaved since their kiss. The newly exposed skin only served to enhance the sharp lines of his jaw and the prominence of his cheekbones.

"It's my soap. I wash my hair with it."

"Well, it smells nice. Real pretty."

He glanced up and caught her gaze reflected in the window. She couldn't speak so she nodded, thinking it would be impolite to let his compliment go unacknowledged.

A slow smile creased his face. "I need my hand."

She looked down quickly, horrified to realize she had yet to let go. "Oh!"

Rachel released her hold, mortification scalding her skin from head to toe. Once Caleb stepped away, she spun around.

He held up his hand. "See, I'm fine."

Already the redness had begun to fade. She'd overreacted.

She cleared her throat. "Be more careful the next time."

His smile grew and light danced in his mercurial eyes. "Yes, ma'am."

She found it difficult to breathe. She needed to escape to her room, but Caleb had stepped back and now blocked her way. She would have to pass him to leave. She didn't trust herself to get that close again.

They stood like that for a moment, staring at each other.

"I think I got it!" Ethan rushed into the room in his nightshirt and boots, waving the harmonica in his hand. He stopped between them, his face beaming, completely unaware of the tension choking the air. Or was that something only she felt? But no, she could see it in Caleb's eyes, as well. She wasn't the only one who'd felt it. The sizzle. The heat.

"What did you get?" she said, thankful for something else to focus on.

"I think I can play a song. I made it up myself. Wanna listen?"

Rachel forced a smile. "Absolutely. Play away."

Ethan raced to the table and pulled out a chair, scrambling to stand on top of it. He motioned to the two of them, pulling the harmonica away from his mouth.

"You have to dance. It's a dancing song."

Suddenly, Ethan's diversion was less appreciated. "What kind of dance?"

"The kind where you—" He waved his hands back and forth, motioning the two of them together. "You know. Dance together."

Caleb's voice sounded behind her. "A waltz?"

Ethan nodded, the instrument already to his lips. He blew a harsh note that made Rachel wince then glared at them when neither had moved. With a huff, he jumped off the chair and stalked toward them. "C'mon."

Ethan grabbed Caleb's wrist and pulled him toward Rachel. He placed Caleb's hand on her waist and then gave her a small push. She stumbled toward Caleb but his hand on her waist kept her steady—while setting her insides on fire.

Ethan climbed back onto his perch and put the harmonica to his mouth. This time, the sound that came out of it was quieter. He stopped and glanced down at them. "Don't forget to dance."

Rachel wasn't sure she remembered how to dance, it had been so long. She hadn't danced since her wedding, really. There had been no call for it afterward. And Ethan's uneven tune did not help matters. Nor did the fact her knees had become as wobbly as a foal's.

Caleb picked up her hand. The other hung limply by her side. "I believe the other one goes on my shoulder."

She stared at his chest, where his shirt opened at the neck. Maybe, if she didn't look him in the eye, she could imagine he was someone else. Someone less likely to put her brain in a dither. Then maybe she could control the insatiable need to step into his arms and let him sweep her around the kitchen as if they were in the middle of a fancy ball, the likes of which she'd only read about.

She placed her hand on his shoulder. Muscle shifted beneath her light touch, sending tremors shooting up her arm. He started to move. She stumbled again, forgetting the steps, her mind and her memory a jumbled mess.

"Easy. Just one step at a time," he whispered, his voice traveling beneath the tone of Ethan's playing.

Caleb's movements were smooth, and soon she found her rhythm and followed his lead. His gracefulness surprised her, a complete contrast to the hard man who had shown up at Robert's funeral and turned her life upside down. Only a couple of weeks had passed since that day, yet it felt as if a lifetime had gone by. She opened her eyes and glanced up to find him watching her.

A rush of desire swept through her. She tried to beat it back but remnants remained, prickling her insides and making her ache.

"Where did you learn to dance?" she asked.

"Picked it up along the way."

The vagueness of his answer piqued her. "Anywhere in particular?"

"Here and there." His steady gaze never left hers, making it hard to concentrate on her questions. He had a way of frazzling her thinking until it twisted around itself and refused to come out right.

Caleb spun her around, drawing her closer, his movements not exactly matching the tune Ethan was attempting to play. It was as if he had a different song going through his head. She wondered what it was, where it came from. Who had he danced with before? Did he have a sweetheart stashed away somewhere? A wife?

The thought struck out of the blue. She had assumed he didn't, but he wouldn't be the first man to wander about looking for work, leaving a family somewhere, going back to them from time to time when the mood struck.

She fought to steady her breath. If he did have a wife and family, likely he would move them here, settle down for good, maybe. Had he already sent them word? Was he simply biding his time until they arrived before breaking the news to her? And where would that leave her when they did? No wife in her right mind would let a widow with a brood of people depending on her stake a claim to her home. Or her husband.

Not that Rachel was looking to stake a claim.

"Are you married?" She choked the words out.

Surprise registered in Caleb's eyes, but it was a fleeting expression like a light breeze that touched down and disappeared before you had a chance to truly enjoy it. "Why?"

Rachel shook her head. "It just occurred to me you might be."

"I have no wife." He said the words, but his gaze skittered away, looked over her shoulder at some point beyond.

She breathed easier upon hearing his answer, but something about his reaction left her unsettled. Before she could consider whether to question him further, the front door slammed open and Brody flew through the opening, his eyes wild and his breath coming in gasps.

Caleb and Rachel jumped apart.

"What are you doing, Brody? You scared the life out—"

"Len didn't come back...went lookin'...he's hurt bad...gunshot...horse threw him...think his leg is broke..."

Rachel grabbed Caleb's hand without thinking. "Help me get the buckboard. Brody, get Freedom to stay with Ethan then meet us at the barn. Go!"

"It's a clean break," Dr. Bolger said, coming out of the back room where he treated his patients.

Unlike Merrick, Dr. Bolger tended to those who still had a pulse.

He wiped his hands on a clean towel then hung it on a hook protruding from the wall. "Should heal up fine providing infection doesn't set in. I'll keep him here until the worst has passed. Safer than trying to get him back to the ranch over rough road and messing up my handiwork." The doctor smiled through his meticulously trimmed gray beard, his blue eyes twinkling.

Rachel slumped against the wall where she had been waiting impatiently for the doctor's verdict. He was a direct man, thorough and not given to sugarcoating matters. If he said Len would be fine, she believed him. It was a relief. Finally, some good news.

Dr. Bolger walked over to the potbellied stove near the window and pulled down three mugs, pouring a generous helping of steaming dark liquid into each of them. The enticing aroma of coffee filled the room. He handed her a mug, and another one to Caleb, who had waited with her quietly, offering comfort if not conversation.

The doctor took a seat at the long table and motioned for them to do the same. Rachel was thankful for the offer, her legs were about to give out. Caleb waved it off, standing sentinel behind her.

"You want to tell me what happened? Len said someone shot off a gun close enough to make his horse rear up and throw him. Can't see any of your boys being so foolish."

Rachel winced as the hot coffee burned its way down her throat. "My boys aren't. Len was out fixing the fence bordering on the Double K lands."

"You think Kirkpatrick did this?"

Rachel scowled. "Not him personally, but one of the hooligans he hired. They're the ones who knocked down the fence last week, I'm sure of it. My guess is they waited until he went to ride back for the night, took potshots at him and knocked him off his horse."

The idea of it twisted her stomach into knots. Shamus's actions were escalating. It was one thing to pressure her into selling her land to repay her debt, but resorting to violence to intimidate her? Well, he could come after her all he wanted, but she wasn't about to stand idly by and watch him hurt innocent bystanders in the process.

"Maybe best you talk to the sheriff," Dr. Bolger suggested, but they both knew it would do no good. As much as Hunter wanted to help her, his hands were tied. He needed evidence, and that was the one thing Shamus was careful to never leave behind. "Stay in town tonight. You can check on Len in the morning. I don't want to see you riding back home in the pitch black if Kirkpatrick has turned his mind to these kind of tactics."

Rachel nodded. She was exhausted, and the idea of riding over rough road in the dark did not appeal to her. She'd get a room at the Pagget and try not to think about the added expense Shamus's actions were causing her over-extended purse strings.

"Thanks for everything, Dr. Bolger. I'm much obliged." She stood on shaky legs, Caleb's strong hand on her elbow a welcome relief. She leaned into his strength.

"Take care of her," the doctor instructed Caleb as they turned toward the door. She didn't hear his response, but his hand never wavered from her arm.

They walked to the hotel in silence. When they arrived, Cletus was at his usual spot behind the counter, half asleep. Caleb took care of procuring two rooms and within a few minutes they were on their way to the third floor.

"Maybe we should tell the truth," she said, dropping her weary body onto the edge of the bed. Caleb had followed her inside, though his own room was across the hall. She hadn't stopped him, glad for the company.

"Which truth would that be?"

She glanced over her shoulder to find him at the window. He'd pulled back the faded curtain and peered down into the street below. The sounds of raucous laughter filtered up from the saloons.

She pushed herself to her feet and turned to face him. "About the deed. We need to let people know. Or Shamus, at least. He had his men hurt Len to make me give up and sell him the land.

Maybe if he knows I don't own it he'll back off. Give up."

Caleb turned away from the window and met her gaze, his mouth pulled into a grim line. She wanted to trace his mouth, brush her fingertips over his lips until his expression softened. Her breath caught. No. She couldn't be thinking like that. She curled her fingers into the palm of her hand and pressed them into her thigh.

"Men like Shamus Kirkpatrick don't give up. They just find another way to get what they want."

"Then what do I do?" Frustration roiled inside of her. "I can't stand back and let him hurt my men!"

Caleb stood silhouetted against the window, the thin lamplight casting him in shadow. For a long, silent moment, he stared at her saying nothing. Finally, he spoke, and she was thankful for it. His intense scrutiny left her weak and made her long to rest her burden on his strong shoulders.

"If people discover you no longer own the Circle S, what do you think they'll say, knowing you're still living in the house with me there?"

His words hit with the force of a runaway horse.

"They'll think I'm…we're…" She swallowed and sat back on the bed, all the fight going out of her. "That I'm earning my room and board flat on my back."

"That's right."

"We could tell them it isn't like that. Set them

straight," she reasoned, but Caleb's response only echoed what she already knew.

"You can't set people straight. Once they put their minds to an assumption there's no changing it."

"They'll think I'm no better than Mama," she whispered. With the runaway feelings she was having for Caleb, maybe they'd be right. Maybe she really was no better than her mama.

He crossed the room and knelt down in front of her, his hand covering hers where it rested on her lap, large and capable against the faded calico of her skirt. The intimacy crossed the line of propriety, but she didn't stop him. The warmth of his touch comforted her.

"We'll keep up appearances," Caleb said. "With Len hurt, no one will question you on hiring extra help. It will buy us some time until we can figure out what to do."

We. As if she had a say in any of this. The land was his, the decisions were his. She was nothing more than a bystander in her own life, waiting for the ax to fall.

She nodded her agreement. What choice did she have?

Caleb remained where he was. She could feel his gaze upon her, though she didn't dare look up to meet it. Defeated, she feared one glance into those hazel eyes and she'd be lost.

"What did your mama do to make you so determined to be nothing like her?"

Chapter Thirteen

Rachel blinked, staring down at his hand where it covered hers. It was a painful subject, an even more painful memory. "My mother was a selfish woman."

"In what way?" He squeezed her hand, sending a shiver up her arm to her heart.

"When I was ten, Pa had to leave to work in the railroads. The winter had been hard on us and we needed the money. While he was gone, Shamus Kirkpatrick started calling. He'd only recently bought the land bordering ours. At first, it was just social calls, but soon I noticed..."

"Noticed what?"

"They stopped visiting in the drawing room and moved it to the bedroom. When Shamus would leave, he'd see me in the kitchen and put his finger to his lips at the same time he placed a coin on the table. Like it was our little secret and I wasn't to tell. After he left, Mama would come out, bright and chipper like nothing had happened. I might have been a child, but I knew what was going on wasn't right."

Caleb was quiet for a moment. "Your mama and Kirkpatrick had an affair."

"It wasn't just an affair, Caleb. It was pure, un-adulterated selfishness. She let Shamus have his way with her like a common whore, putting her own desires before her family, and it destroyed us."

"Did you ever confront her?"

She nodded, squeezing her eyes shut against the ugly memories. It did no good. They kept coming, like waves crashing the shore. "Every time Shamus showed up on our doorstep I felt sick inside. And each time he left, he'd put his finger to his lips to let me know I was to keep quiet. I couldn't stand it any longer and demanded Mama stop or I would tell Pa what she was doing."

"What did she do?"

Rachel opened her eyes at Caleb's gentle prob-ing. She didn't know why he cared, but something about telling the story relieved her. Not that it was any secret in town what had occurred. Shamus had made sure of that.

"Mama begged me not to tell. She said it would destroy our family if my father knew. She said we needed the money and that Shamus had promised to help us out, but he wanted something in return. Mama was a beautiful woman. He didn't care that she already had a husband. That's the way he is.

He just takes what he wants and to hell with who gets hurt in the process."

"And did your mother get hurt?"

"Mama tried to make it sound like a sacrifice, but I saw the way she looked at the other ladies in town and the things they had that she wanted. Shamus gave her those things." Rachel shook her head. "What everyone must have thought. They knew Papa was away, that we didn't have the money to buy such things. The only way for her to get them was by—"

She cut herself off, unable to say the words.

Unshed tears burned her eyes and Caleb's handsome face swam before her. He'd remained motionless while she spoke, his thumb slowly caressing the palm of her hand where he held it.

"What Mama did, she did for herself."

"What happened?"

Rachel took a deep breath and continued. "I told her I was going to tell Papa. It made me sick carrying around the shame of her secret. But Mama promised if I kept quiet, she would never see Shamus again and as far as I know she kept her promise. He never came to our house again. Pa returned a month later, but by then, the damage had been done."

"What kind of damage?"

"The kind that shows up nine months later." Rachel stared down at her lap, unable to meet Caleb's gaze. She didn't think she could stand to see his pity.

"Brody," he said, quickly putting two and two together and saving her from revealing it herself.

Rachel nodded. "He knew Brody wasn't his. It sent him into a tailspin. He couldn't reconcile what she had done. He was angry. When he begged me to tell him what I knew, I couldn't keep her secret any longer. I thought if I told him the truth, maybe we could be a family again."

"But that didn't happen."

Rachel shook her head. "No. It made things worse. I think Pa tried. He loved Mama, but in the end, her betrayal was too much. One day Pa left the house with his gun. I thought he was going hunting, but he didn't return. The next day Foster found him. He'd ridden down to the creek, to his favorite fishing spot and killed himself."

"I'm sorry, Rachel." Caleb's words were simple but they touched her just the same. "You said you had a drawing room…where?"

Rachel shook her head. "We had a different house then."

"What happened to it?"

"Mama burned it down. She wasn't right after Brody was born, and when Pa died, she took a turn for the worse. She languished for a while and by the end of it, she'd near lost her mind. We left her alone to tend to some chores and before long we could see smoke in the distance. We came running. Mama had set the bedroom on fire. I grabbed Brody from his cradle and Freedom picked Mama up like she was nothing and we ran out of the house. But by the time the fire was under control, it was too late. I was glad for it, to be honest. I hated that house. Every inch of it reminded me of what she'd done."

"You never forgave her, did you?"

"I never forgave her and I never wanted to be like her, some wanton creature who lets her desires override her common sense, with no care about who gets hurt in the process."

"Is that why you keep ignoring what's going on between us like it doesn't exist?"

She swallowed; her emotions raw from confession. "There's nothing going on."

"What your mama did, that was wrong and it hurt a lot of people. But us...we haven't done anything to be ashamed of. I don't understand why it's happenin' but I'm dog tired of tryin' to pretend it isn't there. Every time I look at you, I want to kiss you. I've tried to tell myself it's the wrong way of thinking and maybe it is. But it doesn't seem to want to right itself either way."

Caleb's hands moved from hers and slid up her arms, gently gripping her elbows, forcing her to look at him. The shuttered expression he usually wore changed, and for the first time since their initial kiss, Rachel thought she saw him as he really was. Not the hardened drifter who had ridden into town, but the man who had been drifting and needed a place to stop. A place to call home.

"I do feel it," she whispered, the admission

slipping out of her the moment she let her guard down. "But it scares me."

He took in her words and nodded. She could see him mulling them over, but she didn't know his mind well enough to determine what he thought.

"You don't need to be afraid of me."

She didn't know how to tell him it wasn't him she feared, but herself. She feared letting go and giving in to her desires, knowing how catastrophic the results could be. Rachel had too much resting on her shoulders to allow that to happen. But when she looked at him, the intensity of his gaze robbed her of the words. All she could think of was how much she wanted to kiss him, to feel his lips on hers again, to know for one blissful moment that she was alive, that she existed beyond just being a widow or a mother, a sister, a rancher or a boss. That she was a woman.

She couldn't be certain which of them moved first; maybe it was her, her desires pushing past her reluctance, fighting through her fears and taking control. It hardly mattered. The end result was the same. Only this was no gentle kiss as before. Their lips melted together. She opened to him and allowed him to explore the contours of her mouth. He pulled her closer to him until she sat perched on the end of the bed, her skirts sliding up her legs as she straddled his kneeling form. She could feel the strength in his thighs where they pressed against hers and reveled in his touch as one hand slid into the loose bun at her neck and set her hair free. It fell heavy against her back as their mouths and tongues tangled together, wanting and demanding. Needing.

But what he needed from her went far beyond her ability to give. His desire was evident, pressing against her where their bodies meshed together. He wanted more than a kiss. And she wanted to give it to him.

Then the fear she'd pushed away came rushing back. She broke the kiss, pulling back even though every instinct in her body demanded otherwise. "I can't be that woman."

"What woman?"

"The kind who gives her body away like it has no value."

"Is that what you think I want you to do? Just lie back and give me what I want?" He cupped her cheek and forced her to look at him. "You do have value, and I would never expect you to do something you didn't feel right about. Are you telling me you don't feel right about this? You want me to stop?"

Emotions tore about inside of her, shredding her sense and reasoning. Part of her wanted to throw caution to the wind and give in to the feelings she had developed for this man, but the other part of her, the part that feared the unknown consequences, silenced her until she had no answer to give.

"Alright then."

Caleb's hand slid away and he stood, taking with him the warmth of his touch. Her skirts slid back into place. It frightened her how much she wanted him back, to tell him everything in her heart and mind. She'd already lost so much. She didn't know if she had it in her to risk losing anything else. She'd given her heart once, and it had ended badly. What made her think this time would be any different? That if she gave him her heart and her body he wouldn't one day decide he'd had enough and ride out of town as suddenly as he'd ridden in?

"I'm sorry. It's just—"

But he had already turned away, settling his hat on his head.

He paused at the door, tilting his head slightly in her direction. "I'm goin' for a walk. Lock the door behind me and get some sleep. We'll ride back to the ranch in the morning."

Despite the late hour, there was still plenty of activity in town, centered mostly around the saloons. Tinny music and raucous laughter spilled out into the street. Caleb headed in that direction. It had been a long, hard day and he desperately needed a drink.

He couldn't return to the hotel, not yet. If he did, he'd drive himself crazy, thinking about what had almost happened and how much he still wanted it to, never mind the consequences.

Rachel Sutter had become a fever in his blood.

Walking the streets afforded little relief from the feelings she aroused in him. He'd spent the past two weeks trying to avoid her at all costs, then turning around and coming up with any excuse to be near her, until he didn't know whether he was coming or going.

What had he been thinking? He had no right to kiss her, to touch her, let alone anything beyond that. She had no idea who he was, the things he'd done. If she did, she wouldn't let him anywhere near her, and she'd be right to do so. He should have kept his mouth shut and his hands to himself. But Lord have mercy, resisting her took a will stronger than he possessed. Every ounce of his being wanted her in every possible way. And not just physically. The more he learned about her, the stronger his need grew to gather her in his arms and keep her safe from harm. To hear her stories and tell his own. To look toward the future instead of trying to run from the past.

But the past always caught up with him. It had with Marianne, and eventually it would this time. Once Rachel knew the kind of man he truly was, she would want nothing to do with him. In the end, maybe that was for the best, but for now, he needed to figure out how the heck he was going to keep her safe from Kirkpatrick and find a way out of their current predicament.

Without succumbing to these feelings she evoked.

Caleb pushed through the doors of the Jeweled Ace saloon and was greeted by the hum of a crowd, punctuated by low male voices and the occasional bawdy laugh from one of the women hoping to entice a patron to the rooms upstairs. He walked up to the bar and motioned to the man behind it wiping down glasses.

"Whiskey."

A few seconds later he stood nursing the glass, staring down into its amber contents and wondering how much he would have to drink before his current troubles floated away.

Do not let sin reign in your mortal body so that you obey its evil desires!

Caleb scowled at the sound of his grandfather's preaching voice, slamming the contents of his drink back and enjoying the slow burn as it slid down his throat and warmed his belly. He ordered another, out of spite more than anything else, and maybe the slim hope that enough whiskey would curb his thoughts of Rachel, if only for a little while.

"Weren't you supposed to be passing through?"

Caleb toyed with the refilled whiskey glass, turning it around before sliding a glance to his right. Shamus Kirkpatrick leaned casually against the bar as if he owned the place.

Caleb ignored him and turned back to his drink. He didn't answer to the likes of Kirkpatrick.

His silence did not deter the man. "Where you been keeping yourself?"

Caleb took a slow draw on the whiskey, trying to ignore how much he wanted to pound the last breath out of the man who had made Rachel's life a living hell.

Kirkpatrick snorted. "You think I can't find out? Ain't nothing in this town I don't know about."

"Then you don't need me to fill you in."

Kirkpatrick smiled, but Caleb read the menace in his cold eyes. It didn't worry him. Kirkpatrick wouldn't do anything rash. Not here, not with witnesses.

He wasn't that stupid.

"What is it with you and the Widow Sutter?" Kirkpatrick's smile turned into a thin, reedy line. "You'd best not be settin' your sights there. Woman is all but spoken for. Has been for a while."

"Up until two weeks ago the woman was married. I'm guessin' no one spoke for her but her husband."

Kirkpatrick snorted. "That laughingstock could never manage a firebrand like Rachel. She needs a firm and steady hand to tame her."

If Kirkpatrick considered taming Rachel an achievable feat, Caleb needed to rethink his assessment of the man's intelligence.

"And who do you think has spoken for her then?"

"Me."

It was Caleb's turn to smile. "From what I've

seen, she can't abide your presence. Can't imagine she'd be hitching her saddle to your horse any time soon."

"The woman just needs a little convincing. She doesn't know what's best for her. But she can't keep on tryin' to run the Circle S herself. She'll run it into the ground. Either way, I end up with what I want. Only a matter of whether she gets something out of it or not."

Behind him, the piano banged out a lively tune, grating on Caleb's worn nerves. The realization of what Rachel was up against hit him full force. Kirkpatrick didn't just want the land, he wanted Rachel with it, and he had no intention of relenting. Caleb gritted his teeth at the mere idea of Rachel being subjected to Kirkpatrick's attentions, knowing he would keep at her, searching out her weaknesses and picking away at them until she bled.

He couldn't let that happen.

"Leave Rachel alone."

Triumph glittered in Kirkpatrick's eyes. "Rachel now is it? Guess you know the widow a mite better than you been lettin' on."

Caleb bit his tongue. He'd said enough. He tossed back the last bit of the whiskey and slammed the glass down on the bar, tossing a few coins after it.

"Maybe I best pay the widow a visit," Kirkpatrick mused.

"Maybe you best stay out of her way. And mine." Caleb started for the door.

"Bold threat coming from a man with no guns."

Caleb turned and glared at the man, venom sharpening his words. "There's plenty of ways to kill a man, Kirkpatrick. You keep this up, and I'll show you every last one of them."

Fire burned in his veins as he left the saloon and headed back to the Pagget. This situation became more complicated by the minute.

They couldn't reveal the truth about the new ownership for fear of ruining her reputation and having people look at her the way they had her mama. He couldn't allow that. He couldn't chance her being ostracized by the town because of him. It would put her at further risk. And he couldn't return ownership of the land to her without putting her in danger of Kirkpatrick's greed.

He groaned and ran a hand over his face as he stood outside the entrance to the Pagget. Kirkpatrick's designs on Rachel's body, as well as her land, changed everything.

The truth of it slapped him in the face.

He already cared too much to leave her at the mercy of Shamus Kirkpatrick.

Chapter Fourteen

Rachel stoked the small fire until the blaze
caught and held. The hotel room felt even chillier
after she'd undressed and washed using the cold
water in the basin. She would have preferred to
order up a hot bath, sink down into rose-scented
water and forget this day had ever happened, but
she couldn't afford the luxury.

She doubted a warm bath would be able to
erase the feeling of Caleb's hands on her body,
entangled in her hair, his mouth devouring hers.
She shook her head. She had almost given in,
almost let her desires gain the upper hand. She
had broken their kiss, yes, but she hadn't had the
strength to send him away. Not when everything
inside of her wanted him to stay.

In the end, it had been Caleb who drew them
back from the edge, sensing she wasn't ready.
But was she?

Her eyes strayed to the bed and she shivered,

imagining all the things that could have happened. All the things she secretly wanted to happen.

Rachel took a deep breath and tried to shake off the memory, pulling the blanket from the bed and wrapping it around her shoulders. She'd stripped down to her chemise and bloomers.

Outside, the raucous noise from the saloons below drifted up, muffled by the closed window until it became nothing more than a hum in the background.

Rachel wondered if Caleb had ended up in one of them after he left. From her window she'd watched him head in the direction of the main part of town, away from the seedier saloons. She had no idea where he'd gone, and it wasn't any of her business. But curiosity didn't care about what was proper or appropriate.

Something about Caleb kept drawing her in, despite every effort to prevent it. He was like a beacon in the night whilst she was a lost ship looking for land. It was a ludicrous notion. She knew nothing about him, outside of his aversion to small, enclosed spaces. He talked little about himself. But every now and again she spied a deeper well of character, and those were the moments she held close. They were small gems that made her feel less alone in the world.

She groaned at the foolish, romantic notion. She should have learned her lesson on that account. It was that kind of thinking that led her into

one disastrous marriage; she certainly wouldn't
be so stupid a second time around.

Not that it was marriage Caleb had been after
tonight.

She gave the fire one last poke and sat down in
the straight-backed chair she'd dragged in front
of it. The turmoil of the day wore on her and it
wasn't long before she struggled against heavy-
lidded eyes. She tried to convince herself to crawl
into bed, but the warmth of the fire lulled her,
drawing energy from her limbs until moving became more effort than it was worth.

She had no idea how long she slept, or how
long she would have stayed there had the click
of her door not shot through the haze of her tu-
multuous dreamland. She was up out of the chair
before her senses caught up with her.

"Dammit, woman—"

Rachel gave her head a quick shake and stared
at Caleb's irate presence blocking the doorway
to her room.

"What are you—" Her senses fully returned
and the breeze from the open door filtered
through the thin material of her chemise. Her
arms flew up to cover her breasts. "Get out!"

She searched for the blanket she'd had earlier.
It had pooled on the other side of the chair away
from her.

Caleb shut the door but stayed on the wrong
side of it. "I thought I specifically told you to lock
the door. Was I not clear on that account?"

Frozen to the spot by his anger, Rachel sputtered out her defense. "I did lock it!"

Caleb motioned to the door, then to himself on the other side of it, an expression of incredulity written deep into his features. "Apparently not."

Rachel pulled her bottom lip through her teeth. She thought she had locked it. But so many other things had been on her mind. She must have forgotten.

"That doesn't give you the right to barge in." She glanced at the blanket a few feet away. It felt like the other side of the world.

He glared at her. "Kirkpatrick is in town and he's itchin' to talk to you. I wasn't trying to barge in. I was making sure you were safe in case he came callin'. Hardly my fault the thing swung wide open."

Fear slithered down her back, momentarily making her forget she stood there in nothing but a chemise, pair of bloomers and bare legs.

Rachel mustered up a scrap of dignity and lifted her chin. "Could you turn around, please, while I cover myself?"

Caleb sighed but did as she asked. "Fine."

She dove for the blanket and wrapped it around herself like a shield. "Shamus is looking for me? Where'd you see him?"

"The Jeweled Ace." He hesitated a moment, then added, "Seems he has designs on makin' you his wife."

Rachel said nothing. What was there to say "Then you know what he wants from you?"

"Yes." She knew all too well what Shamus Kirkpatrick's designs were. He'd made them perfectly clear even before Robert's death.

"I'm not lettin' you marry that lowlife."

Letting her. The words grated. "I do not need your permission with respect to who I marry, thank you very much."

What was it with men thinking they had the right to order her around? She'd been doing just fine making her own decisions. She had no intention of marrying Shamus, with or without Caleb's permission and regardless of how bad her situation got. She'd live in a cave and forage for berries before she let Shamus put one hand on her.

"Have you finished covering yourself so I can turn around and we can discuss this face-to-face?"

She hesitated. It was easier to converse with his back. When he was watching her, she had to contend with those eyes that bored into her, making her body respond and her heart race. "I'm barely covered and there's nothing to discuss."

He turned around. "Fine, but I'm stayin' in here tonight."

She nearly dropped the blanket. "Have you lost your mind? How much whiskey did you drink?"

"Not enough," he muttered. "If Kirkpatrick is looking for you, I'm not leaving you unprotected."

"He's hardly going to bust into my room and accost me. Unlike some people."

"I did not accost you." He took a step toward her, and her nerves jumped to attention. "And if I recall correctly, you returned my kiss with enthusiasm. A lot of enthusiasm."

The heat from his gaze penetrated the woolen blanket and made the fire pale in comparison. She cursed the way her body reacted to him.

"Well, you still busted into my room!"

"There wasn't much busting required—you left the door unlocked. Stop trying to change the subject. I'm stayin'. I'll sleep by the fire," he said, waving a hand at the chair she had vacated.

The obstinate set to his jaw told her there was no budging him. Unease crept up her spine and lodged at the base of her skull.

"You can't stay here. It isn't proper." What certainly wasn't proper was the sudden ache between her legs that his suggestion brought on. Even more improper was what she wanted him to do to ease it.

"No one will know. I'll leave at first light."

He pulled off his hat and her gaze went to his hands. She remembered the feel of them on her. The pull at her center intensified. She tried to tamp it down, to remind herself Caleb was little more than a stranger to her, but her body didn't believe it. It was as if her body had knowledge of him separate from her brain, as if it knew him in an extraordinary elemental sense.

He stalked toward her, purpose in each step. She wanted to scramble out of his way but her bare feet remained rooted to the spot, her toes curling against the hardwood beneath her. She held her breath, part of her hoping, the other part fearing.

He brushed past her. "Get into bed."

She threw a quick glance after him. Did he mean—

He gave the fire a hard poke. A log tumbled into place and sparks shot upward. "Relax. I'm not going to ravish you."

An irritating rush of disappointment flooded her veins, doing nothing to calm her jittery nerves. The glow from the flames highlighted his razor-sharp cheekbones and picked out the russet tones in the whiskers sprouting once again along his jaw.

"I didn't think you were."

He grunted, the sound indicating he had sensed her jumbled emotions. She hated being so easy to read, every thought and feeling out there for all to see. She wished she could school them the way he did.

Caleb put another log on the fire, his slow movements and deep sigh exposing his weariness. The lines that weather and hard living had etched around his eyes had grown deeper. Not that it made him look bad. If anything, it only added to his handsome ruggedness.

The ache grew deeper still. Lord have mercy,

but she wanted this man. The strength of it scared her to pieces, but there it was. Plain as day. She wanted him, and based on their earlier kiss, she suspected with one word from her, she could have him. Would it be so wrong? Just this once, she could give in to the passion inside of her, fulfill her desires. It was as he'd said, he could leave at first light. No one would know. No one would judge her.

Caleb walked over to the bedside and leaned down, cupping his hand around the lamp on the table next to it. With a quick puff, he blew it out and plunged the room into semidarkness. Every movement he made had an edge to it, an economy of movement that bespoke the type of life he lived. Hard, sparse and dangerous.

It was the element of danger that scared her. And, if she were being honest, excited her. She'd spent her entire life being responsible, doing the right thing by her family, never taking a risk or acting rashly, afraid that, if she did, it would send her down the same path as her mother. She could not afford to court danger now. She had a family counting on her. But what if, just this once, for one night…

It would only be for one night. She would make that clear. Just to work him out of her system so she could focus on more important matters. Her fingers knotted together as she drew in a deep breath to throw out the suggestion before she lost her courage and regained her good sense.

She swallowed, the possibilities swirling in her mind as her need for him battled with the firmly entrenched voice always demanding she tuck her needs away. *Be strong. Be responsible. Don't give in.*

Caleb shucked his jacket and laid it across the back of the chair. She loved watching him move. His fluid grace mesmerized her. When they had danced, the steps had come so easily to him and she wondered how many times he had trod them before, with how many different women.

Even from a few feet away, his nearness surrounded her like an embrace she could fall into. Moonlight and fire cast shadows against him. He reached a hand toward her and her heart jumped at the silent invitation, only to crash down to earth when he spoke.

"Give me the blanket and get under the covers."

The memory of his strong body holding her on the night of the rainstorm rose up to taunt her, bringing with it the overwhelming sense of rightness of waking up next to him, limbs entangled, the weight of his body covering hers, the intoxicating scent of wind and rain and wood smoke that seemed a permanent part of him.

"Why don't you join me?"

She watched the light from the flames flicker over him. His body stilled at her words. He didn't look at her, didn't give any indication he'd heard.

After a long, heart-stopping moment, he spoke.

"It's been a long, trying day for both of us. You best get some sleep."

What? Did he honestly expect her to rest peacefully after she had just propositioned him?

"I just thought—"

"Go to bed, Rachel," he said, walking over to her and drawing the blanket from around her shoulders. The sudden coolness of the air did nothing to douse the burning heat of her body. His fingers grazed her bare skin and need raged through her. She wanted to pull him back, but her boldness had been used up.

The uncompromising firmness of his rejection mortified her. She had offered herself to him like a wanton and he had turned her down. She'd been certain he'd wanted her as much as she did him. Had she misread the signals? Misunderstood what he had said? Perhaps she had been a passing fancy, only of interest at the moment he wished to slack his lust. Perhaps a walk through town and glass of whiskey was the only cure he needed to forget he'd ever wanted her in the first place.

He left her standing alone as he returned to the chair, the chill in the air cooling her ardor if not her embarrassment. A small grunt of discomfort escaped him as he settled. His preference for the unforgiving chair over being with her only served to add insult to injury.

She turned, unable to face him and crawled beneath the covers, keeping her back to him. Tears stung her eyes. She was no stranger to rejection, but repetition did not make it an easier hurt to bear.

Silence permeated the room, broken only by the occasional pop and hiss from the hearth as the fire burned itself out.

"It isn't that I don't want you," he said. His dark whisper taunted her.

"It's fine. You don't have to explain. I know I'm not the kind of woman men want." Hadn't Robert always said so?

"You're exactly the kind of woman men want. But it wouldn't be right. You and me."

"Why not?"

He went silent again and she wondered if maybe he had said all he meant to, but eventually he answered her question. "You don't know me. You don't know the things I've done. If you did—"

"It wouldn't change my mind." She'd tried changing it. Lord knew she'd tried, but her desire for him burned through every inch of her until there wasn't a single part that wasn't scorched. She did not want to want him like this. She'd never felt like this before and she had no defense against it. It made more complications than she cared to manage. But the feelings were there and they refused to budge.

"Yes, it would."

The finality of his words rocked her. What had he done?

Outside, the wind buffeted the window, rattling

the glass in the frame. A draft rushed down the chimney and teased the fire, making the flames lick and dance in the hearth before settling down once again.

She should leave well enough alone. If he didn't want to share her bed, she should be happy about it. Grateful even. He'd saved her from turning into her mama, if nothing else. Saved her from that long ride down a painful road.

Still…

Rachel tried to forget her feelings, to ignore the aching pull deep in her belly. She prayed for deep and silent slumber, to escape the tumult in her heart and mind. Her behavior this evening shocked her. She'd never allowed herself to voice such feelings before, and having done so now left her stupefied. Is this what had happened to her mother? Had desire addled her mind to such a degree she had given into the immoral cravings? A new understanding of her mother began to dawn on her, but she wasn't sure she was ready to forgive.

Sleep continued to elude her and eventually the fire in the hearth burned low. She had no idea how much time had passed. Darkness altered the natural feel of things.

"Are you still awake?" she whispered.

"I am."

Her heart raced. There was something strangely intimate about talking to a man in the dark.

"Can I ask you a question?"

"I suppose." He drew the words out, his tone laced with hesitation.

"Why don't you like small spaces?"

It seemed strange that a man like Caleb would fear anything, let along something so innocuous.

"Doesn't matter."

"Does that mean you're not going to tell me?"

He sighed, the sound drifting between them. "It isn't exactly a bedtime story."

"Sometimes sharing with others can make a burden less heavy."

"Know that from experience, do you?"

She didn't miss the thread of sarcasm sewn around his words. "I'm going by what I've heard."

He chuckled, low and deep. The night clouds broke and a shaft of moonlight slid between the thin curtains illuminating his sharp profile.

"My grandfather was a harsh man," he began, his voice sounding strangely far away. "Pious and self-righteous, he expected his family to adhere to his strict rules and beliefs."

Rachel stopped herself from asking questions, afraid to interrupt in case he stopped. This was the first real glimpse he'd offered into his past.

"When my mother met a drifter and found herself in the family way, my grandfather refused to forgive her. The drifter, my father, didn't stick around long enough to marry her or even see me born. My grandfather said she'd shamed him in the community, and he spent the rest of her life reminding my mother of her sin and making us both pay the price. He told me I'd never amount to any good. Each time I defied him or tried to protect my mother he…" Caleb stopped.

"What did he do?"

"He would lock me in the root cellar. Keep me there for hours, sometimes days." He stopped for a moment. Horror filled Rachel. How could someone do such a thing to an innocent child? He was not responsible for the circumstances of his birth.

"Caleb—" Her heart went out to him and she wished she could hold him, as if wrapping her arms around him would heal the wounds his grandfather had inflicted.

"I remember thinking, 'One of these times he's going to forget I'm down here.'"

"What did your mother do?"

Sadness and regret filled his voice. "There was nothing she could do. My grandfather had her so beaten down she couldn't save herself, let alone me. Eventually it got the better of her. She got sick and lost her will to live. I think she almost welcomed death in the end, just to escape him."

Like Rachel's mother had escaped her own guilt.

Caleb drew in a long breath and continued. "When she died, he refused to bury her in consecrated ground. Said she didn't deserve it. I left that night and never looked back."

"And you've been drifting ever since?"

He didn't answer her directly. She sensed he was now picking and choosing his words more carefully. She wondered why. What had happened between then and now that he held so close to his chest?

"I joined up with the Union Army. I was just shy of sixteen. When the war ended, I took odd jobs here and there."

"Did you ever think of settling down?"

He lapsed into silence and Rachel wondered if maybe she had gotten all the truth out of him she would for one night. She held her breath, waiting.

"Once."

"What happened?"

He shifted in the chair and turned to look at her. The dying embers of the fire cast him in shadows. "You ask a lot of questions. Anyone ever tell you that before?"

She smiled. "No. I never had anyone to ask things of before. Around here, everyone knows everyone else and their business."

"Did they know about your husband's gambling?"

The question pierced. She didn't like to think about it; the shame was still too close to the surface. But she'd dug into his past and he'd complied. Fair was fair.

"I expect they did. No one ever came out and said it to my face, save for Shamus, but I could tell. The pitying looks, the way they would shake their heads." It wasn't just the gambling they'd known about. It was everything. She swallowed, her voice dropping to a whisper. "It was humiliating."

His tone softened. "Guess it hasn't been easy for you."

Tears stung her eyes, but she blinked them away, thankful Caleb couldn't see them. "I don't want your pity."

"I'm not givin' it. You've done right by yourself and those boys. There's not a single thing about you needs pitying. If I was doling out pity, I'd send some in your fool husband's direction for being too blind and stupid to know what he had, and for throwing it away."

His words, blunt as they were, bolstered the part of her that years of neglect had worn down. A wayward tear escaped, drifting across the bridge of her nose and landing on the pillow next to her.

"Thank you. That's nice of you to say."

"Just speaking the truth. Now get some sleep. That's enough jawin' for one night."

Rachel didn't argue with him on that point. All this sharing left a body exhausted. And vulnerable.

Exhausted she could handle. The other one, well, that was something different. She wasn't accustomed to leaving herself open like that. She pulled the blankets around her tightly, as if they could protect her. "Good night, Caleb."

He grunted and stretched out his long legs toward the hearth. Rachel closed her eyes. It was easier if she didn't look at him.

* * *

Caleb shifted his position in the hard chair, wincing. A person was not made to sleep upright like this. He'd take a bed of lumpy earth any day of the week. He forced himself to his feet and stretched, his muscles protesting.

Early morning light peeked from the inch or two between the curtains and caressed Rachel's sleeping form. All but the top half of her head was hidden beneath the blankets, as if she'd wrapped herself up in a cocoon. Her thick braid streamed behind her, stark against the white pillow. Her deep, even breathing told him she'd finally found peace in sleep.

A strange sense of contentment warmed him. Despite turning down her proposition the night before, his need had not abated. It went beyond the physical and reached somewhere deeper, into the marrow of his bones and somewhere even deeper than that.

His heart lurched. He tried to beat back the fear of what would happen when she discovered the truth about him. And she would. He would tell her eventually, whether he intended to or not. She had a way of getting things out of him that he had every intention of keeping to himself.

He wondered sometimes if he had lost his mind. He'd known this woman all of two weeks, but somehow it had been enough. He cared. Too much. There was no way he could turn his back on her now and ride out of town with a clean conscience. But staying permanently was not an option, either.

Caleb pinched the bridge of his nose and closed his eyes. They burned from lack of sleep. He'd been stuck in some no-win situations before, but this one topped them all.

During the darkest hours of the night he'd come to the conclusion that he had to start extricating himself from the tangled mess he'd woven. This morning he would go down to the bank and make arrangements to pay off Rachel's debt to Kirkpatrick. She would hate him for taking such liberties without discussing it with her, but he knew she'd only refuse his help. But there was no way he could leave Salvation Falls knowing Kirkpatrick had any hold over her.

Once the payment came through, then he could start removing himself in other ways. He took one last look at Rachel sleeping quietly in the bed. The pull to join her, to take her up on last night's proposition nearly floored him. He turned swiftly and left the room, knowing the second part of his plan would be much more difficult to execute.

The bank manager was not eager to let him in so early, but his incessant pounding wore the man down. He was even more reluctant to process his payment of the debt, however, and it didn't take long for Caleb to realize whose pocket the man lived in. He didn't doubt the manager's next stop would be wherever Kirkpatrick had holed himself up for the evening to inform him of recent developments.

As Caleb left the bank and made his way back to the hotel, he knew he had to tell Rachel immediately. If not, she might find out from someone else, and given her aversion to his help in this regard, he didn't want to add any fuel to the fire.

Chapter Fifteen

❦

"You see, the thing is," Sheriff Donovan said, glancing out the window down into the alley below, "I had a man in Laramie ask around about you."

"That a fact."

Caleb dried his face with a towel and tossed it onto the bureau next to the wash basin. The sheriff had shown up a few moments earlier, looking for Rachel as well, but they were both to be disappointed. When Caleb arrived back from the bank, Cletus informed him that she'd set out a quarter of an hour earlier. He assumed she'd gone to check on Len, but before he could leave, the sheriff arrived and decided to speak with him, instead. He wished Donovan would say his piece and get on with it. He needed to find Rachel to let her know what he'd done.

"Turns out there wasn't a hotel in the whole town with a man registered by the name Caleb Beckett. Not one. What do you make of that?"

Caleb shrugged and struggled to control his urge to run away. He didn't want the sheriff poking around in his past.

"I reckon that means I didn't sleep in a hotel."

"Odd, don't you think. You were there how long?"

Caleb wavered between the truth and a lie. He decided to keep with the truth. It would be easier to keep it straight in the end. And he had enough strikes against him at the moment without adding anything else to the mix.

"About a week."

Donovan nodded and lifted a quizzical dark eyebrow. "And you what? Bunked out in the livery? Slept with your horse?"

"Never been one for hotels." Not exactly a lie, albeit not the actual truth the sheriff was fishing for.

The sheriff's gaze skimmed over the bed with its unwrinkled blankets before returning his attention to Caleb.

"You're in one now."

"Didn't want to leave Mrs. Sutter alone, not with Kirkpatrick harassing her."

The sheriff stiffened. "I heard there'd been trouble. What's he been doing?"

"Guess that's up to her to say if she wants to tell you." There was no reason to bring Donovan into the fold. There was nothing he could do. The sheriff was bound by the law, and Kirkpatrick made a fine practice of dancing inside its boundaries, or ensuring that, when he stepped outside of them, it never came back to roost at his door.

As if realizing he'd get no further information on that matter, the sheriff returned to his original line of questioning.

"What can you tell me about Sinjin Drake?"

Caleb schooled his reaction to the hated name. "Nothing."

The sheriff smiled. "Nothing? You sit at a card table with one of the fastest draws and sharpest shooters this side of the Mississippi and you got nothing to say about the man?"

Caleb shrugged. "What did your man have to say about him?"

"Not much. Yet. He sent a telegram. He'll be back in a day or two with a full report. I expect by then he'll have plenty to say."

"Well, good luck," Caleb said, not really meaning it. He walked to the door and opened it. Recognizing the dismissal, the sheriff followed, stopping at the threshold.

"Just so you know, I happen to care a great deal about Rachel Sutter, and I'm not going to take too kindly to someone steppin' in and causing her grief. She's had enough of that to last a lifetime."

Caleb wanted to tell Donovan he had no intention of hurting her, but that was a promise he couldn't make, no matter how much he wanted to.

"Where'd the money come from?" Kirkpatrick demanded. "I don't give a lick what cockamamie story that outlaw told Henry Little. Robert couldn't win himself a card game if you stacked the deck in his favor and tried to lose."

Rachel glared hard at Shamus Kirkpatrick. Her mind reeled as she took in what he had told her, caught between anger and relief. Her debts were paid off. She was free. At least of Shamus. But by doing this, Caleb now left her indebted to him.

"What makes you think he's an outlaw?"

"I recognize the type. Now, where'd the money come from?"

She didn't press Shamus further on his assessment of Caleb. Though she didn't believe him an outlaw—what kind of outlaw didn't wear guns?— she knew there was something dark in his past, more than he had already told her.

A part of her wished she could have seen Shamus's face when the news was delivered.

The other part remained angry as a hornet's nest at Caleb for going behind her back. Maybe she was better off owing him than Shamus, but it didn't lessen the impact that he hadn't even thought to consult with her. He'd just gone ahead and made the decision as if she had no stake in the outcome. At least Caleb had nothing to threaten her with. He already owned her land. She had nothing left to lose.

Memories of last night flooded her mind. How desperately she had wanted to experience his touch, his taste, the pleasure of being in his arms. She'd offered herself to him, and he'd turned her down. Rachel swallowed hard. There was still something she had left to lose, something far more personal than her land. But at least it would only be she who suffered, and not her family.

"It's none of your business where the money came from," she said, pulling her thoughts away from last night. "All that matters is my debt to you is paid. You've got nothing to hold over me now."

"Don't I?" Shamus straightened and smiled—a cold, calculated stretch of the lips that reminded Rachel of a rattler about to strike.

Her heart stilled. *Don't say it. Don't say it.*

But it was too late. She'd pushed too far. Triumph sparkled in his pale blue eyes, eyes so much like Brody's it shot a chill straight through her. Any understanding she had garnered with respect to her mother's actions dissolved in that moment.

"Did you hear?" Shamus asked, his smug grin growing wider. "I hired me a new ranch hand last night."

"No…" But the word changed nothing.

"Seems Brody takes bein' the man of the house serious-like. Wants to prove himself. Said you needed the money and I paid a good wage."

Ice crystallized in her veins. "You leave him be."

Shamus shrugged. "Wasn't my doin', darlin'. He came to me of his own free will looking for honest work. Who am I to turn the boy away? Seein' as he's my son and all."

Bile rose in her throat. This wasn't happening.

For Brody's entire life, Shamus had denied his birthright, though he made enough veiled threats to let her know he was well aware of her brother's parentage. Now, when she had nothing left to fight with, no one left to turn to, he struck. And hit his mark with deadly accuracy.

"What do you want?"

"You know what I want."

She clenched her teeth. "The ranch."

He shook his head. "Price has gone up." His gaze traveled down her body, leaving a sick feeling in the pit of her stomach. "You know, you look a lot like your mama."

"I am not my mother." She had promised herself she would never follow in her mother's footsteps, but Shamus had Brody and Caleb owned her land. Rachel had nothing else to bargain with.

Maybe she was like her mama after all.

"I'll give you a few days to ponder that," Shamus said.

She wanted to tell him he could wait until hell froze over, but she didn't have enough bravado left in her to convince him she meant it. She stood, mute, as Shamus turned and walked away.

"What were you thinking?" Rachel whispered, leaning across the table at him. Though the restaurant at the Pagget was sparsely populated, she kept her voice low.

Caleb knew she wouldn't be pleased, but a small part of him had hoped her relief over having Kirkpatrick out of her life would override her displeasure. Given the potent mix of anger and indignation edging her voice, he'd been wrong.

She continued to glare at him. He wouldn't hold his breath waiting for a thank-you once the shock of what he'd done wore off.

"You're free and clear of him now," he added.

She laughed bitterly. "Do you honestly think that will stop him? And what will people think, you paying off my debt and living in my house? They'll think I'm earning it on my back! The one thing I was trying to prevent, if you'll recall."

Caleb glanced around at the other patrons. A few had cast them sidelong glances when they first entered the restaurant but no one appeared to pay them any mind now. Still, he kept his voice down. This was not a discussion he wanted overheard.

"I made it clear the money came from Robert's winnings in Laramie. I was merely the messenger as you were busy tending to Len and overseeing his care."

A haggard waitress appeared at his elbow and refreshed his coffee with a thick mixture he'd barely swallowed down the first time. Lord liftin', what did they do to the coffee here? He'd tasted better sludge left on the campfire overnight.

Rachel waited for the waitress to leave before she continued. "You had no right. I told you I would handle this on my own. Why didn't you tell me you were planning this?"

"You would have told me no." Which should have been his first clue that any attempts at gallantry would be met with umbrage.

He had hoped, foolishly so, that sharing some of their pasts and admitting their feelings had helped bridge the gap and made her realize they were on the same side. The last thing he wanted was for her to feel in his debt.

Maybe he had underestimated the importance of her feelings. He wished it didn't matter, but he was embarrassed to realize it did. Not that he understood what had developed between them any better than she did. It'd come on with such speed and intensity he'd had no time to duck or maneuver around it. Walls he had built thick and wide around his heart were no defense. Rachel had found a weak spot, and the more time he spent with her, the more she chipped away at it. At this rate, there would soon be nothing left.

If he had any sense at all, he would leave. Her debt was paid. Kirkpatrick would no longer be a problem. He could sign over the deed now, saddle up Jasper and leave town.

So, why didn't he?

"I did what I thought was best. Now you can hate me and glare at me till the sun sets, but what's done is done. We might as well make the best of it."

Rachel stood abruptly, bumping the table. The thick coffee oozed over the edge of his mug and puddled on the blue checked tablecloth beneath it.

"*You* make the best of it," she said in a harsh whisper. "Robert, Shamus, you. You're all alike. You think you can take over my life like you have some right to it. Well, you don't."

The comparison rankled him. "I am nothing like Kirkpatrick or your dead husband."

"What you are is a complication I didn't ask for and don't want." She took a deep breath, the shakiness in her voice verifying the tenuous grip she held on her emotions. "I am sorry if my actions last night gave you the impression I was willing to let you have your way in all respects. Let me assure you, I am not. I do not care what your intentions are or were, you do not have the right to make decisions about my life."

"That's not what I was trying to do. I just thought that—" What? Did he think she would fling herself into his arms, relieved and grateful? Maybe a part of him had. He had done it for her, dressed it up in the purest of motives, but somewhere under the surface, he had hoped it would improve his standing in her eyes. A foolish attempt given that he had every intention of leaving.

Didn't he? The answer was no longer clear.

"You didn't think! Not about what I wanted. You have no idea what you've done. No idea the position you've put me in. Now, if you will excuse me," she said, turning before he could get enough of his wits about him to stop her. "I am going home."

She left the restaurant, her shoulders squared,

not even the slightest bend showing in her spine. The navy blue homespun skirt swished about her legs with each irate stride. Only her anger remained, lingering in the air around him.

What had she meant when she said he had no idea the position he'd put her in? What part of the puzzle was he missing?

One thing was certain, he had every intention of finding out.

By the time they left town and headed back to the ranch, Rachel's stomach writhed like a nest of eels. Not even the serenity of the forest could calm her fears. In the span of twelve hours everything had flipped on its ear.

Shamus had Brody.

He had struck the lowest blow possible, taking the only thing that mattered to her, the only thing she would give up everything for. Her family.

Brody. What had he been thinking going to Shamus? But she knew exactly what her brother was thinking. He figured that with Robert gone it was his responsibility to see them out of this mess, even if it meant working for the enemy to pay off the debts.

Her brother had no idea the mess he had stepped into. She had tried his whole life to protect him from the truth. If Shamus told him he was his true father, what then? Everything would change, and not for the better. Brody had been looking for a father figure his whole life. Robert had proven woefully inadequate. What if Shamus tried to fill that role? He could turn on a certain slimy charm when he wanted to, convincing you he could perform miracles. He'd fooled her mother into believing him. Would he fool Brody in the same way?

Perhaps if she hadn't seen him destroy her parents' lives, she, too, would have been taken in by him. But she saw through his slick veneer to what he really was. A monster.

Now it appeared the monster was ready to destroy her family again, and Rachel had no ammunition to stop him. Even so, if she gave in to his lecherous demands, Shamus wouldn't get her land. Everything she once owed Shamus, she now owed Caleb. The question was—what did Caleb want in return?

The buckboard jolted as the wheel slipped into a rut and then climbed out, the horse straining at the task.

Why had Caleb paid the debt? What was the advantage? He already had everything. Her land, her home. She'd tried giving him her body but he'd turned her down, though he claimed that had nothing to do with how much he wanted her. But morning had a way of shedding its harsh light on things, and Rachel realized the intimacy they'd shared by revealing their pasts had been nothing more than an illusion created by the night.

Caleb may have lusted for her physically, but he had made no claims of love. The thought slipped into her mind unbidden. She tried to shake it out, but the word stuck. Love. Something she had longed for her whole life. She thought she'd found it once, but she had been sorely mistaken. She would not be duped like that again.

Last night was nothing more than two people caught up in a moment, reaching out to find temporary respite from the chaos of the past two weeks. Soon, the shine of this new life on the ranch would wear thin and Caleb would realize what a scramble it was. Then what? He'd leave or he'd send her packing. Either way, there was no future for them together.

The thought left an empty hollow in her chest. In the short time he'd been with her, Rachel had become accustomed to Caleb's presence, looked forward to it as much as she fought against it. She did not want to fall for him. He was a drifter with a haunted past, an edge of danger and secrets he would not reveal. It was a heartbreaking combination and she'd do well to be rid of him.

But knowing that and wanting it, she discovered, were two entirely different things.

Caleb pulled Jasper up even with the buckboard. "Still angry about me paying off the debt, aren't you?"

She glanced up at him, her hands tightening on the reins. Shamus's threats wore a fresh track in her mind. She wasn't sure what she felt more—fear or anger. Maybe they were one and the same. She had yet to tell Caleb about Brody's defection. She'd stormed out of the restaurant before she could.

"You have no idea the situation you're dealing with, Caleb. You should have stayed out of it."

"Can't do that."

She turned in her seat slightly to face him, giving the horse enough rein to take his lead. "Why not? What is it to you whether I owe money to Shamus or not? It's none of your concern."

The morning sunlight filtered through the trees and touched his face, illuminating the sharp edges and grim set of his mouth. "It is my concern. You're my concern."

"I am not—"

"You are. And don't get me wrong. I don't like it. Last thing in the world I wanted was to show up here and be puttin' down roots. I tried that once and it ended in a real bad way. I know this ain't the kind of life I get to have, and so be it."

That was the second time he'd mentioned trying to settle down, but each time the subject arose his expression closed down and she knew the subject was off limits.

"Then why are you doing this? Letting us stay, paying off my debt? Why do you insist on involving yourself in my life like you have some right to be there?"

"Because every time I turn around you or one of your family keeps gettin' yourself into a situation needing my help. Maybe the men you encountered in your past were the kind to turn a blind eye to such a thing, but I can't. I've got some small scrap of honor left and it's about all I've got, so don't go askin' me to just ignore it because my actin' on it puts your britches in a knot."

Rachel's eyebrows lifted of their own accord. His voice was filled with anger and frustration, as if it had been she who put this burden on him. Of all the cotton-pickin' nerve!

"I am not the one who made you sit down at that table in Laramie to gamble. And I certainly never laid the responsibility of bringing Robert home at your feet. You took that upon yourself after you cleaned him out of every last thing we owned." How dare he make it sound as if this situation were somehow her fault? If anyone was an innocent victim in all of this mess, it was her!

The horse snorted and shook his head. Rachel loosened her hold on the reins, realizing in her anger she had pulled them taut.

"I didn't say this was your fault. I'm just sayin' that maybe if you stopped snapping like a turtle every time someone tried to do something for you, you wouldn't find yourself in such a mess."

"Oh!" He may as well have just branded her completely incompetent. "Let me tell you something, *Mr. Beckett*—"

He rolled his eyes at her formal address, and she swore if her hands weren't busy holding the reins, she would have reached across and poked him in those damnable hazel eyes.

She pulled in a harsh breath. "You are the most

insufferable man I have ever met. You waltz in and take over and then have the audacity to claim honor made you do it, as if that somehow excuses your heavy-handed behavior. Well, let me tell you what your honor has done. It has left me with nothing. Shamus has Brody now. And I cannot use the debt repayment as leverage to get him back because you have gone and paid it off. So do you know what I get to use now, Caleb?"

"Rachel, I—"

"I get to use my body. I get to prostitute myself like my mother did. So thank you. Thank you so much for all the help your honor provided. I hope it makes you feel better."

She snapped the reins and urged the draft horse to move faster. Unlike Old Molly, this one had some pep and it picked up speed with little effort. Rachel ignored the rattling of her teeth as the buckboard bounced and jostled with every rut and bump in her path. Maybe if she went fast enough, she could outrun the trouble that had grabbed hold of her life.

To his credit, Caleb let her go and it wasn't long before she left him far behind. It was a relief when she saw her home appear on the horizon.

Even if it wasn't hers any longer.

Jasper snorted and shook his head, to loosen the hold Caleb had on the reins. He didn't like traveling at such a slow pace, but he knew it was better this way.

Though his insides begged him to go after her, he would let her blow off some steam while he tried to digest what she had told him. He was afraid if he went after her now, he'd do something even more foolish, like propose they get married so Kirkpatrick would never be able to lay a hand on her.

His guts lurched at the very idea of Kirkpatrick touching her. Of her being forced to submit to him in order to get her brother back.

The thought of marrying her, however, that crazy idea had an unsettling sense of home to it. But he knew better than to get too close to those kinds of thoughts. He'd attempted marrying once before and still bore the scars, both physical and emotional, of that particular disaster. If he'd had any doubt he wasn't the settling kind, Marianne had made it perfectly clear when she'd turned her back on him. He didn't need to be dragging Rachel into his hell. No matter how much his heart tried to tell him it was worth the risk.

Besides, he doubted Rachel would even consider a proposal from him at this point. He wasn't sure what had occurred to put Brody in Kirkpatrick's clutches, but somehow Rachel blamed him. He'd give her some time to cool her heels then he'd set about figuring out what had happened and how to fix it. One thing he knew for sure, he'd be a dead man before he let her barter her body to Shamus Kirkpatrick.

Caleb sensed the intrusion only seconds before

the pounding of hooves reached him and riders surrounded him.

He pulled back on the reins, stopping Jasper cold so that he reared slightly in protest. He swiveled in his saddle, quickly counting four men.

And four guns leveled directly at his chest.

Chapter Sixteen

Caleb's hand pressed against his hip where his gun used to be. Nothing. Not that it mattered. With two men in front and two behind, it was unlikely he'd be able to shoot his way out unscathed.

He was suddenly thankful Rachel was angry at him. At the rate she'd driven off, she'd be almost home by now. Safe.

That was all that mattered.

He held himself silent in the saddle. There was no point asking these men what they wanted. He could hazard a guess.

Kirkpatrick had sent them.

Caleb had known that as soon as Kirkpatrick discovered who'd paid off Robert's debt there would be repercussions. He wished he'd had a chance to see Kirkpatrick's face when he heard the news. It would have made the four-to-one odds worth it.

One of the men in front, with a jagged scar

crisscrossing his cheek, motioned with his Colt.
"Get down."

Caleb hesitated, quickly scanning for any possible avenue of escape. But, fast as Jasper was,
even he couldn't outrun a bullet.

As if to punctuate the point, a gun was cocked
behind him.

"Don't try anything stupid."

Caleb didn't have any intention of being stupid.
He eased himself off Jasper and looped the reins
around the pommel. Someone moved behind him
and he stiffened. A loud smack against horseflesh
sounded and Jasper took off into the woods.

"This is gonna be easy," the nasally voice from
behind stated. "He ain't even wearin' no gun.
What kinda man don't wear a gun?"

The kind who has already killed his fair share,
Caleb thought.

Scarface smirked. "Looks like Lady Luck ain't
travelin' with you today."

Caleb was pretty sure Lady Luck had lost track
of his whereabouts a long time ago. "That a fact?"

His nonchalance seemed to irritate Scarface.
His beady eyes narrowed. "You honestly think
Mr. Kirkpatrick was gonna let you get away with
interferin' in his plans?"

Caleb shrugged. "Can't say I gave it much consideration."

"Well, you're gonna be wishin' you had,
stranger. 'Cause he don't cotton to such disre-

spect. Told us to teach you a little lesson about mindin' your own business."

"Then why don't you quit jawin' like an old woman and get on with it."

The man behind him lunged. Caleb spun and managed to stop his approach with a left hook, but by then the other three had dismounted and rushed at him. For the first few minutes survival instinct took over and he didn't feel the weight of the blows. But, bit by bit, his body tired and the pain made itself known. He knew he was going down, but not without taking as many of these miscreants with him as possible.

One already lay in the middle of the path. Another staggered away, leaning against a tree and holding his ribs. Caleb would have liked to do the same. His ribs pained like crazy, as did his quickly swelling eye. Blood streamed into the other eye from a cut on his forehead until eventually he was swinging blind, doing his best to ward off the hits coming his way and get in a few of his own. For a fleeting moment there was a glimmer of hope that he might prevail, but then something hard and heavy crashed down on the back of his skull. As his mind fought the rushing blackness, his battered body openly embraced it.

His knees hit the ground with a jarring thud.

His last thought was of Rachel. Had he given her enough time to arrive home safe and sound? And who would protect her if he didn't make it back?

* * *

"Rachel, how come Mr. Beckett's horse came home alone?"

Ethan stood by the door, peering through the screen and pointing.

Rachel dried her hands against her skirt. She'd spent the better part of an hour throwing herself into her chores trying to forget her argument with Caleb, but it was no use. The more she ran over it in her head the more she came across as...wrong.

The idea galled her.

With the heat of the moment gone, she knew she had been wrong to blame him for all her problems. Yes, he should have checked with her first, but it was as he said: he was only trying to help. She couldn't remember the last time someone had done that.

No wonder her manners were so rusty.

Rachel walked over to the door and placed a hand on Ethan's shoulder as she looked out. Under the gnarled oak in the front yard, Jasper gnawed at the freshly growing grass, his reins dragging along the ground.

Caleb was nowhere to be seen. Fear crept up her spine. He would never leave Jasper saddled and unattended after the long ride from town. She scanned the horizon, hoping to see some hint of him or a clue to why he wasn't here. There was nothing.

"Stay here," she said, stepping around Ethan.

She walked toward Jasper, calling him quietly

so as not to startle him. He glanced up briefly then resumed munching the grass.

Rachel took hold of his reins. There was no sign of Caleb in the barn or along the pathway that led into the woods. Her gaze ran over the horse. His saddlebags were still attached; everything was as it should be, except for the missing rider.

The growing fear seeped into her bones. She had taken off, annoyed and angry, assuming he would be right behind her. But he should have been here by now, even going at a sedate pace.

Where was he?

"Stay in the house," she called back to Ethan. She had no idea what had happened but she wasn't taking any chances. She mounted the horse and turned him around, heading for the line of trees.

Half an hour later she dismounted and ran across the uneven path toward the figure sprawled unmoving on the ground.

"Caleb!"

His back was to her. She rounded him and dropped down. Shock made her rock back on her heels.

"Oh, Lord."

His face was a bloody mess, covered in cuts and bruises, and she guessed beneath his clothes would be even worse. One ungloved hand bore raw knuckles. His hat lay off to the side.

Rachel leaned forward and gently rested a hand against the side of his head. When she pulled her hand away it, too, was covered in blood. His hair, matted against his skull, had turned dark with the stain. Stark terror froze her bones. She couldn't move. All she could do was sit there and stare at the blood on her hand. This was her fault. She should never have left him behind.

"Caleb, please…say something."

Tears sprang to her eyes but she blinked them back, taking a deep breath. She needed to stay calm, to keep her wits about her. There would be time to give in to her emotions later, after she got him home.

"Caleb…"

One eye fluttered. The swelling prevented it from opening all the way. "Hey."

Relief swept through her, turning her bones to liquid. She covered her mouth with her hand, stifling a sob. She couldn't lose control. Not yet. Later perhaps, but right now she had to get Caleb home.

"What happened? Where are you hurt?"

"Kirkpatrick." He winced, his voice thick with pain. "And everywhere."

"Can you stand?"

"Guess I'm gonna have to."

He didn't move.

"Caleb?"

"Think I'm gonna need some help."

Rachel slipped an arm beneath his, angling her body to help him up. It took several tries before she finally had him about as upright as he was going to get. He called Jasper in a raspy, pain-filled voice and the horse walked over.

She kept her hands on his back as he slid his foot into the stirrup and pulled himself up onto the horse. A grunt of pain punctuated the effort. Jasper stood blessedly still. With careful movements, Rachel swung up behind him.

She reached around Caleb and took the reins. "I can do it," he said, but didn't fight her when she ignored him. She took a quick look to her left and right, fearful that whoever Kirkpatrick had sent may still lurk in the cover of the thick trees, but saw nothing but the forest. With a nudge of her heels, Jasper started. She hoped the horse knew enough to take them home, given that she couldn't see around Caleb's broad back, and he couldn't see through swollen and bloodied eyes.

The trip seemed to take forever. Rachel tried to concentrate on each step the horse took, telling herself it was one step closer to home. One step closer to having Caleb tended to. If she let her mind stray much beyond that track, fear and guilt would take over and she would break down.

She kept talking to Caleb to keep him conscious, afraid that if she didn't he would fall off the horse and do more damage to his already beaten body. Finally, she half dragged, half carried his large form through the door. It was no easy feat, but fear fueled her actions, though she did her best to hide it from Ethan. Which seemed ridiculous considering the shape Caleb was in, battered and staggering like a drunkard.

"Ethan, run out and get Freedom. She's in the smokehouse. Tell her to bring whiskey. Hurry!" The boy swallowed once, turned and ran. Rachel hated seeing the terror in his eyes. She knew how much he feared losing anyone. But she had no intention of putting Caleb on that list. He would not die. He couldn't. She wasn't ready for him to leave her, and definitely not in this way.

Rachel managed to get Caleb into her bedroom, rid him of his sheepskin jacket and heave him unceremoniously onto the bed. The soft mattress cushioned his fall, but not enough to keep pain from marring his battered features.

"I will kill Shamus for this," she muttered, and in that instant she believed it. If he had shown up at her door she would have grabbed the rifle hanging above the coat pegs and made him answer for this atrocity. This was the last straw!

It was one thing to come after her. It was something else to come after her family.

She straightened and blinked.

Family. When had Caleb become family?

She couldn't say, but he had. In a matter of weeks he had woven himself into the fabric of her life until she found it hard to imagine what it would be like without him. He couldn't die. He simply couldn't. She looked down at Caleb, who hovered somewhere between consciousness and oblivion.

"Don't die on me." Maybe saying the words out loud would give them more power.

"Do my best," he mumbled.

"Promise?"

His mouth twitched but he remained silent, his hand lifting slightly to cover hers. She stared down at the torn skin and pain welled inside of her. She lifted her head to stare at the ceiling, fighting back the threat of tears.

Not now. Just a little longer. She could cry later, she promised herself.

"Can't get rid of me that easy."

"Good."

She took a steadying breath and turned her mind back to the task at hand, unbuttoning his shirt. The well-worn cotton twill was soft to the touch and frayed at the edges from wear and washing. She peeled it away, pushing it back from his shoulders then did the same to the top half of the long johns underneath.

Bruises had already begun to form, discoloring his well-muscled skin. Without thinking, she ran her fingertips lightly over his warm skin. He flinched slightly.

"Sorry."

"It's all right," he said, his voice thick with pain. "I like it when you touch me. Gives me something else to think about."

He managed a weak smile, wincing when it pulled at the cut on his lip.

"Quit talkin'," she said, trying to ignore the

thrill his words gave her. This was hardly the proper time. "And quit thinking about me touching you."

"Can't."

"Can you sit up? I need to get your clothes off."

"Music to my ears."

Rachel closed her eyes. Her face burned despite the gravity of the situation. He was not making this easy. How was she supposed to concentrate on what needed doing if he kept putting those images in her head?

"Maybe you shouldn't talk. Conserve your strength."

"For when you get my clothes off?"

The vision of his strong hands exploring her body made her falter. She glanced at the bedroom door.

Lord have mercy, where was Freedom?

Caleb didn't need two good eyes to know he'd managed to fluster her. He hadn't meant to, but the verbal sparring took his mind off the pain throbbing through every inch of his body. He gritted his teeth. Even through his pain, as she struggled to get him out of his clothes he couldn't help but enjoy the sensation of her hands running along his body, gently peeling away the torn and bloody material. She'd stripped him down to his underclothes before Freedom bustled into the room all business.

By then, Rachel was breathing hard. He wasn't sure how much was from the exertion of trying to maneuver him and how much of it was from his constant commentary about getting him out of his clothes.

"Good lawd liftin'," Freedom said.

He squinted though the eye that was only partially swollen shut. "That ugly, huh?"

Freedom gave him a rueful smile. "Guess you ain't too bad."

Laughter rumbled in his chest. "I think I'm a hard day's ride from *ain't too bad*."

Ethan's head poked out from behind Rachel, who had started tearing strips of bandages from the sheet Freedom brought in. "Does it hurt?"

"It sure don't tickle," he said. No sense lying to the boy. He had eyes. He took in a deep breath, wincing as his ribs screamed in protest. He turned his head toward Ethan. "You think you can take Jasper down to the barn and help Foster brush him down and feed him?"

Having something to do, something useful, brightened the boy's expression. "Yes, sir."

Rachel glanced down at him, appreciation glowing in her dark eyes. He tried to smile, but the motion became increasingly difficult.

He heard the uncorking of a bottle and prayed it was the whiskey Rachel had requested. The amber liquid would numb his body, and he needed the relief. Not just from the pain. He didn't want the added humiliation of certain areas of his anatomy taking on a mind of their own while Rachel administered to his wounds.

"Help me get him up on the pillows," Rachel said to Freedom. "I'll get him under the arms, you swing his legs around."

Caleb wished he'd had a long, hard swig of the whiskey before Rachel leaned over him, her soft breasts pressing into his chest as she slid her arms beneath his and worked with Freedom to haul his body lengthwise on the bed. He nearly passed out from the pain of it. It was a shame he didn't. Parts of him were stirring in ways that were about to get real embarrassing, real quick if he didn't get a handle on things.

He turned his head and whispered into Rachel's ear before she could pull away. "You want to preserve what's left of my dignity and throw a blanket over me?"

She lifted her head and looked at him, then followed his gaze. Her eyes widened in understanding. She reached down for the quilt and draped it over his lower half then turned to Freedom.

"Think you can whip up some of those poultices you used when Stump cut himself on the barbed wire last year?"

"I'll get right to it," Freedom said. She settled the whiskey bottle in Caleb's hand. He grasped it like a lifeline. "Take what you need. There's more where that came from."

Caleb was glad to hear it. Between the pain, both exquisite and excruciating, he had a feeling he would need a whole lot more.

Chapter Seventeen

The whiskey worked its magic, numbing his body and freeing it from the worst of the pain. Freedom had brought in a poultice and set it next to the bed within Rachel's reach. As poultices went, it didn't smell too bad. She had mixed in a healthy dose of sage and thyme. The scent made his stomach rumble.

"Did Kirkpatrick's men say what they wanted?" Rachel had sat down next to him on the bed. Her gentle ministrations eased some of the hurt, but caused a whole different kind of ache that no amount of whiskey would smother.

"Said he wanted to teach me a lesson," Caleb said, taking a swig of the amber liquid. Maybe conversation would keep his mind from straying. Not an easy accomplishment, given that Rachel kept touching him, carefully washing his body and cleaning his wounds. She'd sent Freedom to tend to Ethan and get started on supper, leaving them alone.

He tipped the whiskey bottle up and took another swallow, choking it down when Rachel's damp cloth slipped beneath the blanket to his hip. He reached out and grabbed her hand.

She scowled at him. "You've got blood and cuts and bruises all over you. I need to get you cleaned up."

Caleb raised his eyebrows, no easy feat through the swelling and abrasions littering his face. "You start cleaning in that general direction and we're going to be risking something else entirely." Not that he was in any condition to do anything about it, and given how he and Rachel had left things, he doubted she would oblige. Just as well.

Getting close to him was a mistake.

Rachel pulled her hand free and continued to wash his wounds. "Don't be foolish. You're weak as a babe. Besides," She smiled, and for the briefest moment he forgot about the pain, inside and out. "I should take advantage of this."

"Take advantage of what? Me lying prone on the bed, barely a stitch on and unable to defend myself?"

"I'm guessing that's not a predicament you find yourself in too often."

"Not exactly." He couldn't afford that kind of weakness or vulnerability. Although, at the moment, he could definitely see it did have a few merits. He closed his one good eye as she placed the warm cloth gently against his aching ribs and drew it downward to his hip again. "In my line of work, that kind of predicament gets a man killed. And I'm somewhat partial to living."

"What line of work is that?"

He realized his slip too late. Her touch had a way of breaking down the walls he'd built up until they lay crumbled to dust at his feet. Between the whiskey and the pain he didn't have the wherewithal to come up with a plausible lie. He coaxed his mind to work, covering up the truth with smoke and shadow, hoping it would be enough.

"I'm a drifter. That kind of life means a man needs eyes in the back of his head."

"Oh. Of course."

He could tell from the tone of her voice the reminder of his past did not sit well.

"But I'm done with that now. There comes a time when a man needs to stop driftin'."

She smiled at him, but even through the liquor-induced dullness, he could tell it wasn't genuine. She didn't believe him. He couldn't blame her. Given all she'd been through in her life, he guessed she wasn't predisposed to trust people.

He had a steep hill to climb to convince her that drifting was in his past. He wanted to stay. Not just in Salvation Falls, but here at this ranch, with her. He'd realized the truth as Kirkpatrick's men left him bleeding on the forest floor. He didn't want to leave Rachel. She was the first thing he'd thought of when he woke in the morning and the last image he held tight before drifting off to sleep. Being near her filled him with something he'd yet to define, but it felt good and he didn't want to let it go.

It was new territory for him.

Before, when he'd been ready to marry and settle down, it had been different. Marianne was a virtuous woman from a respectable family. Beautiful and agreeable, he'd grown a strong affection for her. He knew she'd make a good wife and mother, a pleasant companion to come home to after a long day in the field. A woman who would stand by him, no matter what.

But then his past came to call, and he realized how wrong he'd been. It had cut deep, but now he wondered what had hurt worse- the betrayal of the woman he'd cared for, or the loss of a life he'd always longed for? After finding Rachel, becoming a part of her life, he had a sneaking feeling it was the latter.

The question was—what was he going to do about it? And would any of it even matter when Rachel learned the truth about him?

"I need you to roll over so I can wash your back."

Rachel did her best to turn him without aggravating his injuries, but it was no easy feat. Even with the benefit of the whiskey, she could tell moving in certain ways pained him.

She dragged the cloth down Caleb's back. His skin was warm and smooth to the touch, but the smoothness was marred in several places by scars that had been there before today's events. Some had faded with time until they were barely noticeable. Others still seemed new, the skin puckered and pale against his tanned skin. The bruising only added to the sense that he had seen more than his share of violence in his thirty odd years.

"Did you get these in the war?" She slid her hand down his back without the cloth. He tensed at her touch and she reveled in the sensation of muscles shifting beneath her fingertips. "Sorry. Does that hurt?"

"No. It feels good, your hands on me."

His head lay on the pillow, turned toward her. With his eye swollen almost shut, she wasn't sure if he could see her or not.

His admission flustered her at the same time it flattered. She was not accustomed to it. "Is that where you got this one?" She touched the puckered white skin on his lower back. She guessed it to be a bullet wound but couldn't fathom how he had gotten it. It would have meant he'd been shot in the back.

"It's not important."

Rachel rinsed out the cloth and set it against the scar. Though it was well healed she gently cleansed it, as if she could wash away the pain it had once caused.

"I would think getting shot in the back was very important."

"It was a long time ago."

"Not so long." From the way he evaded her questions, she guessed his memories of it were as fresh and cruel as the scar. She shouldn't probe. He had been through enough without her heaping questions on him. But she couldn't help herself. "Tell me about it."

Silence stretched between them. Rachel continued to rub his lower back where the muscles had tensed, waiting.

"I killed a man," he said.

Whatever she had been expecting, that wasn't it. "Oh."

His muscles eased, as if confessing to such an act of violence had lifted a weight from him.

"I didn't want to. I wanted—" He stopped, grimaced then began again. "I was starting a new life. I had a fiancée, a piece of land. I planned to settle down, start a family."

His confession startled her. She tried not to react to the thought of him with another woman, a woman he was willing to give up his drifting ways for. A woman he wanted to make his wife and have as the mother of his children. A woman who was not her.

"One of the young men in town wanted to prove himself. He got drunk and challenged me, tried to get me to pull my gun."

Rachel's attention peaked. Since the day he had arrived in Salvation Falls she had never seen him wear a gun. She didn't even know if he owned one.

"What happened?" She hungered for details of his life before she met him. The mystery of the man, of what haunted his hazel eyes, held a lure she could not deny. Something about the loneliness reflected there spoke to her. She understood. She'd lived with the same emptiness every single day. At least, until he entered her life. And her heart.

"I was leaving the livery. He was coming out of Pandora's Box—"

"Pandora's Box?"

"Whorehouse." He moved his head slightly in her direction. "Beg your pardon."

"I think my sensibilities will withstand the mention of a whorehouse."

"He challenged me again. I ignored him. Told him to go home. But youthful pride wouldn't let him. His friends were watching and he'd been boasting. I tried to walk away."

She ran her fingers over the scar. "And he shot you in the back. That's the act of a coward."

"It was the act of a fool."

"What happened to him?"

Relaxed muscles turned rigid beneath her touch. She let her hand drift between his shoulder blades in an effort to soothe him.

"I heard him cock the gun. I didn't get turned around in time to dodge the bullet, but I got a shot off as I went down. It hit him in the heart. Killed him instantly. I staggered over to him, hopin' maybe my shot had been as bad as his.

But I knew better. Hell of a thing watching the life fade out of someone's eyes." His voice had taken on a faraway quality; he was lost in the past and the whiskey and things he couldn't change.

"What choice did you have? You thought he was going to kill you."

"No. That's the thing in those situations. You don't think. You aim and you shoot. There's no time to think. You react, or you die."

He made it sound as if he'd been in many similar situations.

"My wound wasn't serious, but fever set in. By the time I came out of it a few days later, the doc told me it'd be better if I left town. The boy's family was causing a ruckus and the sheriff figured staying would only make things worse."

"But it wasn't your fault. You tried to walk away."

He didn't seem to hear her.

"What about your fiancée?"

Foolish jealousy bubbled inside of her.

"I went to her family's home but they refused me entrance. Said she wanted nothing to do with me." He fell silent, as if he needed a moment to let the ugly memory settle. "I left town and drifted. Been drifting ever since."

"I'm sorry you had to go through that."

She had wondered what had caused his drifting ways. Was he simply a man who didn't care to stay in one place too long? Or had it been something else? Knowing it had been due to betrayal and a broken heart left her with much to think about. He had been ready to settle down, to start a life with a wife and a family. She'd had it right from the start.

He wasn't a drifter, merely a man who had been drifting.

Regret and sadness filled her. Why couldn't they have met years earlier, before she'd made the blunder of her first marriage? Before Shamus's desperation to get her land turned him to violence against her family. Would they have stood a chance? Would they have met and fallen in love like normal people?

The loss of what might have been cut through her, and she swiped at a rebellious tear as it slid down her cheek, followed by another, until her emotions refused to be bottled up any longer. Soon they streamed silently down her face as the full impact of what had happened this afternoon pummeled her heart and mind. She had come so close to losing Caleb. When she had gone in search of him, she'd prayed with everything in her to find him alive and unhurt. Finding him lying on the ground, she'd feared the worst, that her prayers had gone unheard and she had lost him forever, before she'd had the chance to tell him how she felt.

Before she had the chance to admit she loved him.

The idea of letting her heart have its way, giving over to the desires he stoked, terrified her.

Anything could happen, and the loss of control scared her. What scared her more was the thought of never getting the chance to see where this might take her, how it could change her.

She knew there was much about this man she still did not know, but despite a violent past, he was a good man. An honorable one. He'd proven it to her every day since he'd arrived in her life.

It broke her heart to think she had finally found someone who made her feel this way, only to know their days were numbered.

Shamus had injured Len, taken in Brody and now attacked Caleb. Where would it end? How many people would he hurt to get what he wanted? Would he come after Freedom next? Little Ethan? She had to protect her family.

She had no other choice. She couldn't change what was to come.

She glanced down at Caleb. His breathing had evened and she knew he was asleep. She leaned down and pressed her lips against the warm skin on his back, lingering there for a moment, soaking in the feel of him, his scent.

For the moment, she would live in the present.

It was all she had left.

Thrashing awakened her. Rachel hadn't meant to fall asleep. She'd only lain down next to him for a minute, to ease the burning in her eyes and her churning mind.

Caleb had killed a man in self-defense and been turned out of the one place he had wanted to call home. Those he had loved had rejected him for doing nothing more than protecting himself. Where were these same people when the kid had been badgering Caleb? Why hadn't they cared enough to stop it then?

And why had the young man chosen Caleb?

Was it that he'd felt threatened? He was tough, but that wasn't all there was to him. It wasn't who he was. Life had hardened him, but he wasn't a hard man.

Rachel reached out and laid a hand upon his bare shoulder to calm him.

He continued to mumble incoherently, but every now and again a word would catch her attention.

"Killed him…didn't…my fault…"

Rachel pushed herself up to a sitting position and touched Caleb's face, careful to stay away from any of his wounds. The poultices had been removed an hour ago, replaced by Freedom's homemade salve. In the morning, she would whip up another batch of poultices.

The lamp still burned at the side of the bed, creating a dim glow. She studied Caleb's face. Whatever magic Freedom used had worked miracles. Though the cuts and bruises remained, the swelling had lessened considerably and the angry redness had receded. Neither did his skin feel so hot to the touch. Relief loosened the tightness in her muscles. The fear he would survive his wounds only to be taken by fever lessened a little.

"Shh. Settle down. Everything's fine. No one blames you."

She regretted bringing up his past. She'd had no right dredge up old memories. Lord only knew she was well aware of the pain they brought. It had been a purely selfish need to know more about him. And what had she learned? He'd loved another woman. Loved her enough to want to make a life with her.

The revelation ruined her theory that Caleb would tire of this type of life. She should have known better. The moment he'd arrived he'd thrown himself into life on the ranch, working hard without complaint. It seemed to give him a deep satisfaction, as if he were born to it.

His eyes remained closed, but he gripped her wrist firmly, placing her hand against his heart. A strong and steady beat thumped beneath her palm.

"I'm sorry."

"There is nothing to apologize for."

But her words, meant to comfort, only seemed to plague his cloudy mind even more. "No...not okay. I need to...have to make right..."

If she needed further proof of his sense of honor, she had it now. A man had tried to kill him, shot him in the back like a coward and ruined his future. Yet Caleb harbored a sense of guilt and responsibility for having taken the man's life in his own defense.

"Caleb, you need to wake up." She rubbed at his chest, wishing now they had put his clothes back on. Instead, they had stripped him bare to ensure that no wounds that needed tending were missed. They'd placed a towel over his private parts, but with all the thrashing about, Rachel guessed it was long gone.

She looked down at herself. She had undressed down to her chemise when she'd lain on the bed to rest. Her clothes had been covered in blood and poultices, and soaked with water. At the time, it had seemed practical to avoid dirtying the blankets with them. It would just make more cleaning for her to do later. But now...

She glanced up at Caleb who had grown silent. Both eyes were open—though one more than the other, and he stared at her. His thumb caressed the inside of her wrist where he held it, sending tight shivers up her arm.

"You were dreaming," she said. Her quiet whisper in the hushed night air gave a sense of immediate intimacy. "And you talk in your sleep."

Caleb's brow furrowed as if remnants of the dream still lingered there, but now, awake, he couldn't quite piece them together. "What did I say?"

"That you were sorry. About shooting the young man, from the sounds of it. You seemed to want to make things right. It's my fault. I shouldn't have brought up such bad memories."

He looked at her for a long moment as if there was something he wanted to say but he couldn't quite find the words. She waited, but instead of speaking he closed his eyes and took a deep breath. When he reopened them, it was something else entirely she saw there. Something that made her even more aware of her state of undress. She may as well have sat next to him naked, the way his gaze traveled over her. She shivered. Caleb's hand slid from her wrist to gently rub her arm, only making it worse.

"Cold?"

She shook her head. If anything, an uncomfortable heat had kindled deep inside of her, pooling low in her belly.

"That's unfortunate. I was going to suggest you crawl under the covers with me if you were."

His voice, low and enticing, caressed her gently. She leaned in closer. Her hair, long since freed from its knot, draped over her shoulder, creating a curtain between them and the rest of the world.

"Perhaps I am a little chilly."

His hand drifted up to her neck. His touch held a powerful magic. Seductive with promise, it took away the loneliness that had become an intrinsic part of her life. She wanted desperately to give in to the sensation, to believe in it.

"You're injured."

"Looks worse than it feels."

She didn't believe him. "We shouldn't…"

His fingers slipped to her collarbone. She closed her eyes against the ache building inside of her.

"Shouldn't what?"

"I'll hurt you if we—"

"No, you won't."

"But the cut on your head…the bruises and—"

His hand slipped beneath the flimsy material of her chemise and skimmed the swell of her breast, cutting off her feeble protest. She took in a sharp breath and closed her eyes, letting his touch fill her. The ache at the juncture of her thighs became painful, demanding release. She squirmed slightly, trying to relieve it.

"My head is fine," he said, pushing the blankets out of the way. "The cuts and bruises look worse than they feel for the most part. Ribs are a bit sore, though. Might want to watch out for those."

Rachel averted her gaze. "We can't—"

"Last night, you invited me into your bed."

Had it only been last night? It felt as if a lifetime had passed between then and now.

She continued staring at the far wall, unable to look down at his nakedness no matter how much she wanted to. She'd already had an eyeful earlier and the effect had yet to wear off. Long lean muscle, smooth skin, tanned in some areas, pale in others. She'd tried to keep a practical mind as she washed his wounds but it had been impossible. He was a fine specimen of a man and, despite her best attempts; she was not immune to his rugged beauty any more then than she was now.

"You turned me down last night, if you'll recall."

"With great reluctance," he countered. "And

now, much regret. After nearly being killed this afternoon, I see the error of my ways."

"And what error would that be?" Her heart pumped faster in her chest.

"The kind of error where I realize life is too transient a thing to waste time denying the fact I am falling for an incredibly beautiful, albeit stubborn, woman. And the idea of not being with you is more painful than anything Kirkpatrick's men could do to me."

She dared a quick sideways glance. His eyes flashed with desire strong enough to permeate the low light. She let her gaze drift lower, over the light smattering of hair on his chest, to the ridges on his belly. Then lower still until she realized there were some parts of him completely immune to both the beating he had taken and the whiskey he'd had.

Heat flushed her face.

"Crawl over me."

His words jerked her gaze back to his. "Crawl...? What?"

"Trust me." Caleb placed firm hands on her hips and directed her closer.

Rachel let herself be led but shook her head. "I don't understand."

He smiled at her and she continued to let him guide her as he pulled her across his groin until she straddled him. Beneath the slit in her drawers she could feel his hardness.

"Makin' more sense now?"

She nodded, but the knowledge did little to quell the sudden nest of butterflies jumping around in her belly. Nor did it do much to assuage the ache emanating from where their bodies now touched. She squirmed slightly. Caleb's hands tightened at her hips and he let out a quiet groan.

She froze. "I'm sorry. Did I hurt you? I told you this was a bad idea." She tried to move off him but he held her firm, his strength, after all he'd been through surprising her.

"Not in the way you think. That was a good kind of hurt."

She understood his meaning, the pressure of him against her a painful pleasure.

She worried her bottom lip. She was completely out of her element. Her experience in this regard was woefully inadequate. Robert had rarely come to her bed, and when he did, the ensuing event lasted only long enough for him to take his pleasure and leave. She'd never particularly enjoyed the act. It left her dissatisfied, feeling as if she was being shortchanged without fully understanding how or why.

Her lack of knowledge embarrassed her. She'd been married for eight years. It was likely Caleb was expecting a woman with certain skills. He was about to be sorely disappointed in that respect.

"I'm sorry." Humiliation caused her voice to hitch. "I don't know what to do."

Caleb tried to raise his eyebrow but the cut above it made him stop and wince. "At all?"

Was there a more mortifying conversation to have with a man? "I…I know what goes…where. I just…this…" She waved her hands at their bodies, trying to ignore the heat building where they joined. "I don't know what to do like this."

"Ah," he said.

She looked away, unable to stomach the disappointment she knew she'd see in his expression. "I'm sorry. I can get off. You probably don't want—"

Again he held her firm when she tried to move. "I'll show you."

Chapter Eighteen

He smiled at her, and the expression, despite being marred by cuts and swelling, was filled with a gentle compassion that took her breath away.

"The first thing you do is lean down here closer to me."

She did as he instructed, placing her hands on either side of his head. Their chests were mere inches apart. So close she could feel his body's warmth reaching out, pulling her in.

"Now what?"

"Now you touch my face."

Again, Rachel did as he indicated, letting her fingers lightly skim his cheek. The bristle of new whiskers brushed roughly against her skin, sending a riot of sensation up her arm and down into her belly, causing the nest of butterflies to take flight.

"And then?"

The current between them hummed with desire.

"Now you lean down just a little further and kiss me."

She leaned in, her thick hair falling around them, and gently kissed the corner of his mouth that hadn't been injured. Caleb remained still as she worked her way across his lips with slow, soft kisses. She'd reached the middle when his tongue flicked out and caught her open mouth. She sucked in a breath of surprise, froze for an instant, then responded in kind, letting her own tongue caress the smoothness of his lips before tentatively delving inside and finding its mate.

She stopped thinking then, about what she did or didn't know, and let the swirl of emotion and need carry her. She had been wrong. She did know what to do. She just hadn't known she knew. She gave in to the pleasure, delighting in his touch, the way his hands skimmed her body, slipping beneath her chemise and running along her bare back.

Soon, the kiss was not enough. She needed more. The desire that had been building within her since Caleb had ridden into her life demanded to be set free, and Rachel could no longer deny it. And she didn't want to.

His touch inflamed her, cutting through the cool air and setting her on fire. She sank into him, rejoicing as she settled her weight upon him, rocking against him, blocking out the pain and loneliness of her past.

He nibbled her neck where her pulse leaped beneath his ministrations. "Should I stop?"

She should tell him yes. She was newly widowed. He was a stranger. But she couldn't find the words and none of it seemed to apply any more. She had been waiting for this, she realized, since his first touch, the first fiery glance. Everything had been leading up to the inevitability of this moment.

"No. Don't stop. Don't you dare stop."

Rachel pressed into him, arching her back. Caleb inhaled sharply.

"Do you know what you do to me?"

She did. She just didn't believe it. She had been so determined to not turn out like her mother, she had cut off any thoughts about her own desires or the pleasure they could bring, fearful they would turn her into a wanton. With one touch, one kiss, Caleb erased those fears. With him, it felt right, and how could anything feel this right and still be wrong?

She ached everywhere for him.

He reached for the edge of her chemise and pulled it over her head, tossing it aside, leaving only her drawers as a barrier between them.

"Wait," she whispered, and crawled off him, letting her legs slip over the edge of the bed. Shyness overtook her as she shimmied out of her drawers, and she wished the lamp had been extinguished.

"Lord, you're beautiful."

The reverence in Caleb's tone made her brave. She crawled back onto the bed, settling herself over him. The feel of his hard length, smooth and strong beneath her, sent a shiver through her entire body.

She didn't want to wait. She wanted him to fill her, to bury himself deep inside of her; her need for him was almost savage in its intensity.

She pressed herself into Caleb, his readiness for her apparent. "Please…"

"There's no rush, sweetheart."

But there was. It seemed she had been waiting for this her whole life, the sense that she belonged somewhere, with someone. She was afraid if she didn't grab it now, it would somehow slip through her fingers.

Caleb's hands blazed a path along her rib cage, stopping as he reached the curve of her breast. The roughness of his palm against her bare skin made her pulse leap. He pressed a hand against her back, lowering her to him. He pulled her nipple into his mouth, and her breath shattered in her throat. Sensation spiraled through her. His hand slipped from her breast and slowly roamed the contours of her body, over her thighs, along the curve of her hip, around to span her bottom and position her against him.

His hands were everywhere, then his mouth, slowly exploring every inch of her body. Despite his injuries, he made the most of what he could do until Rachel hovered on the precipice of insanity, wanting to dive over the edge and let it swallow her whole. She squirmed, unable to be still, desperate for more. Each small move she made caused him to wince, but she figured out soon enough that it wasn't from the pain of his wounds.

The knowledge made her bold.

"Can we rush a little?"

She wasn't sure how much longer her body could withstand this madness. He fired things in her she didn't have a name for, didn't understand.

"Is that what you want?"

She nodded. "I can't stand it much longer." Was it supposed to be like this? A heady blend of need and desire storming through her like a tempest?

"Lift up a little."

She did, letting his hands on her hips guide her, then slowly, maddeningly, his length filled her and she relished the sense of completion, of oneness.

She shifted and settled against him, arching her back. His hands settled on her hips and for several long seconds they remained as they were, unmoving. But soon the need for more returned and a deep instinct made Rachel move. Beneath her, she felt Caleb's body tense. He pulled away slightly then filled her again. Pleasure flowed through her, each wave crashing harder than the next, pulling her under.

She had never experienced anything like it. She placed her hands over his where they held tightly against her hips and let her head fall back, her hair tickling the bare skin on her back. Her breath came in gasps and she became oblivious to everything but the thrilling sensations as she rocked her body back and forth against him.

Caleb's own breathing grew labored and the groans coming from him rode a fine edge between pleasure and pain. Somewhere, in some far-off corner of her mind, Rachel wondered if she should stop, if she was hurting him, but she had lost the ability to control herself. The sweet indulgence of their bodies moving together became the only thing that mattered.

She needed this, needed it in a way she couldn't articulate. She let her body have its way; she let it take her where it needed to go. Caleb surrounded her, encompassed her, filled and fulfilled her. And when she thought the intensity of her feelings would be the end of her, they crashed through, shattering inside of her as Caleb found his own release. His body shuddered beneath her, his fingers digging into her flesh.

In that moment, Rachel finally found a place where she belonged.

She only wished she'd found it sooner instead of now, when her time to enjoy it was about to be cut drastically short.

Caleb jerked awake and pushed himself into a sitting position, his sore muscles screeching in protest. Something had woken him from a sound sleep, but what?

He glanced around Rachel's bedroom, his home for the past three days. As far as accommodations went, it wasn't too bad. The room was spacious, a definite plus. He didn't think his beaten body would welcome the hard ground for a mattress. He had steady company to keep him occupied. Ethan had taken to sleeping on the cot in the kitchen but stopped by regularly to keep Caleb abreast of everything going on around him, and Freedom applied her poultices religiously until his cuts and bruises faded considerably.

But best of all, each night, under the guise of watching over her patient, Rachel crawled into bed next to him. Their first night together dogged his memory. The feel of her hands on his body, the way she'd moved against him, abandoning herself to the pleasure. He'd wanted to make love to her again, to lose himself in the sweet bliss her body provided, but he wasn't sure his performance would be up to par, all things considered.

He chuckled quietly, remembering their conversation of yesterday afternoon.

"Don't be looking at me like that," she said, setting a load of freshly laundered undergarments on top of her bureau and opening one of the drawers.

"Like what?" He caught a glimpse of her lacy underthings, a detail about her that seemed incongruous with the no-nonsense woman she was. But he suspected that, beneath all her practicality, beat the heart of a true romantic.

"Like it's a hot summer's day and I'm a cold drink of lemonade."

Tart but sweet. He smiled at the comparison. "Can't help myself. You're the prettiest thing I've seen in a long time."

She scoffed and closed the bureau drawer. "That hit to your head has obviously addled your brain."

Caleb patted the bed next to him then held out his hand. "Why don't you come over here and tend to my wounds. I seem to have one particular ache that needs—"

She swatted at his hand, but not before he saw the blush coloring her cheeks. He loved how his teasing flustered her.

"You can stop that thinking right now. Your... ache...is just going to have to remain unattended."

For a brief moment he feared she regretted what they had done, but then he saw her sly smile. "At least until you're properly healed."

Caleb grinned, thinking back on the promise of those words, but before he could contemplate what it all meant a shot reverberated through the early morning calm.

He scrambled out of bed. Each muscle protested as he grabbed his pants and struggled into them. A quick glance out the window revealed nothing more than rolling hills leading up toward the mountains. A line of trees stood sentry on the tops of the hills, obscuring his view of anything beyond. Instinct told him the shots came from that direction.

He shoved his feet into his boots and threw on his shirt without bothering to button it as he rushed through the newly built section of the house into the kitchen. There was no sign of Freedom or Ethan. Or Rachel.

Where was she now?

Another shot echoed in the distance.

He took off at a run. Each step slammed into his stiff body like a battering ram. His legs dragged but he pushed on, forcing his body to move, feeling stronger with each step as his body became accustomed to movement once again.

Another gunshot cracked the air. Whoever was doing the shooting was taking their time getting the job done. His hand automatically went to his hip. His step faltered.

He had no gun.

He stopped suddenly as he reached the top of the next hill that led down into a small valley below. Rachel stood alone, a gun in her hand. Thirty feet away a glass bottle sat on a stump, still intact.

He watched her, confused, taking in deep, gulping breaths, his still-bandaged ribs reminding him of each blow they'd taken. Rachel lined up her shot again, but her stance was off and her shoulder had dropped. She pulled the trigger. Caleb knew it would hit the left side of the stump before the wood splintered and littered the brown grass surrounding it.

"Doggone it!" She lowered the gun and closed her eyes.

"What are you doing?"

Rachel jumped and the gun came up again. Caleb had the presence of mind to step aside. Not that she was likely to hit him at the rate she was going.

She lowered her arm and fixed him with an exasperated glare. "What are you doing out of bed?"

"What are you doing trying to kill a defenseless bottle?"

He made his way down the hill to stand beside her. They had enough problems without her shooting herself in the foot or accidentally taking out one of the ranch hands. Or worse—Ethan. Bullets didn't have much of a conscience when it came to who they hit.

"What does it look like I'm doing? I'm practicing my shot."

"Your shot?" From what he'd seen she'd be lucky to hit the broad side of a barn before next Christmas.

Something crossed her expression, flirting with the grim line of her mouth and darkening the chocolate-brown eyes a man could easily lose himself in. But it left as quickly as it appeared, and Caleb didn't have time to determine its meaning.

"Put the gun down, Rachel. You don't need to know how to shoot."

"Yes, I do. Shamus has not backed down, even with the debt paid. Things are worse than before. I need to be able to protect my family."

"I'll protect you." The words were no sooner out of his mouth than he realized the strength of that conviction. He'd do anything to keep her safe.

"How? You don't even wear guns."

Anything but that.

"That's what I thought." She turned back toward the untouched bottle and raised the gun again, taking another shot. This one pinged off a distant tree.

"It's complicated," he told her. If she only knew. But if she knew, he wouldn't be standing here now. If she knew, she would have left him to Shamus's men and washed her hands of him. And he would have deserved it.

She spun back around. This time, mercifully, the gun remained at her side. "I understand you feel bad about shooting that young man and I understand you don't want to wear your guns because you can't stand the guilt of killing someone else. That's fine. This feud with Shamus isn't your problem to take on. It's mine. I'll deal with it."

Caleb glanced down at the gun. "And just how do you plan on doing that? You going to shoot the man? Kill him in cold blood?"

"Cold blood is the only kind he's got."

He took a step closer, unable to believe what she was telling him. He thought they'd come to an agreement of sorts, albeit an unspoken one.

But he'd thought she understood. They could have a future together. A future she wanted to throw away to kill Kirkpatrick.

"That's not the way to solve things, Rachel. Trust me."

"Like I said, this isn't your concern, Caleb."

But it was. Everything about her concerned him. She held him here as tightly as if she'd wrapped herself around him and grown roots. He could no sooner leave her than he could cut out his own heart. It shook him to admit it, but there it was.

"You really think you can kill a man?"

"I have to protect my family." The vehemence in her voice told him she had the determination to carry out her threat. But it took more than grit to watch a man die by your own hand. He ought to know.

"You go through with this and you'll end up hanging from the end of a rope. Who will care for Ethan if that happens?"

Rachel faltered at his words. The weight of the gun pressed into her palm. After seeing what Shamus's men had done to Caleb, she'd decided it had to end. She couldn't stand idly by and watch Kirkpatrick destroy her family. The time had come to act. She had to protect them. But in her rashness, she hadn't thought beyond the act itself to give the consequences much weight. She didn't want to be deterred by the details. Now, Caleb made her face them and what it would mean if she went through with her plan.

"And what about Brody? He's a hot-headed young kid who makes even more impulsive decisions than you. Who's going to guide him through life, turn him into a responsible man? And what about Freedom? She's like family to you, but I can guarantee the color of her skin won't make it easy if she has to go out into the world and start all over again. Same with Foster because of his age. You think killing Kirkpatrick is going to fix things? It won't. If anything, it'll make things a heap worse."

His words pummeled her, forcing her brain to work past the obstacles he threw in her path.

"I...I can claim it was self-defense," she said. It was a weak argument, but not without merit. "Hunter knows Shamus has been harassing my family. He'll believe me."

"Donovan can believe what he wants, but in the end, he's a man bound by law and my guess is he has too much honor to turn his back on that even if it means holding you accountable for your actions."

"But Shamus deserves to pay for what he's done!"

"And you think this is the way to do it? Have you ever watched a man die, Rachel? Because I can assure you that once you do, you won't ever look at anything the same way again."

"Is that why you don't wear your guns? Because you had to watch that young man die? That wasn't your fault. He left you no other option."

Caleb shook his head, the pain of the memory etched into the lines of his face. "I made a promise to myself I wasn't going to shoot another man and I mean to stick by that."

"Not even to protect yourself? If you had been wearing your guns, Shamus's men would never have been able to jump you."

"I won't do it." Fierce determination clasped around each word.

"Well, I will. I'm going to kill him." Not wound him or wing him. It had to be a direct hit, a fatal shot.

She wouldn't get a second chance.

Caleb took a step closer until there was little space left between them. "Are you seeking justice or revenge?"

Rachel's teeth clamped down. How dare he suggest such a thing! But a niggling worm of doubt crept into her heart. Could he be right? Was she trying to prevent him harming them in the future, or was she trying to make him pay for the past? Both had become so tangled and twisted in her mind she wasn't sure she could recognize the difference any longer.

"He's destroyed my family once already," she whispered, unwanted tears springing to her eyes. Caleb's image, rough and tired from his ordeal, swam before her. "I can't let that happen a second time. I can't lose everyone I love again."

Caleb reached out and took the gun from her, slipping the weight of it into his own hand. Rachel glanced down, not wanting him to see her weakness. "Am I included in that everyone?"

One recalcitrant tear slipped out and splashed against the hand holding the gun.

She stared at it, the truth welling up inside of her, battling with her fear and begging to be released. "You are."

His free hand lifted and cupped the side of her face, forcing her to look up and meet his eyes. The curtain shielding his emotions had been pulled back, and in their hazel depths she could see the promise of a different kind of life, the kind filled with love and companionship, laughter and hope. The kind of life she'd always dreamed of, but that had remained heartbreakingly beyond her reach.

"Then marry me."

Chapter Nineteen

Rachel blinked, unsure she had heard him correctly.

"What?"

"I love you, Rachel Sutter. I tried not to, honest I did. You were an unwanted complication. But every day I spent with you made me realize I had to have you, and now every time I try to imagine my life without you I don't like what I see. It's empty and joyless and—" He stopped and shook his head.

"You want to marry me?"

His thumb brushed against her cheek and sent rivulets of warmth and pleasure rushing into her bloodstream.

"I want to spend my life with you. I want to wake up in the morning and find you there. I want to go to bed at night holding you in my arms. I want to watch you raise our children, and see Ethan and Brody turn into men. So yes, God help me, I want to marry you. Tell me you don't feel the same way."

She couldn't. And even if she did, he'd recognize it for the lie it was. Her heart soared at his declaration, and even though she had yet to say the actual words herself, she felt them through every inch of her.

But she had believed in this dream once before and suffered eight years of misery as a result. She'd been wrong about Robert and she'd known him most of her life. She'd only known Caleb a short while and though she had no doubts she loved him, what did she really know about him? His past was like the river flowing through her land during spring thaw—murky and dangerous.

The part of her that had been burned in the past wanted to retreat back into the safety of nothingness. It wanted to shove these new feelings down into the dark recesses where she had kept them safely locked away. But it did no good. Caleb had found the key. The locks were gone, the bars rolled back. He had reached inside of her and shone a light deep into the dark.

"You might as well say the words," he told her, a smile kicking up the uninjured corner of his mouth. "I can see it in your eyes. And I know you, Rachel. I know you would have never given yourself to me if you didn't love me. I know it with the same certainty I can feel the sun on my face right now."

"I do," she admitted, without saying the words. She didn't know why she hesitated. It wasn't as if holding them back would save her now. The emotion took over every last inch of her body, mind and soul. But if Caleb was dissatisfied with her choice of phrasing, the smile on his handsome face gave nothing away.

"And you'll marry me and together we'll find a better way to rid ourselves of Kirkpatrick that won't leave you swinging from the end of a rope?"

She smiled and nodded. Did she dare hope? Could there be another way, a better one? She couldn't say. Certainly none came to mind. But if one existed, she was going to take it. She'd waited a long time for happiness to find her. Now that it had, she didn't want to let go. She wasn't sure Caleb would let her, even if she did.

"Good, because I'm rather partial to this neck." He pulled her to him and pressed his warm lips against her throat, gently nibbling the length of it before making his way to her mouth. "I'm right partial to all of you, really."

He kissed her then, a kiss imbued with the promise of a better life. Rachel placed her hands against his solid chest and swayed against him, overwhelmed by her commitment and the future she now dared hope for. His kiss made her limbs weak and her head spin and for the moment carried all her fears and worries away.

She gave in, letting herself go, even though deep down a dissenting voice told her it would never be that easy.

* * *

"I can't sleep," Rachel said, her voice traveling out into the dark room. She'd crawled into bed next to Caleb once again, but tonight was different. He had asked her to marry him and she had accepted. The gravity of what that meant had slowly begun to sink in. He was hers. Forever

It frightened her how quickly she'd grown to rely on his presence and the comfort he provided. It was a part of love she hadn't considered before, the strength you drew from another person, knowing they were there providing support when you needed it most.

She pushed herself up on one elbow and looked down at him. The faint glow of moonlight illuminated his fading bruises. They weren't nearly enough to detract from his handsomeness. Rugged and elemental, there was something about him, something indefinable that pulled at her. He had given her a place to belong.

"It's been an interesting day," he said, lifting his arm so she could snuggle next to him. She melded her body to his, careful not to add too much pressure to his bandaged ribs.

The man didn't have a spare ounce of flesh on him. Every last inch was worked into tough sinew, hard muscle and bone. She could feel all of it, given that he continued to sleep without a stitch on, claiming he was more comfortable that way. She'd protested the first night, but not since.

"Better?"

She nodded, her cheek rubbing against his chest.

It amazed her the way his touch could ignite her body, push everything else away until only the two of them existed. Their pasts, their problems, the future, all faded into the background, like a hazy memory she couldn't quite recall.

"Sleepy yet?"

"No," she said. Sleep was the last thing on her mind at the current moment, with his hand stroking her shoulder, slipping beneath the loose neck of her nightdress.

"You want to talk?"

Rachel pressed her lips against his bare chest. "Not really."

Laughter rumbled deep in his throat and a thrill shot through her. She loved the sound. She'd experienced so little of it in the past years it was like a balm to her soul.

Caleb's hand slid slowly downward, pulling the gown as he went. She lifted enough to let it slide past her rib cage then down over her hip. When it fell beyond his reach, she kicked it off, freeing herself from any barrier between them.

She stretched against him, thrilled at his sound of pleasure as her hand slid down his hard belly, then lower still until his breath caught.

"Woman, that kind of behavior is going to get you into a heap of trouble."

"Maybe I like trouble."

She continued to stroke him, luxuriating in the way her touch made him harden, the way his body tightened and tensed. When his breathing became shallow, she let go and straddled his hips the way he had shown her before. Beneath her, the ridge of his mounting desire pressed into her. She moved against him, a heady sense of power surging through her. He wanted her.

His gaze feasted hungrily upon her body with such intensity, the ache between her legs increased. She rubbed against him, the friction sending a spiral of pleasure shooting through her.

She gasped. "Oh! Caleb…"

"I'm right here." His hand moved to her belly, moving upward with deliberate slowness until he gently cupped her breast. She arched her back so she filled his palm. The hard calluses brushed her nipple and she released a sigh of pleasure, letting her head fall back as she gave in to it.

The moistness between her thighs grew. Heaven help her, but she loved and needed this man with such ferocity it was almost too much to bear. Tonight, there would be no holding back. He loved her. The knowledge thrilled her, amazed her. And tonight she would give him all she had.

Caleb raised himself into a sitting position, his hands moving to circle her back, his lips trailing a fiery path from her collarbone, up her neck until they found her mouth. With an intensity at once gentle and passionate, he kissed her, his lips and tongue igniting a passion inside of her that threatened to overwhelm.

Without breaking the kiss that was slowly

driving her to the brink, Caleb pulled her down, turning them until she lay beneath him, his body covering and surrounding hers, her legs still wrapped around his hips. She pushed herself against him and was rewarded with a deep growl.

"If you keep that up this will be over before we even get started."

She heeded his warning, not wanting this night to end, not yet. She let herself explore his body, taking in every inch and committing it to memory. The angles of sinew and bone, the scars that crisscrossed his skin, the hint of stubble growing on his chin and the smattering of hair on his chest. The curve of his buttocks and the strength in his long legs. She outlined his hands with her finger and caressed his face with her lips. Finally he settled more firmly in the cradle of her thighs and gently entered her, filling her until the need built to a fevered pitch.

Caleb drew the moment out, lowering his mouth to hers, filling his kiss with naked desire until neither of them could stand the wait another minute. The slow rhythm of their movements created a friction that drove her to madness then beyond. Pleasure and tension grew inside of her, leaving her incoherent. All she could do was grip Caleb's muscled arms as he rose above her and hold on for all she was worth, moving with him until he, too, lost control and the wave of desire rose, crested and washed over them.

Rachel had no words for the oblivion that filled

her with a sense of completeness she had never known. Her mind melted into it and her heart soared. She felt the love they shared, the trust she'd willingly given him. She had dreamed of love, but she had never dreamed it would be like this.

"I love you," she whispered, as Caleb collapsed on top of her, holding her tightly to him, deeply afraid it would all come to an end far too soon.

"You are my heart," he said, his voice quiet and plain in the still night. He settled his body to one side and fitted her against him. "I'm going to be wanting to do that again before morning light."

"Good," she mumbled, already feeling the sleep that had eluded her earlier approaching. It took no time at all before the heat of his body and her sated exhaustion drew her into a satisfied slumber.

Caleb opened his eyes as Rachel turned in her sleep and nestled against him, her small body curling into his and awakening the rest of him. Tonight, she had held nothing back. Though he was still sore from his injuries, he welcomed the oblivion her body provided and reveled in the love her heart gave.

Their lovemaking had left him exhausted, yet exhilaration filled him at how she had responded to his touch. She was a wonder. A constant whirl of contradictions he could barely understand.

Every time he thought he had her figured out, something new would crop up.

One moment she was shy and uncertain, the next bold and fearless. She amazed him and scared him and made him glad his drifting days were over. It was time to stop, to set down roots. Time to make a life he could be proud of. A happy life.

Tonight he'd held that life in his hands.

But the idyllic image soon faded. It wasn't all sunshine and roses. Shamus Kirkpatrick had to be dealt with and Caleb didn't delude himself into believing that would be an easy task. Men like Kirkpatrick didn't give up easily, if at all. Most likely he would go down swinging and try to take as many people with him as possible.

It would be Caleb's job to ensure none of those people included Rachel or her family.

He turned his head, feeling the pull of his sore, beaten muscles, and kissed her gently on the forehead, letting her warmth seep into his aching bones.

Rachel stirred, rubbing her nose against his arm. There was something comforting about having her next to him. The feeling went beyond wanting her, exploring deeper until it settled into the very core of him.

But his happiness was marred by the prospect of what he needed to do. He had to tell her the truth. The whole truth. Not the bits and pieces he'd doled out here and there.

She deserved to know everything. Sheriff Donovan didn't appear likely to stop digging until he uncovered Caleb's secret. Eventually he would stumble across it, and when he did he'd make a beeline for Rachel.

She deserved to hear it from him first.

He closed his eyes and tried not to wonder what she would do. He'd been down this road before. But Rachel was not Marianne. Rachel had a strength to her he'd not seen in most men. Maybe she would understand. Maybe she could look beyond his past, the things he'd done, and find a way to forgive and accept him.

Caleb rested his cheek against her forehead and breathed deeply. The scent of violets lingered on her skin. Violets and—

Smoke?

His eyes shot open.

The acrid scent filtered into the room. Caleb bolted upright and took a deep breath. The smell wasn't strong enough to be in the house, so where?

His sudden motion woke Rachel. Her slow, languorous movements were a testament to how depleted she was after their lovemaking.

"What...?"

He reached over and squeezed her arm. "Get dressed."

She stopped mid-stretch and opened her eyes. "Get—? What's going on?"

Caleb had already thrown his legs over the side of the bed and groped in the dark for his clothes.

"I smell smoke."

Rachel froze for a brief moment, then the reality of what he'd said sent her scurrying in the dark for her own clothes. She relit the lamp next to the bed, but by then, Caleb had already dressed.

Rachel's gaze shot to the window. "The bunkhouse! Foster!"

She threw on her discarded nightdress and dressing gown then ran past Caleb before he could stop her. He tore after her. As he passed through the kitchen, he motioned to Ethan, who rubbed one eye and stared at them with the other, still half asleep.

"Stay put," Caleb ordered. He had used a similar command on Rachel once. He hoped Ethan paid more attention.

Outside, Rachel screamed Foster's name. The lamp bobbed in the distance, illuminating her as she ran toward the flames, her nightdress billowing out around her. He didn't bother trying to call her back. It would have been a wasted effort.

The door of the bunkhouse swung open and the old man staggered out in his faded red long johns, his white beard a stark contrast to the dark night. He fell to his knees a few feet from the door, his body racked with coughs. Rachel reached him and fitted her body beneath his arm, pulling him away from the burning building.

In the distance, the shouts of Stump and Everett echoed through the still air as they made their way down the hill. The clang of buckets behind

Caleb caught his attention. Freedom, her billowing white nightgown swirling about her legs, ran from her own cabin, two buckets in each hand.

Seeing Rachel had Foster taken care of, Caleb ran to the water pump to start filling the buckets. The effort pummeled his ribs. Freedom gently pushed him aside and took over, using her weight to drive the handle down and keep a steady stream pouring from the spout.

"You should get back to bed afore you make yourself worse."

Caleb shook his head, ignoring her suggestion. Being in bed was partly to blame for his current state of soreness. He called to Everett and Stump as they arrived. "Start a line!"

They worked together as a synchronized unit as flames licked up the side of the bunkhouse, devouring it. Silence prevailed except for the occasional order shouted by either himself or Rachel. Bit by bit, the fire dissipated, but by the time it was extinguished, the bunkhouse was destroyed.

Freedom rubbed her hands together, breaking the silence as they stood and stared at the damage. "I'm gonna go heat up some water. We'll all need to wash up before bed. C'mon, old man," she said, taking Foster's arm. "We's gonna get you looked over."

Caleb picked up a shovel that had been leaning against the chicken coop and started tossing dirt on the still-glowing embers.

"I'll go get some more shovels," Everett offered, wiping his sooty forehead with an even dirtier sleeve.

Around them, the night had grown quiet now that the roar of the fire had been quenched. As Caleb glanced at Rachel in the distance, he stopped what he was doing. Something had caught her attention. He could tell by the way she stood, her posture rigid. Caleb's gaze swept the horizon, but all he saw was the gnarled old oak.

Caleb drove the edge of the shovel into the ground and took a step toward her. "Rachel?"

She ignored him and headed for the tree. Before Caleb had taken more than a few steps, Freedom flew out the front door, her white nightdress streaming behind her. "Where's li'l Ethan? Where's the boy?"

Rachel's head swiveled first to Freedom then back to Caleb. Even from this far away he could see the fear in her dark eyes illuminated by the stark moonlight. She gathered her nightdress in both hands and took off at a run. Caleb snatched the lantern next to him and followed.

"Ethan!"

As he ran after her, Caleb's tired brain put the pieces together. She was heading for the old well. Terror gripped his insides.

"Get a rope," he called over his shoulder. Stump took off for the barn at a run.

When Caleb reached the boarded-up well, Rachel was already on her stomach shoving pieces of

broken wood aside. Had she done that, or Ethan?
Caleb dropped down onto the ground next to her.

"Ethan!"

"I'm down here!"

Rachel's breath caught. "Are you hurt?" Strain
edged her voice and Caleb wondered just how
much they were to endure this night.

"No," came the whimpered reply. "But the
w-water's c-cold."

Relief swept through Caleb. Ethan was still
alive. He hadn't drowned.

"Lord have mercy," Freedom muttered, her
eyes staring up toward the heavens. "Thank you,
Jesus."

Caleb wasn't about to thank anyone until he
had Ethan safe and sound and out of the well.

"Hang on, I'll get you out," he called down
the dark, narrow shaft. He tried not to think of
how. The notion of lowering himself into this tight
hole made sweat bead on his forehead and trickle
down his back.

Next to him, Rachel's whole body shook. Freedom had moved next to her and wrapped a comforting arm around her. Caleb reached out a hand
and squeezed Rachel's. It was ice cold. "He's
okay. Don't worry. We'll get him out."

She nodded, her lips pursed tightly together.
He could tell she wanted to offer Ethan comfort,
but was afraid that if she opened her mouth all
that would come out was a wail. She looked at
him with desperate, pleading eyes.

Eyes that begged her to save him. "I'll get him out."

Stump arrived, out of breath, and tied the long rope around a tree, while Caleb worked the other end into a makeshift noose and pulled it over his head, securing it under his arms. Rachel clawed at the remaining slats, breaking them off and tossing them aside until the hole was large enough for Caleb to fit through.

"I'm coming down to get you Ethan. Hang on."

"Hurry!" The boy's plaintive plea cut through Caleb with the sharpness of a razor's edge.

He turned to Rachel as Stump dug his heels into the ground and held the slack in the rope as Caleb began to lower himself down. "Hold the lantern close to the edge to throw some light in."

The rope cut into his flesh and made his bruises pulsate with pain, the pressure hitting directly on the sorest part of his ribs. He tried to breathe through it, but even that hurt. He prayed Stump could hold his weight. If not, he would go barreling down on top of Ethan, likely killing or injuring them both.

He tried to take another breath. The tight shaft closed in on him. Had it grown narrower? His breath came in short gasps. Could he do this?

Sweat streamed down his back as he braced his feet against the mud wall, searching in the dark for the wood and stone reinforcements built around it. The mud crumbled beneath his boot as he dug in then searched again.

Beneath him he could hear Ethan crying quietly.

There was no choice. He had to do this. Nothing could possibly be worse than crawling back up to the opening and telling Rachel he had failed. That his fear had gotten the better of him. She would never forgive him.

He would never forgive himself.

"Hang on, Ethan. I'm almost there." In truth, it was too dark to tell how far he had left to go before reaching the bottom. The light from the lantern did not penetrate this far into the endless black. Only Ethan's sobs hinted he was drawing closer.

His boot splashed against the water. Ethan's small hand grasp at his foot. "A few more feet then stop," he called up. Rachel's face filled the small opening of the well, blocking out the moon.

"Is he okay?"

"Seems fine."

"I'm cold!"

Rachel's laugh was pitched with giddy relief. "You get yourself out of this well and we'll see if Freedom can't whip you up some warm cocoa."

Freedom's booming voice filled the narrow shaft. "Crazy fool way to spend your time, young man. What were you thinking diving down this well?"

"I—I wanted to help. I thought I could get some water from here to put the fire out."

"How many times have I told you to stay away

from the old well?" The sternness in Rachel's voice was a mixture of relief, anger and love.

"Lots," Ethan mumbled, but Caleb suspected he was the only one close enough to hear.

"I'm almost there, Ethan."

Caleb's breath caught as Stump lowered him further. The icy water crawled up his legs until he was half immersed in the pool. "Alright," he called up. "Hold there."

The rope stayed taut and Caleb reached around until he found Ethan and gripped his thin shirt. The boy was shivering.

"You hurt?"

"N-no, sir. Guess I'm in trouble, huh?"

"I think maybe a little." He pulled Ethan to him. "I want you to put your arms around my neck and your legs around my waist. Think you can do that?"

There was the sound of splashing followed by a pair of cold, thin arms snaking around him. His ribs ached something fierce when Ethan's legs hugged his middle. Biting down, he accepted the pain. He'd take anything to get Ethan safely out of the well.

"Ready?"

"Ready," Ethan whispered through chattering teeth, his cold face pressed into Caleb's neck.

"Pull us up," he called, keeping one hand gripped on the rope and the other arm around Ethan. Bit by bit they moved back up the shaft. Caleb tried to hurry the process by digging his feet into the side of the well and propelling them upward. He couldn't get out of this dank, dark hole fast enough. What little strength he had left this night faded with each passing minute, along with his focus. He could feel his breathing grow erratic. He'd been here before. Soon the fuzzy blackness would overtake him. He couldn't risk that. He couldn't allow them to fall back into the well.

Forcing his mind away from his fear he concentrated on Ethan, on the solid feel of the boy's arms wrapped around his neck, on the stabbing pain in his ribs where Ethan held on for dear life, on the way he shivered from the cold.

After several long, insufferable moments, the hole at the top of the well grew larger and Stump's arms reached for the boy. Then Caleb was over the edge, falling to the hard ground, gasping in air still scented with smoke.

Ethan was safe. They'd made it.

Next to him, Stump and the women admonished and rejoiced as they checked Ethan over, ensuring that his claims to be unhurt were true. Caleb couldn't move. His limbs had gone numb, his lungs still begged for air.

The fear had left Rachel's voice. "Take Ethan inside and start heating up a hot bath—"

"And cocoa," Ethan piped in.

Caleb smiled from where he lay sprawled on the ground, his heart still pumping hard inside his chest. The kid was none the worse for wear.

He listened to their voices as Freedom led Ethan back to the house and Stump took the supplies back to the barn, leaving him alone with Rachel.

Her face filled his gaze. Worry, relief and a host of other emotions were scattered across her features. "Thank you. You saved his life."

"It was nothing."

"It was everything." She touched his face, her warmth chasing away the cold that had seeped into his bones. "Are you hurt?"

"I'm fine," he said, lying. Tonight had done his injuries no favors, but he'd do it all again without hesitation. Rachel leaned down and kissed him, her mouth soft and pliant against his. Caleb reached up, burying his hand deep in her hair, holding her to him.

She broke the kiss and rested her forehead against his. "We should get inside. We both need to get cleaned up."

He nodded his agreement, though he was quite certain he could have stayed here for the rest of the night, kissing her like this, feeling her close to him. She was a balm to his wounds, both inside and out.

How funny to think that he'd ridden into this town hell bent on getting out as fast as humanly possible, and now he was planning on staying for a lifetime. It was strange how fate worked its magic.

A whiff of smoke wafted on the breeze and up

from his clothing, reminding him that not all fate had in store would be easy.

Caleb wasn't deterred. He'd never been on good terms with easy anyway.

Chapter Twenty

Rachel stared at the charred remains of the bunkhouse. In the early morning light, its unsalvageable state was a testament to how close they'd come to losing Foster. The roof had caved in. The skeletal remains of the bunks were barely recognizable. Only the small woodstove had escaped intact.

She looked back at the house. She'd left Caleb sleeping soundly. He'd been exhausted after last night's ordeal. Guilt wended its way into her thoughts. She shouldn't have enticed him last night, intent on enjoying him. It was too soon. His injuries had not fully healed. Between their lovemaking, fighting the fire and pulling Ethan out of the well, he had pushed himself beyond his limits.

But the events of last night told her one thing. Despite his fear of small spaces and the pain in his body, he had acted without hesitation to put out the fire and save Ethan. She could count on

Caleb to do whatever was necessary to keep her family safe. She stared at the pile of burned rubble at her feet. That was all she needed to know.

The fire had been no random act. Foster had heard noise outside the bunkhouse before the fire started. He'd thought it had been animals rooting around and didn't pay much attention. It had been animals, but of the human variety. And there was only one person who would stoop to such tactics. The same person who'd jumped an unarmed man in the woods. The same man who'd purposely injured one of her ranch hands.

Shamus Kirkpatrick.

Rachel's eyes still burned from the smoke and the scent clung stubbornly to her hair. She'd been too tired to wash it last night before crawling into bed and curling up in Caleb's embrace, thankful for the comfort she found there.

She knew it would be one of the last times she experienced it. After she did what needed doing, there would be little comfort available.

Shamus Kirkpatrick needed to be stopped. He had targeted the bunkhouse because he believed Caleb slept there, likely based on information he'd pried out of Brody, who wouldn't have realized the consequences of what he'd said. Caleb had become a threat, one Shamus wanted eliminated. And in the process people had nearly died, including little Ethan.

For a brief, idyllic moment, Rachel had allowed herself to believe she and Caleb could face this problem together, but last night proved how wrong she'd been. The time for talk and reasoning had ended. Shamus's actions left any hope in that regard smoldering in the cinder and ash. The time had come to end this once and for all.

The thought of leaving Caleb was a sharp knife in her heart. She accepted the pain, knowing she had no other choice. Shamus had grown desperate. How long before his attacks left someone dead? And what about when he discovered it was Caleb who owned the land? If he had been intent on eliminating Caleb as a threat before, learning about the deed would only increase his efforts.

Rachel couldn't take the risk, no matter the cost to her. First, she needed to talk to Brody, convince him to come home, where he belonged. She took one last look at the house and headed north to the closest point where her land and Shamus's converged. Everett had mentioned seeing him near there the day before. She hoped he'd show up again today.

"What are you doing here?"

Brody slid from his horse and marched over to Rachel when the bird call she had taught him as a child caught his attention. Remaining hidden in the trees and tall grass, Rachel stayed close enough to her own land in case she had to make a run for it if one of Shamus's thugs saw her. Finally she found Brody as he rounded up a few strays. He did not look pleased to see her, a fact that left a gaping hole in her heart.

"I came here to tell you to come back home." If she was going to go through with her plan to eliminate Shamus as a threat, she wanted Brody safely out of the way. She didn't need him getting caught in the middle.

"Well I ain't goin', so you might as well go back." Brody crossed his arms over his narrow chest and tilted his chin at an arrogant angle. He looked so much like Shamus it made her want to cry.

Rachel bit down on her tongue to keep from lashing out. Part of her wanted to pull him by the ear all the way home but the other part knew such behavior would only alienate him further, sending him straight back to Shamus as a sign of defiance. She took a deep breath, changing tactics.

"Did you know the bunkhouse burned to the ground last night?"

Brody's stiff posture slackened. "What? Which one? Was anyone—"

"No. Almost, but no. Foster got out in time. I'm surprised your boss didn't tell you about it, seeing as it was his doing."

"No, it wasn't." His denial came fast and hard, shooting out at her. "And he isn't my boss. He's my father."

Shock froze her words on her tongue. For whatever reason, Shamus had decided he no longer needed to hold on to the secret of Brody's parentage. Instead he had attempted to sever her last tie with her brother.

"He can't be trusted, Brody."

Her brother scoffed at her words. "At least he didn't lie to me like you did. You've known all along he was my pa and you didn't say anything. You wanted to control me. All this time worrying and fighting to make ends meet and it was all here for the takin'!" He swept his arm wide to encompass the land around them.

His words, fed to him by Shamus, were as effective as a sucker punch to the gut. "It wasn't ours to take, Brody. Do you think I like our situation? I don't. But if you think for one minute Shamus Kirkpatrick is going to share all his worldly possessions with us out of the kindness of his black heart, then you're a fool. He doesn't care about anyone but himself."

"He's my father!"

"Then where was he all these years? Why didn't he come to claim you after Pa died? Or after Ma passed away and we were left on our own, struggling? He'll use you as long as you're useful to him then he'll toss you aside."

"You're lying." Brody's pale blue eyes burned bright with anger and indignation. He'd waited his whole life for a father figure and now she was trying to tear it away from him.

"I'm sorry I kept this from you, Brody. Maybe you're right, maybe you should have been told. But Mama made me promise to keep it a secret. She didn't want Shamus to have any claim on you.

And for your whole life, he was perfectly happy not to. How did he explain that away?"

Brody shifted. "He said he just found out."

Rachel made a sound that landed somewhere between a snort and a laugh. "Then he lied to you, Brody."

"He said you'd say that, try to make him look bad. But it's true. Said it wasn't till I was grown he realized the resemblance and knew the truth. He said one day I'll inherit this. Then we won't ever have to worry about money ever again."

"We don't need the money. Not that badly."

"Well, I do. I'm tired of scraping by and goin' without. I'm tired of watching you and Ethan give up things you want. Of Stump and Len and Everett working their fingers to the bone because we can't afford to hire more help." He jabbed his finger into his chest. "I'm the man of the house now and I won't be treated like a child that needs protectin'. Go home, Rachel. You're not my mother and you ain't my boss. I'm my own man now. Being here is my decision and I won't change it just 'cause you don't like it."

He turned his back on her and, in a few swift strides, reached his horse and mounted. Rachel's heart broke when he didn't look back once as he rode off. Those might well be the last words they ever spoke to each other. After she killed Shamus, Brody would have one more thing he'd never forgive her for.

And even if he did, it might be too late.

* * *

Caleb squinted against the sun, absently stroking his knife down a piece of kindling. He'd been sitting on the step leading up to the porch and brooding long enough for a pile of chips to collect at his feet and dot his woolen trousers.

He and Rachel were getting married. Of all the events of the past couple of days, that was the one most deeply embedded in his heart. She had agreed to marry him.

He should be elated. Part of him was. But the other part...

He shook his head. He had to tell her the truth and he had to do it now. There was no way around it. He could not, in good conscience, allow Rachel to marry him without knowing.

He had meant to tell her this morning, but when he awoke she was already gone and no one seemed to know where. He'd been sitting here ever since, waiting.

Her absence worried him. She'd taken the burning of the bunkhouse and Ethan falling down the old well hard. It was another sign Kirkpatrick had no intention of slowing down his assault. Caleb had promised her they would work it out, find a way to stop him, but in the morning light things looked no more promising than they had when he was lying in bed, staring at the ceiling long after Rachel had fallen into an exhausted sleep.

He couldn't think of a single way to convince

Kirkpatrick to stop. The knowledge made him sick. And knowing he still had to tell Rachel the truth of who he was, what he'd done, didn't make things any better.

The door behind him opened and closed. He glanced over his shoulder to find Freedom looking down from the top step, a load of laundry balanced on her hip. She nodded at his hands. "What's that supposed to be?"

He turned what was left of the wood over in his hand. "A very sharp stick."

Freedom made a clucking sound and walked past him, holding the laundry basket high so as not to hit him in the head with it. When she reached the large basin set up for washing, she set it down and turned to face him.

"Rachel done told me you plan on marryin' her."

"That's right." If she'd still have him.

"You worried it might be too soon after losin' Mr. Sutter? 'Cause it ain't," she said, not waiting for him to answer. "Woman in these parts can't be putting stock in propriety and the like. Survival holds more weight than manners. Ain't no one gonna blame her if she up and marries fast after him bein' buried."

Caleb slid his knife back into the sheath at his waist. "I'm not worried about that."

In truth he'd given it very little thought. Maybe he should have.

"Then what's got you so tied into knots you been takin' it out on that piddly little stick?"

"Anyone ever tell you its bad manners prying into someone else's personal business?"

"Can't imagine I'da listened if they had."

He tested the sharp tip of the stick with the pad of his thumb. "I've got a past."

She shrugged off his admission. "We all got a past, Mr. Beckett. I's got one, Rachel's got one. Even little Ethan's got one. Everyone's got a story to tell."

"Maybe so."

The question was, did anyone else's story start with a peaceable game of poker and end with a cold-blooded murder?

"Well maybe now'd be a good time to be discussin' that past with Miss Rachel," Freedom said, nodding at the hills to the northwest. Caleb turned and saw Rachel in the distance walking toward the house. Her shoulders sloped inward as if the burden she carried was on the verge of defeating her. It killed him that he had to add to that.

He hesitated, the way a man would before being led to the gallows, putting off the inevitable for as long as possible. The green calico dress she wore caught in the breeze, pressing against her. It was one of his favorites, the color enhancing the dark brown of her eyes. Eyes he had become lost in, and, as it turned out, found himself in.

He didn't want to give that up. It was cowardly of him, but the idea of losing her...well, he might as well drive the whittled stick straight through his heart and save her the trouble.

He wondered if Freedom would be so keen for him to reveal his past if she knew the truth. But she didn't. No one did, save a handful of people present in Laramie when the late-night shooting took place. And as far as any of them knew, it was Sinjin Drake who'd done the killing. None of them had ever heard the name Caleb Beckett.

But it wouldn't stay that way. Not with Sheriff Donovan poking around, refusing to let the thing lie. The sheriff knew Robert Sutter hadn't been wearing his guns, a truth that continued to scrape across Caleb's conscience every day and in his dreams each night.

How long would Donovan keep silent with what he knew? Caleb shook head.

They couldn't start their life together on a foundation of lies. He needed to tell her.

He stood, brushing the curly pieces of wood from his trousers as she drew nearer.

"Guess maybe I's be needed down in the smokehouse," Freedom said. "Probably be there a good long time, too, jus' in case you's was wonderin'."

Caleb nodded without taking his eyes off Rachel's approaching form. When she reached him, she walked straight into his arms without stopping. He embraced her, turning his head to breathe in her scent and press his lips to her temple. Her skin was warm from the morning sun.

"Brody won't come home." The words muffled against his shoulder were painted thick with hurt. "Shamus told him he's his father. Now Brody's angry at me for keeping it a secret. Said I was trying to control him. I just wanted to protect him, that's all."

Caleb closed his eyes. That's all he had been doing, too, but like Brody, he didn't hold out much hope Rachel would see it that way.

"He'll come around. Give him some coolin' off time." He pulled back, just enough to see her face. Her eyes were dry but rimmed with red. It was likely she'd cried half the way home, her brother's rejection a raw wound that would take time to heal. "You were just trying to do what was best for him."

Would she feel the same way?

She sniffed, then nodded, though the sadness in her eyes told him she wasn't ready to fully believe him.

"Rachel, I need to talk to you about something," he said, letting the words out before he talked himself out of it yet again, delaying the inevitable. "It's important."

"Okay." She pulled out of his arms and walked into the house. Caleb paused a moment and prayed this would not be the end. But likely God had given up on him a long time ago and he was just wasting his breath.

Inside the house, the inviting aroma of baked apples filled the kitchen. Pies lined the window sill, waiting for the evening's meal. He wondered if he'd still be here by the time the dinner bell was rung.

He walked over to the arched door that led to the newly built section. The work was done, the room ready for use after a good cleaning to remove the dust and clear out the debris.

"Where's Ethan?" she asked. The cot he now slept in had been made in a haphazard fashion, the quilt hauled up over twisted blankets and George the bunny perched on top of the pillow as if it were a throne.

"Foster took him to deliver lunch to Everett and Stump."

For once, Caleb was glad not to have the boy around. He didn't want Ethan to hear the confession he needed to make. He wasn't sure he could handle the devastation in the young boy's eyes after he'd spent weeks treating Caleb like a hero. It was bad enough that he had to witness the change it would make in Rachel.

It was strange how it took him a lifetime to find a place that felt like home, and now his own past and the things he'd done conspired to take it away. Part of him wanted to keep living a lie. But he knew it would never work. The truth would fester inside of him, eventually poisoning everything good between them.

She deserved to know the truth, to make her decision to marry him with all the facts at her disposal. She hadn't known what she was getting into when she married Robert, and she'd paid the price. He wouldn't put her through that again.

"What did you need to talk about?"

Caleb turned around to face her. How did he tell her? Where did he begin?

"My name is Caleb Beckett."

Her brow puckered as she tried to make sense of what he was telling her. "I know."

"But until I came here, until I met you, I hadn't used that name for a long time. So long I can't even remember." Rachel had brought it back, brought him back to be the man he'd wanted to be before life and circumstance and his grandfather had changed the path he walked.

"I don't understand. What name did you use?"

"Sinjin Drake."

Chapter Twenty-One

Rachel's body went rigid as Caleb's words took hold. "What? No."

"I can explain, if you'll let me. I—"

She shook her head. "You're Sinjin Drake?"

"I used to be."

Pain, raw and ugly, glistening in her dark eyes. He wished now he had told her the whole story when he'd first met her. At the time, he thought he was doing her a service, given all she had to bear, but at least then she would have had the luxury of hating him from the start. She wouldn't have fallen in love with him, and he wouldn't have had the possibility of a future with a good woman he loved dangled in front of him before being snatched away. He'd been a fool to think he could outrun his past. To think it wouldn't be waiting for him at every turn.

"You lied to me?"

He didn't try to deflect her question. What defense did he have to offer? He motioned toward the table, reaching out for her. "Sit down."

Rachel stepped away from him, her hands clenched at her sides so tightly he could see the white ridges of her knuckles.

"Don't touch me."

Caleb let his hand fall away, the chasm in his heart deepening. He recognized the revulsion in her gaze. He had been down this road before. At the time, he thought he couldn't hurt worse. He had been wrong. Losing Marianne was nothing compared to the agony he experienced now.

"Rachel, please, sit. This isn't going to be a short story."

She hesitated then gave a short nod, keeping enough room between them so he couldn't touch her. With deliberate movements, she lowered herself into a chair at the table. Caleb pulled out another and sat in front of her.

"Sinjin is my middle name. My grandfather gave it to me to remind me of where I came from. That I was borne out of sin and was no better than that. It's the name he called me. When I left my grandfather I took the name he'd given me. I was determined to live up to his low opinion. I was young and angry and didn't care much whether I lived or died."

He remembered those days with a strange sense of detachment. It had been a long time since he'd revisited them in his memory. He had simply accepted who he was, what he was. That is, until he came here and started wishing things could be different. Until Rachel reminded him of the dreams he'd once had, of a good life filled with someone who loved him.

"I told you I fought in the war."

She nodded, refusing to look at him.

"During that time, I garnered myself a reputation as a sharpshooter. Afterward, I used that skill to pick up work. I was a Pinkerton for a bit, road gunner for Overland Stage, even did a stint as a marshal once. Each of those jobs built my reputation as a fast draw, and being young and cocky I didn't care. I didn't stop to think how it would affect things down the road. Didn't realize people would want to try and build their own reputations by destroying mine."

"By killing you."

"Yes." Caleb had never gone looking for trouble, but it found him nonetheless. He'd been twenty-three when a man called him out for no other reason than to be the one to outdraw Sinjin Drake. Caleb had tried to talk sense into the man, but the fool wouldn't relent. He was dead before his body hit the litter-strewn streets of Laredo.

"I drifted around after that, changed my name a lot to try and put some distance between me and my reputation. I thought I had finally outrun it when I met Marianne. I shouldn't have been surprised it caught up with me." He glanced down at the table where his hand rested. His gun hand. "After that, I gave up. I left Caleb Beckett buried in the past. Figured sooner or later I'd die by the gun, and maybe that was all I deserved."

Rachel took a deep breath and looked up. He could read nothing in her expression.

"Why did you kill Robert?"

"I—" He hesitated. This was the question he'd been dreading. The answer he knew he had to give. "We were playing cards. The stakes were high. When his money ran out, he put up the deed to the ranch. I tried to stop him, told him no card game was worth losing your home. But he wouldn't listen. Said he would win the next hand and I'd be sorry."

Rachel let out a derisive snort and mumbled something under her breath he couldn't make out.

"When he lost the hand, he went crazy. Cursing and swearing, he threatened to make everyone at the table pay. He accused me of cheating then suddenly pushed back from the table and—"

"And what?"

He hated this. Hated reliving this moment. Remembering the stark desperation in Sutter's eyes.

"He reached for his gun. I reacted...out of instinct and—"

"And you killed him."

"Yes."

He hadn't hesitated. His reflexes had taken over and he'd drawn. In one swift motion he'd aimed and fired, and a man's life was ended.

Rachel's gaze fell away and returned to her lap. She rubbed absently at the buttery yellow flowers dotting the soft green skirt. Caleb wished he could end the story there, but he'd promised her the truth.

"There's more."

Rachel looked up and Caleb wished she had left her gaze on the flowered pattern of her dress. Pain and betrayal had turned her eyes the color of midnight.

"What more can there be? You shot him, then you came here, the deed to my ranch in your hand. You made me love you. Made love to me. The whole time..." She shook her head. "What else could there be to tell me?"

Caleb pushed the words out before they locked in his throat. "He didn't have a gun."

Rachel froze, trying to make sense of what Caleb was telling her.

"But...you said he drew."

Caleb's voice lowered to a whisper. "I said he made the motion."

"I don't understand." Or she didn't want to. Her head had already figured it out, but her heart refused to believe it. Because believing it would mean the man she loved was a cold-blooded killer.

Caleb continued. "Your husband didn't have a gun. He'd sold it that afternoon to raise money for the game. He must have forgotten, or...I don't know. It was well past midnight by then and he sat in shadow. When he reached for his gun I—"

"Shot him."

"Yes. I'm sorry." The broad expanse of his shoulders crumpled inward and he dropped his face into his hands. "God help me, Rachel, I'm sorry."

Anger burst through her as every moment they'd shared since he first rode into town flashed through her mind. All the opportunities he'd had to tell her the truth had been there for the picking, but he'd ignored every one. He'd let her go on thinking he was someone he wasn't, someone she could trust, someone she could love.

All that time he'd been lying to her.

All that time he claimed to be Caleb Beckett, in truth he'd been Sinjin Drake. The man who'd killed Robert.

She had fallen in love with her husband's murderer.

"How could you do this to me?" As if it was all his fault and she'd had no part in it. As if she hadn't craved his touch, or needed to hear the sound of his voice or see his warm smile. It was easier to think that way for the moment. She might feel differently later, but she would deal with it then. Not now. Now she had all she could handle.

Caleb straightened and looked at her, his eyes pleading for a forgiveness she couldn't muster. The killing she could almost understand. He had acted out of instinct, a sense of self-preservation honed over years of being a target and needing to survive. She knew what a hothead Robert had been. How he reacted when desperate and angry.

But to not tell her? To live each day knowing what he had done and never telling her? It was the ultimate betrayal. How did she forgive him for that?

She didn't know if she could.

"Rachel, let me—"

She held up her hand, cutting him off. She'd heard all she could stand. "I need you to leave. I know this is your land and I have no right to it, but I need you to leave all the same until I can make other arrangements."

He stared at her for a long moment. She could feel his gaze upon her but couldn't meet it. She waited until it dropped away before she looked over. His gaze had fallen to his hands—hands that had killed Robert. The same hands he'd gently explored her body with, teasing her skin, delving inside of her.

She closed the door on her memories. They no longer mattered.

"I'll get my things," he said, standing. His voice held no surprise, as if he'd known all along what the outcome would be, the damage it would cause.

He had been right.

"I'm sorry," Caleb said, his hand resting on her shoulder. She should have brushed him off, moved beyond his reach, but she didn't. She needed to feel him, to savor one last touch before it was lost forever.

"It doesn't matter." They were just words now. They didn't change the truth.

His hand slipped away. He paused when he reached the doorway, his head turning far enough for her to see the strong lines of his profile, and for one last torturous moment, she remembered the touch of his lips on hers and the sense of home she'd found there.

It had been nothing more than an illusion.

Pain lanced her heart and she closed her eyes, unable to watch him leave.

The door hit the frame, announcing his departure. Sobs choked Rachel's throat. She tried to fight them back but the pain was too great, refusing to be buried or pushed aside. She doubled over and let it come, hugging her arms across her middle.

Caleb nursed the drink in his hand as he rested his elbows on the bar. He hadn't had decent whiskey since he'd left Laramie, and the watered-down liquid in front of him was a sorry substitute. It hardly mattered. Even the strongest drink wouldn't numb the pain of losing Rachel.

He'd come within a hair's breadth of happiness, but it had all been a lie. He'd known it from the beginning. What he didn't know was why he fooled himself into believing it could ever be otherwise. He was a murderer. He'd finally lived up to his grandfather's low opinion. It brought him no satisfaction.

He touched the deed to her land where it rested on the bar. The saloon was all but deserted at this hour, though he knew business would pick up soon. He planned on being long gone by then.

But first he had one last item of business to take care of.

"Heard you wanted to see me."

Sheriff Donovan hooked a foot on the rung of an empty stool next to Caleb. He didn't sit down, an indication that he had no intention of staying.

Caleb swirled the remaining whiskey in his glass then finished it off. It barely burned going down. He set the glass on the bar and, with one finger, slid the land deed toward Donovan.

"What's this?" The sheriff picked up the piece of paper and glanced at it, doing a double take when he realized what he was holding. "What are you doing with this?"

"Sutter lost his land in Laramie. To me."

Donovan's weight shifted and he sunk hard onto the stool. "You own the Sutter ranch? You have owned it all this time?"

Caleb didn't bother answering the obvious. "I need you to give this to Rachel. I've signed it back over to her."

This was enough to pull the sheriff's attention away from the paper in his hand. "Why don't you give it to her yourself?"

"She doesn't want to see me." The admission drove nails into his heart.

"Had the sense you two were right cozy up there."

"We were," Caleb admitted. "Until I told her I'm the one who killed her husband."

Donovan stiffened and his hand automatically went to the gun at his hip, his fingers playing against the handle. The sheriff was a smart man. It didn't take him long to make the connection. It was a testament to his courage that his hand remained on his gun. And testimony to his intelligence that he didn't draw.

"You're Sinjin Drake?"

Caleb nodded and, with little preamble, gave him the same story he'd relayed to Rachel three days earlier. It didn't get any easier to tell the second time around.

"The law cleared you?"

"You know they did." The sheriff had investigated Robert's death. In another town on another day maybe Caleb would have hung for it, but the law in Laramie had been happy to send the notorious gunslinger on his way, get him out of their town and the body with him. Sweep the whole thing under the rug as if it had never happened.

"I take it Rachel wasn't quite as charitable."

"Would you have been, in her shoes?" Donovan didn't answer, his silence summing up what Caleb already knew. What he had done was unforgivable.

He stared down at his empty glass, tilting his head at the deed. "You'll see she gets this?"

"I will. Take it this means you're leaving town?" Caleb noted the hopeful sound in Donovan's voice. He was a good man. Probably the one Rachel should have chosen all those years ago. How different her life would have been.

"I have one more thing I need to take care of."

"Kirkpatrick?"

"Kirkpatrick." Caleb turned to the sheriff, his coat falling open to reveal the guns strapped to his hips.

"You plan on confronting him, or killing him?"

Caleb didn't answer.

"You'll swing for it, regardless of how vile the man is. If you go out there and intentionally kill him there isn't anything I can do to help you."

"I'm not asking for your help."

If killing Kirkpatrick kept Rachel and her family safe, he'd gladly accept the noose. What did he have left to live for, anyway? Without Rachel, the rest of his life stretched out like a vast wasteland. He'd spent his life living by the gun. Every time he tried to leave that life behind, it tracked him down. Maybe this was the way it was supposed to be. Maybe everything he had done up to now simply led him to this moment.

"See that Rachel's taken care of."

The idea of her with another man made him sick, but she deserved someone to lean on, someone to share the burden with. Someone better than him. She could do a lot worse than Hunter Donovan. Despite that, Caleb couldn't help but hate the man a little for being able to step into the life he wanted for himself.

Donovan folded the deed and slipped it into the front pocket of his shirt behind his badge. He sat silent a moment before speaking again.

"Maybe I'll ride out to see Rachel today."

"I appreciate it."

"In fact, maybe I'll even forget you and I had this conversation, or that I saw you wearing those guns."

Caleb looked at Donovan, but the sheriff was staring at the glasses lining the shelf behind the bar.

"It's even plausible that, after you finish your business with Kirkpatrick and ride out of town, I'll remember you had left much earlier than you did so as to make it impossible you could have met with him at all."

"Don't do me any favors."

"Ain't doing it for you." Donovan stood and headed for the door. "I'm doing it for Rachel. She might hate you now but it will pass. And when it does, I don't want her stewing in guilt or crying over your grave."

Caleb didn't want that, either, though a small part of him embraced the idea that she would still care enough to miss him. He would miss her, too. He would feel her absence keenly with every breath he took, from this day forward. "Do what you have to."

"You, too."

Caleb waited for the sheriff to leave, took one last sweeping glance around the saloon, empty save for a couple of tired old whores and a drunk in the corner. They wouldn't remember him, their memories conveniently vacant. He could kill Kirkpatrick, ride out of town and keep on going as if he'd never seen or heard of Salvation Falls.

Except that he had, and whether he swung from a rope or rode out of town a free man, he left here a ghost.

Chapter Twenty-Two

The damp white sheet flapped around Rachel like a ghostly specter as she struggled to peg it onto the clothesline. She'd thrown herself into helping Freedom with the laundry, anything to escape the unending regret at her angry reaction of three days ago.

Her eyes still stung from the amount of crying she'd done.

The tears had come from a mixture of hurt and frustration. She felt betrayed by Caleb's lies, trapped by his confession and angry at herself for acting so rashly, ordering him out of his own home.

She knew even before he disappeared over the hill that she should go after him and bring him back, but pride had choked the words in her throat where they withered and died. Now each passing moment of his absence carved a separate scar onto her soul.

She tried to justify her actions. He had lied to

her. Lain with her, touched her in a way no man ever had or ever would again. All the while he'd known the truth and kept it from her. For the first day, this bolstered her anger and kept her from falling apart, from riding into town and begging him to come back. But by the second day, her self-righteous indignation began to erode as the niggling voice in her head kept asking questions she didn't want to face.

Hadn't she done the same thing to her brother? She'd kept their mother's secret about his true father from him his entire life, justifying her actions by saying it was for his own good. He was better off not knowing. She was only trying to protect him, and maybe herself, if she were being honest.

How was that any different than what Caleb had done?

It wasn't.

She tried to console herself with the fact she would have lost him anyway. Facing down Shamus was a one-way trip. She would end up dead or incarcerated by the end of it, a sacrifice she had been willing to make if it meant her family would be safe. But those plans now lay in tatters, another casualty of Caleb's truth. Without him here, there was no one to look after her family. In sending him away, she had destroyed her only chance to protect them. What would she do now?

She hoped keeping busy would slow the tumult of emotions twisting through her and allow her to make sense of things, but so far no answer made itself known. She had painted herself into a corner and could see no way out.

"He did what he thought was right," Freedom said, her voice filtering up from behind the line of sheets.

Rachel gritted her teeth. She had told Freedom what happened, needing the older woman's strength to lean on and any guidance she had to give.

"He should have told me right from the start," Rachel said, trying to salvage the remnants of her anger and wrap it around her heart to shield against the pain.

"And what would you have done if he had?"

"I would have told him to leave!" Right at the beginning, before she fell in love with him, before she knew what it was like to have a man love her back. Before her heart broke into so many pieces there was no hope of putting it back together.

"Can't kick a man off his own land," Freedom pointed out.

Rachel groaned and let her head fall back until the warmth of the sun bathed her face. Freedom was right. She'd had no right at all, not in a legal sense. But to her, the deed was little more than a piece of paper. It didn't matter whose name was on it, this land was hers. It was in her blood and her bones. She couldn't imagine life without it, or where she would go if Caleb returned and demanded she leave.

"Maybe he kept his peace because he figured

you'd had enough pain without dishing you out a second helping. Maybe he jus' wanted to love you and not complicate the whole thing with—"

"—the truth? Yes, pesky thing that truth." She ought to know. She'd kept her own secrets, and now Brody held her accountable in the same way she held Caleb. Being angry at him made her the worst kind of hypocrite. Though, in truth, in the dead of night when she allowed herself to examine her motives, she wondered if she wasn't angrier at herself for sending him away than at him for giving her reason to.

She tossed the sheet over the line with enough force that it slipped off the rope and landed on the grass below.

"Don't be takin' your anger out on my clean laundry. You got yourself into a pickle sending Mr. Beckett away and you'll jus' have t' figure out a way to make it right."

Rachel picked up the sheet and gave it a sharp snap, sending pieces of grass flitting into the air. "I know you're right. I just don't know how I'm going to do it. I was awful to him, and maybe I had a right, but maybe he won't see it that way. You can't make amends to someone who isn't interested in hearing your apology."

"Only one way to be knowin' how interested he is in listenin'. But first, why don't you go see to the visitor comin' at us and leave my laundry alone afore you double my work."

For a brief moment, Rachel's heart soared with

hope, but it was short-lived as she peeled back the edge of the sheet and quickly recognized Hunter's tall form sitting straight in the saddle.

A chill swept through her. The last time he'd come here it was to bring news of Robert's death. She slipped a peg onto the sheet to hold it in place and started to walk toward him. He pulled up on the reins and slid from the horse. His hat shielded his eyes, but she recognized the grim line of his mouth and braced herself for what was to come.

"Afternoon, Rachel." Even his voice sounded forbidding. She tried to steady her breathing. She wasn't sure she could handle any more bad news.

"What is it?" She couldn't make herself ask *who*. Brody and Caleb were both unaccounted for, and she knew there was no bracing herself for the loss of either one of them. If that was what Hunter had come to tell her, he may as well dig her grave now. She'd taken as much as she could carry.

Hunter stopped in front of her and reached into the pocket of his shirt. He pulled out a piece of folded paper and handed it to her.

Rachel recognized the paper even before he set it in her outstretched hand, but she unfolded it anyway and glanced down at the familiar words. It was the deed to her land. Returned to her.

"Where did you get this?"

"You know where I got it."

Hunter was right, but that knowledge did nothing to stop her heart from pounding against the walls of her chest until she feared it would break every last one of her ribs. Caleb had promised that so long as he drew breath Shamus Kirkpatrick would not harm her or her family. And he was a man who kept his promises.

She squeezed her eyes shut. "Was he wearing his guns?"

"He was."

Fear assaulted her from every angle. Caleb was going to confront Kirkpatrick. And he didn't expect to return.

"Why didn't you stop him?"

"Ain't a crime to be wearing guns, Rachel. I had no cause to arrest him."

Desperate, she grabbed for the only piece of information she thought might help. "But he killed Robert!"

Hunter dipped his head then nodded. "I know."

"He—he's Sinjin Drake!" Anxiety raised her voice several octaves until she barely recognized it. Why was Hunter being so calm? What did she have to do to get him to get back on his horse riding after Caleb, to haul him to jail where he'd be safe?

"I know who he is and I'm guessin' he told you what happened just like he told me. Beckett didn't do anything any other man wouldn't have done in the same situation. Only difference being Beckett was a much faster draw than most men. Even if Robert did have his guns the outcome would have been the same, and the fault would have still been his."

"He's riding to his death!"

"Man's got a right to ride where he feels the need to go, Rachel. I can't stop him. No crime has been committed." Hunter pointed at the deed now crumpled in her hand. "He wanted you to have that and he wanted you safe. That's a hell of a lot more than I've been able to do. If Kirkpatrick isn't dealt with, who knows what else he'll try, and I won't be able to stop him. Let Beckett take care of this, Rachel."

A scream of frustration burst out of her, bringing Freedom running. Rachel shook her head at the other woman's questions, unable to articulate answers beyond her fear and anger. This was her fault. She'd been so hell-bent on killing Shamus, seeing it as the only way to stop him—and maybe it was—but now Caleb had taken the job from her and was riding out to confront the man. If it was just the two men facing each other, maybe she wouldn't be so scared. But Shamus never sullied his own hands with the dirty work. He'd have a posse of thugs to do it for him. Caleb wasn't riding into a one-on-one showdown, he would be facing a gauntlet of men who would love nothing more than to gun him down the moment he set foot on Shamus's land.

And there was nothing anyone could do to stop it.

Or so Hunter claimed.

With another shout of frustration, Rachel shoved the deed into Hunter's chest with enough force to set him off balance. She used this to her advantage and bolted past him to his horse, throwing herself up onto it and grabbing the reins before he could stop her.

"Rachel!"

She ignored him, jerking the horse around. It reared up in protest, forcing Hunter to stumble back to avoid the kicking hooves. Rachel dug her heels into the horse's sides and bent low over its neck, leaving Hunter cursing after her. The wind pulled at her skirts and her mind raced with possibilities, none of which offered her any peace.

She prayed she wasn't too late.

This was her fault for acting in anger, for lashing out and sending Caleb away. If he died— whether by Shamus's hand or hanging for his murder, his blood would be on her hands. She had wasted her days hoping he would return without her swallowing her pride and going after him.

Honorable fool that he was, he'd respected her insistence that he leave, and then he'd upped the ante by not coming back.

Now she might lose him forever. Her heart staggered at the prospect.

She urged the horse to move faster and let the wind whip the tears from her cheeks.

She couldn't lose him. Not like this. Not at all.

"Finally come to your senses and decided to leave town?"

The gun hidden beneath Caleb's jacket burned

against his hip and his palm itched to use it, if for no other reason than to erase the smug expression of victory from Kirkpatrick's face.

He wouldn't be smiling for long, Caleb reminded himself. Still, the idea of killing churned his guts. Ending a life was never an easy thing, even if the life belonged to scum like Kirkpatrick. Any other time he'd pulled the trigger it had been because trouble had come looking for him. This was different.

He steadied his mind. There was no other way. Kirkpatrick wouldn't listen to reason or be talked out of taking what he wanted. So long as he lived, so long as he wanted her land, Rachel and her family were in danger.

"I'm leaving," Caleb allowed. "But you and I have a little business to conduct first."

Kirkpatrick scowled and arrogance glistened in his eyes, reminding Caleb of a snake. "I can't imagine what we have—"

He didn't get a chance to finish. Caleb recognized the twitch of the man's hand, the shifting of his weight. He was going for his gun. Caleb drew, and in one fluid motion held the gun level with Kirkpatrick's chest.

The Colt weighed heavy in Caleb's hand. Like fate. Like destiny.

Like death.

Something flickered across Kirkpatrick's face as his hand moved away from his holster. Surprise. Respect, perhaps. But not fear. Men like

Kirkpatrick never conceded defeat. They always assumed they would come out on top, regardless of the odds.

"You really that stupid, Beckett? You honestly think I'd let you get this far onto my land without having this room surrounded by my men? You won't get out of here alive. The second you pull that trigger you're a dead man."

Caleb nodded. He knew the hand he'd been dealt. "But you'll be dead first."

Kirkpatrick's eyes hardened. "You ain't got it in you to shoot me. You're just some insignificant drifter with a conscience who thinks he needs to rescue—"

"I buried my conscience a long time ago." The fact that Rachel Sutter had resurrected that conscience didn't bear mentioning, at least not now.

"You expect me to believe that?"

"Ever hear of a man by the name of Sinjin Drake?"

Kirkpatrick's eyes widened enough to let Caleb know he had. For once, his notoriety served him well and he was thankful for it. Part of him wondered which name would grace his tombstone. It hardly mattered now.

"What about him?"

"You're lookin' at him."

Some of the smugness left Kirkpatrick's expression, but not much.

"Before you get too cocky, there's someone here I think you might like to talk to." He barked out an order to one of his men waiting outside his office. "Bring in the boy."

Caleb's stomach dropped as, a moment later, one of Kirkpatrick's henchmen, the one with the scar stretching down the size of his face, entered the room, pushing Brody in front of him.

"Quit shovin' me, Titus!" Brody pulled his shoulder away from the man and glared at him, but his gaze quickly swung back, stopping short when it reached Caleb and his raised gun. "What's he doin' here?"

Caleb cursed his hesitation. The words he'd told Rachel echoed in his head, mocking him.

You don't think, he'd said. *You aim and you shoot. There's no time for thinkin'.*

Truer words were never spoken. When you gave yourself time to think, you started to second-guess yourself. You started to realize the gravity of what you were about to do, and in those moments everything was lost.

He should have shot Kirkpatrick the moment he issued his order. He'd known who Kirkpatrick meant by *the boy* but the sudden fear of Brody getting caught in the crossfire stilled his trigger finger. The hesitation had cost him. Now he had more than his own life to contend with.

The thought of what Rachel would do if anything happened to Brody did not even bear thinking about. Her devastation would be so palpable it would reach clear into the afterlife and haunt him beyond the grave.

Kirkpatrick smiled, a slick, hard grin. Caleb wanted to backhand the expression off the man's face, but if Brody caught the magnitude of the situation, he gave no indication. The foolish kid probably thought Kirkpatrick had his best interests at heart. Caleb knew from experience this man didn't possess a heart. He'd chew Brody up and pick his teeth with the bones, and not think twice about it.

Kirkpatrick motioned for Brody to come to him. "Ever hear of a man named Sinjin Drake, son?"

"Stay where you are, Brody." But Brody ignored Caleb, edging his way toward Kirkpatrick, his eyes never leaving the gun in Caleb's hand.

"Read about him in some dime novel. Said he's an even faster draw than Hickok—" Brody stopped, his eyes growing suddenly wider as realization sunk in. "This ain't—"

"But it is," Kirkpatrick said, placing a hand on Brody's shoulder and bringing him closer, strategically placing him in the direct line of fire. "Seems your sister had some strange taste in men."

"He said his name was Beckett." Brody spit the words out, the glare he'd saved for Titus earlier now aimed at Caleb.

"You need me boss?" Titus had remained near the back door. In his peripheral vision, Caleb watched him edge closer to the exit after hearing who he was up against. Now that Caleb had a gun in his hand, Titus wasn't nearly as bold as he had been the afternoon he'd attacked him in the forest.

"Nah, but stick close, Titus," Kirkpatrick said, his grin firmly in place. He had the upper hand now, and he knew it. Caleb couldn't shoot him without endangering Brody, and they both knew he wouldn't do that. "Just in case Mr. Drake here gets any funny ideas about leaving. Alive, anyway."

Brody's head swiveled around. "What do you mean, alive?"

Seeing the two next to each other, the resemblance was unmistakable, but it was apparent in Brody's reaction that he lacked the cold ruthlessness of his father. He was sullen and moody, prone to a mouthy bravado he'd yet to grow into, but he was no killer. His sister's influence had been substantial, and at his core, Brody was a good boy. Killing was not in his nature.

"Well, I'm not sure if you noticed, son, but the man has a gun on us. Seems he's intent on killin' me. Thinks I had something to do with all those shenanigans going on over at your sister's place."

Brody lifted his chin, but fear had begun to seep into his eyes. "He ain't had nothin' to do with that. He told me so himself. They were just accidents."

Caleb slowly arched one eyebrow. "You don't say? So four of his men, Titus included, accidentally jumped me in the woods? And the bullets shot at Len's horse just magically appeared out of the air? And what about the bunkhouse? Struck by lightning, perhaps?"

"Shamus had nothing to do with the fire at the bunkhouse." But Caleb could see the change in Brody's eyes, hear the question threaded through his words.

Kirkpatrick tightened his grip on Brody's shoulder. "Don't listen to his propaganda, *son*. He's just trying to trick you. I can hardly be held responsible because some old coot fell asleep with a lit smoke, now can I?"

But doubt had already crept in. Brody may be impressionable, but he wasn't an idiot. "Foster doesn't smoke."

"Then one of the other men likely—"

"No. They wouldn't be that careless." Brody tried to pull away, but Kirkpatrick held firm and jerked him back, pulling his gun from the holster and jamming it into Brody's ribs. As much as Caleb wanted to shoot, he couldn't get a clear shot, not without risking harm to the boy.

"Stay put, boy. You aren't going anywhere."

"B-But you're my father." Realization dawned on Brody's face as he spoke the words and Caleb's heart went out to him. He didn't deserve that kind of hurt.

"And you're a disappointment as a son, I don't mind sayin'. Always jawin' on about helpin' your sister and wantin' to visit a whore's bastard like he was your brother. Only purpose you can serve now is being my ticket out of here."

"That's not going to happen," Caleb said. He couldn't let Kirkpatrick leave. He'd come here to kill the man, to protect Rachel and her family. Letting him leave with Brody in tow was not going to happen. If he grew desperate enough, Kirkpatrick wouldn't hesitate to throw Brody into the line of fire, or kill him himself. It was a risk Caleb couldn't take.

One way or another, it ended here, in this room.

Tears stung Rachel's eyes, causing her vision to waver and blur as she ran Hunter's horse hard and fast across the rough terrain. Part of her feared she was pushing the animal past its limits—it had already made the ride from town to her ranch—but the horse had a strong will, and as hard as she pushed it, it responded in kind.

When she reached the Kirkpatrick place, she pulled up near one of the outbuildings and slid from the saddle, grabbing Hunter's rifle from its scabbard. She crouched low at the corner of the building and surveyed the land between her location and the main house. Her heart sank at the sight of Jasper waiting patiently near the porch. She was too late to stop Caleb from confronting Shamus.

The sound of male voices forced her to shrink back against the side of the building until the rough wood bruised her back through her shirtwaist. She wished she'd donned a pair of Brody's old trousers to do chores in this morning. Her skirts were an impediment she didn't need, but there was no changing that now. She waited until the voices faded, taking deep breaths to control the wild beating of her heart. It did little good.

She peeked around the corner again. Everything appeared clear. With a speed she hadn't known she possessed, she ran toward the house, one arm cradling the rifle, the other holding up her skirts. She slid to a stop at the corner of the house and hid to the side where she could see up over the edge of the raised porch to the door beyond.

She wished now she had taken Shamus up on one of his many offers to entertain her. She had no idea of the layout of the house, or where Caleb and Shamus might be. She needed to get inside and find them. Sitting here, waiting for someone to emerge filled her with a sense of helplessness.

Rachel turned around, maintaining her crouched position and sidled along the side of the massive house. When she reached each window, she stretched upward and peered through the glass to the room beyond, trying to build a floor plan in her mind. It wasn't until she reached the back of the house that her search was rewarded. Voices filtered out through a partially open window.

"You best be putting your gun down, Drake.

Don't think his being my kin will prevent me from killing the boy."

Rachel's blood froze in her veins. Shamus had Brody!

"I don't doubt it." Caleb's calm voice reached out and wrapped around her. She held it tight against her heart to ward off the fear. She had to do something. She couldn't just stand by and allow Shamus to hold Brody hostage like some kind of human shield!

"Put your gun down, Drake, and I'll let the boy go."

But Rachel knew Shamus better than that. He'd used the name Drake when referring to Caleb. He was a lot of things, but he wasn't an idiot. Shamus would never give up an advantage, especially not one that kept him from getting a bullet through his black heart from a man notorious for being a fast draw and accurate shot.

She didn't dare peer through the window, afraid if she did, Shamus might see her, or that Brody would, and in his fear give her away. Right now, she still had the element of surprise. If she could get inside, perhaps she could use that. She had to at least try. Especially now with Caleb on the verge of being disarmed. She didn't doubt he would set his gun down if it meant keeping Brody safe. The fact that it would put him in harm's way would not deter him in the least. That was the kind of man he was. He'd shown her his true self every day they'd been together, from the first moment they'd met to the last few seconds before she'd sent him away. She silently cursed herself for letting her hurt and anger override the truth about Caleb.

He'd kept pertinent details of what had happened in Laramie from her, true. But he'd never lied about who he really was. If anything, by giving her his real name, he'd told her more truth than he had most people. He'd opened up to her and shown her his heart, and he'd taken hers and treated it with kindness, doing his best to protect her from pain.

He'd lied no more to her than she'd done to Brody.

Yet she'd sent him away.

Maybe she deserved this outcome now. But one thing was certain, Caleb and Brody did not, and she refused to make them casualties of her own rash behavior.

Rachel crept along the side of the house, back to the front porch. A quick sweep of the area showed no one around. Were they all inside? Would she have to outrun a gauntlet of men to reach the back room?

She shored up her courage. It didn't matter. She'd do what she had to.

The door opened easily and she slipped through, looking around. A hallway to her left led in the direction she needed to go. She tiptoed quietly, wincing with each creak of the floorboards.

"Hey there, girlie."

Rachel started and swung around, raising the rifle in one swift motion, her finger on the trigger. Everything happened too quickly for her to think. She took in the man's scarred face, his close proximity and reacted. The recoil from the shot knocked her hard into the wall.

"Son of a—" The man fell and scrabbled against the floor, his feet slipping on the hardwood as he tried to find purchase. One hand grabbed his arm as he regained his footing and ran in the opposite direction.

For a brief second, Rachel stood there stunned, her shoulder throbbing where the kickback had slammed the rifle's stock into her. Then she realized the impact of what she'd done. She'd lost her element of surprise, the only thing she had in her favor.

The shot reverberated up the hallway and echoed outside the door to the room. Caleb straightened, having just pushed his gun across the floor. Every instinct of self-preservation screamed at him to dive and pick it up, but it was out of reach of both him and Kirkpatrick now, having slid beneath the opulent desk.

There was a brief, muffled curse, then silence. A hint of alarm brightened Kirkpatrick's cold eyes before he quickly regained control.

"Sounds like maybe we have ourselves an uninvited guest."

The words were barely out of his mouth when

Rachel burst into the room, rifle held high. "Drop your gun, Shamus. Drop it, or I swear to God I will kill you!"

Caleb cursed under his breath. As much as he had longed to see Rachel once more, this was not the time or place he would have chosen.

"Rachel, get out," he said. She was still close enough to the door to save herself and leave him with one less body to be concerned about. She ignored him, walking farther into the room until she was an equal distance between him and Kirkpatrick.

"I'm not leaving." She wouldn't look at him, but he could see her hands trembling and the pallor of her skin. Not a good sign. He knew what a poor shot she was. She was just as likely to hit Brody as she was Kirkpatrick. Caleb's mind raced with all the possibilities of what could happen, none of which had a happy ending.

"Brody, are you okay?"

The boy nodded, but Caleb could tell from the way he clenched his jaw he was holding back his fear.

"Boss?"

Kirkpatrick's gaze slid to the window. "Titus, get the rest of the men and get your butt in here!"

Caleb didn't like the escalating edge to Kirkpatrick's voice. It spoke of desperation, and desperation led to rash decisions, which led to dead bodies. And now Caleb had one more body to protect and no gun with which to do it.

"She shot me in the arm, boss."

"I don't care if she shot you in the head. Do what I tell you!"

There was a silence on the other side of the window, then, "Me and the other men…we figured we ain't goin' to prison again."

"If you don't get in here now, prison will be the least of your worries."

But Kirkpatrick's threats had lost their luster. Titus had made his choice, and it seemed his henchmen considered it a better idea to get out while the getting was good.

"Sorry, boss."

"It's all over, Kirkpatrick. Let the boy go." Caleb kept his voice calm. He could sense Kirkpatrick's mounting anger and anxiety. He prayed Rachel wouldn't add to it. To her credit, she'd stayed stock-still since speaking to Brody. Her gaze continued to bounce between Kirkpatrick and him.

A smarmy smile crested Kirkpatrick's face. "Oh, it ain't over by far, Drake. I have no intentions of letting you out of here so I can spend the rest of my days lookin' over my shoulder."

"Your days are numbered as it is, Shamus," Rachel said, and from the steel in her gaze, Caleb believed her. She may be terrified, but she was determined. She would protect her family at any cost.

"You might want to remember, I got the boy." Kirkpatrick tightened his hold on Brody, but the motion caused him to react. Brody jerked away, the sudden movement throwing Kirkpatrick off balance long enough for him to slip out of his grip and run to Caleb.

Caleb pushed Brody behind him, using his body to block him from Kirkpatrick's line of fire. "Get out, Brody. Do it now." For once, the boy did as he was told without argument, leaving just the three of them.

"Guess you've got nothing now," Rachel said.

Caleb eyed the desk where his gun lay out of reach. Dread flooded his bloodstream. He couldn't kid himself. In a shootout between Rachel and Kirkpatrick, he knew her lack of skill left her at a distinct disadvantage. And with Kirkpatrick growing desperate, there was no telling what the man would do.

Caleb met Kirkpatrick's gaze. A sick smile edged upward into his cold eyes and in that moment, his intent was clear.

Kill Rachel.

The muscles in Kirkpatrick's arm bunched, and Caleb knew he had run out of time. His body was in motion before he could consider the consequences, his only thought was of Rachel and reaching her before the bullet did. He dove toward her, wrapping one arm around her and grabbing the rifle with his free hand. He didn't have time to aim. He pulled the trigger and dropped it as it recoiled.

Twisting his body as he fell to the ground, he

pulled Rachel beneath him. It all happened in seconds. Less than that.

Fire burned across his back as the gunshots echoed through the room, loosening every tightly held memory of every man Caleb had ever killed. But in that moment, as he hit the floor and knew the next shot would take his life, he realized it had never been about death. It had been about choice.

Life or death.

He hadn't wanted to kill those men, not one of them. He'd done everything in his power to convince them to walk away. They had refused. Their choice had been death. Caleb had defended himself in the only way he could.

He had chosen life.

And now, he chose Rachel's life. He wouldn't let her die, as long as there was breath left in his body.

Another shot rang out. Caleb turned his face and buried it in Rachel's hair, breathing in the scent of violets for the last time as he braced himself for the impact of the bullet that would finally end his life.

Chapter Twenty-Three

Warm sun and a light breeze slowly coaxed Rachel from the deep sleep she'd enjoyed. Bit by bit, she became more aware of the sounds around her. The normal sounds of her everyday life. The birds chirping, Freedom humming in the kitchen and somewhere in the distance, the men arriving at the main house for breakfast.

The smell of freshly brewed coffee and bacon cooking made her stomach growl, but she put off opening her eyes, unwilling to embrace the day, wishing desperately to return to the solace of the night.

Something nudged her.

"Open your eyes."

She did as she was told, squinting against the sunlight filtering in from the window near her bed. Above her, Caleb's face settled into view as he leaned over her. His smile deepened the lines etched into the corners of his eyes.

Relief swept through her. He was still here. He

hadn't left her. Shamus's last shot had done nothing more than graze Caleb's shoulder. It was the last evil thing the man ever did. As Caleb covered her, another shot had rung out, but it hadn't been from Shamus. Hunter had followed her, only minutes behind. He'd arrived as Brody burst out of the house. Rushing in, he'd reached them as Shamus was about to make his final shot. Hunter beat him to it. Rachel had heard Shamus's surprised grunt, then the sound of his body slumping to the floor.

It was over.

Caleb's fingertips lightly touched her shoulder where her nightdress had slipped off to reveal the bruise the rifle stock had left. "How do you feel?"

"Better. I won't break. I promise."

Caleb shook his head, and the worry eased from his hazel eyes. A quiet breath lifted his chest. She could have stayed there all morning staring up at his handsome face and the depth of emotion mirrored there.

"What were you thinking, going after Kirkpatrick?"

"I was thinking I could stop you before you tried anything heroic." Her admission shocked him, though he managed to keep his expression calm. She shrugged. "I didn't get there in time. I wish I'd killed him," she said, the memory of him holding a gun to Brody still filling her heart with fear and anger.

"You're no killer, Rachel." Caleb brushed a lock of hair from her brow.

She reached up and took his hand, bringing it down to rest against her heart. "Neither are you."

His mouth twisted. "I've killed a lot of men. Your husband included."

"Robert got himself killed. You were only defending yourself. I'm sorry Robert's dead, but he brought it on himself. It isn't your responsibility. I'm sorry I made you feel as though it was. I was angry you hadn't told me."

"I wanted to, that first night I met you in the restaurant. But it had been a hard day, and the news of the deed had been too much. I figured I'd best wait before I hit you with the worst of it. When I realized the problems you had with Kirkpatrick I didn't want to leave you unprotected. If I'd told you then, you'd have kicked me off your land without hesitation."

It was true. His presence had disturbed her from the first moment she'd laid eyes on him in the church. It had scared her, the sudden and powerful draw toward him. Fear and uncertainty had made her want to push him away.

"It wasn't my land."

He conceded the point with a tilt of his head.

"I wanted to tell you—" He stopped and shook his head, his gaze drifting to the window. "No. That's a lie."

"Caleb?"

When he looked back, pain had replaced

worry, hardening his features, tightening the skin over his sharp cheekbones. "I didn't want to tell you. Not when I saw how much he had hurt you. How much you were still hurting. I didn't want to add to it. And after a bit, I didn't want to leave you alone."

"You wanted to protect me."

A bitter smile flitted over his mouth before disappearing. "I wanted more than that." Desire burned in his eyes, driving straight to her core, making her nerves dance to life. But that wasn't the only thing she saw. There was something else. Something deeper.

She started to shy away, afraid to hope, but courage found her in the nick of time. "What did you want?"

He curled her hand in his and lifted it to his mouth, kissing the sensitive skin on the inside of her wrist. "You."

"You had me." Thoroughly. Completely. In a way that left her body singing and her mind reeling.

He chuckled and the spark ignited in his eyes. The hope she'd kindled deep in her breast flamed to life.

"It wasn't just your body I wanted, although—" he looked at her, all of her, his gaze a physical touch "—it is a delectable little body."

She blushed. "What else did you want?"

He leaned down and kissed her forehead. "Your mind. I love the way it works."

"What else?"

His mouth hovered over hers. She ached for him to take it, to taste him once again, to be swept up in the pleasure his kiss could bring. But he did not oblige. His smile deepened and that was almost enough, to see the worry and the pain beaten back until it barely existed.

He moved past her mouth, pulling the blankets down to her waist. He lifted the front of her nightdress where the buttons had come loose at her neck. A thrill burned through her body as his mouth pressed down over her heart.

"I want this most of all," he whispered against her skin. "Tell me it's mine. Tell me I haven't ruined things past fixin'."

Rachel sifted her fingers through Caleb's thick hair and urged him back up. Her hands explored the planes and angles of his face, the straight line of his nose, his prominent brow. There was so much about this man she loved—inside and out. Yet words failed to adequately describe the overwhelming emotions he brought to life within her.

She pulled him down and savored the moment when their lips met and their breath mingled. She relished the sensations that coursed through her as he answered her kiss with his own, his lips gentle and coaxing, teasing and true. Every emotion she had kept locked inside poured out of her into her kiss, every answer he needed given through taste and touch.

"I love you," she whispered as his mouth explored the line of her jaw. The pulse at her throat beat wildly. Again, words paled in comparison with her feelings. How could something so simple convey everything he meant to her? He had lifted her up, restored her sense of self, put to rest all her fears. He had cared for her and stood by her and made her feel loved and special and important.

He had made her believe she deserved to feel all of those things. She couldn't imagine her life without him.

"Please stay."

Caleb lifted his head and gazed down into the face he had come to love with such completeness it should have frightened him. It didn't. The only fear was in losing her, in walking away and never holding her in his arms again, or knowing the pleasure of her kiss, or delighting in her sharp mind and beautiful smile.

In Rachel he had found a woman of courage and strength unlike any he had ever known. She was a wonder to him. A wonder he wanted to spend the rest of his life discovering.

"On two conditions," he said, stretching out on the bed next to her.

Rachel rolled on her side to face him, one hand slipping beneath her cheek. "Conditions?"

"That you agree to love, honor and obey—"

"—cherish," she said, talking over him.

He smiled. "Guess that last one was too much to hope for."

"Do you want an obedient wife?"

"I'd rather have you."

"I'm already yours. What's the second condition?"

"We tell Ethan to start calling us Ma and Pa. He needs a proper family. I don't want him thinking we're just people who took him in and can send him away when we see fit."

"Agreed," she whispered, a sheen of tears covering her eyes. "Now kiss me before I embarrass myself and turn into a watering pot."

"Happy to oblige." He gathered her in his arms and kissed her until they were both breathless. Until the noise and hustle of the outside world fell away and only the two of them remained. He kissed her until the sense of home he'd always longed for filled him, settled in and took root, and he knew it would be a long time past forever before it let him go.

"I love you, Rachel Sutter."

"Beckett," she said, lavishing little kisses across his face. "Rachel Beckett. You might as get used to calling me by what's going to be my proper name."

"Rachel Beckett," he said, finding her mouth once again.

It sounded like home.

* * * * *

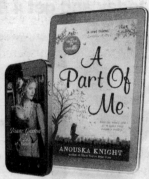

MILLS & BOON®

Why not subscribe?

Never miss a title and save money too!

Here's what's available to you if you join the exclusive **Mills & Boon Book Club** today:

✦ *Titles up to a month ahead of the shops*
✦ *Amazing discounts*
✦ *Free P&P*
✦ *Earn Bonus Book points that can be redeemed against other titles and gifts*
✦ *Choose from monthly or pre-paid plans*

Still want more?

Well, if you join today we'll even give you
50% OFF your first parcel!

So visit **www.millsandboon.co.uk/subs**
or call Customer Relations on **020 8288 2888**
to be a part of this exclusive Book Club!

MILLS & BOON®

Why shop at millsandboon.co.uk?

Each year, thousands of romance readers find their perfect read at millsandboon.co.uk. That's because we're passionate about bringing you the very best romantic fiction. Here are some of the advantages of shopping at www.millsandboon.co.uk:

* **Get new books first**—you'll be able to buy your favourite books one month before they hit the shops

* **Get exclusive discounts**—you'll also be able to buy our specially created monthly collections, with up to 50% off the RRP

* **Find your favourite authors**—latest news, interviews and new releases for all your favourite authors and series on our website, plus ideas for what to try next

* **Join in**—once you've bought your favourite books, don't forget to register with us to rate, review and join in the discussions

Visit **www.millsandboon.co.uk**
for all this and more today!

MILLS_WEB